TRADE OF THE TRICKS

The Tricks' Brand

David Noe

Cover by Kevin S. Halter
Book design by Julie L. Casey

ISBN 978-0692461129

Printed in the United States of America.

For more information, visit

www.amazingthingspress.com

or
authordavidnoe.weebly.com

DEDICATION

There are those in my life who have spurred my imagination. They have prompted my mind to wit. They have helped shape the unseen worlds and the residents therein. They are the Imagineers! They are a selfless group who seek to fertilize creativity for the sake of itself. They live in those dimensions. They goad to fruition those foolish enough to think of writing things down. They provide nourishment, sunlight, even sanctuary for a wandering seeking soul. Gifts of building materials, they happily and arduously provide, and I take advantage of those gifts. I build castles and armies. I create life!

Yet, there have been those who contrive selfishly to darken the path. They set roadblocks. They cry foul. They mock and laugh and hate. There have been those, too. They have no name. Their minds cannot conceive of one. I have worked diligently to avoid or exorcise these demons from my life. It has cost me time. Upon occasion, it has robbed me of the muse. This book is a refutation of them.

To the Imagineers! Long may they prosper! This book is for them! They are family and friends, online friends and professional inspirations, even you, the reader of this book. Be an Imagineer. Help spread the words.

INTRODUCTION BY ROGER MCKENZIE

I'm not going to bore you with a long introduction. The Trade of the Tricks doesn't need one. It speaks for itself quite well. Besides, if you're like me, you don't read these things anyway. You jump right into the story!

But, if you are the sort who reads these things, I would like to say a few words about Dave Noe. He's an idea guy. I can't remember a time as Managing Editor at Charlton Media when he didn't have an idea ready! It's in his blood. He can't help himself.

He's a writer, and the energy and love of what he does shines through every page. Every paragraph. Every word.

Trade of the Tricks is Dave's first novel, and it's a very interesting take on the whole super-hero scene. In fact, he turns it on its ear. But I've come to expect that from Dave. He does that a lot.

He doesn't look at the world quite like the rest of us. He sees twists and turns and avenues most of us never notice… until Dave points them out to us. Trade of the Tricks is no exception. I've written super-hero comic books since the late 1970's. I thought I'd seen… and written… it all in that time.

But I was wrong. I hadn't seen, Trade of the Tricks. But enough about me, AND Dave. If you're reading this, you're missing the sheer fun awaiting you. Get on with it already!

One final thing, though, before I go. As I said earlier, this is Dave's first novel.

You can bet it will not be his last.

—Roger McKenzie, April 2015

(Roger McKenzie broke into comics in 1975. He has

written for Marvel, DC and many independent comicbook companies. He is currently the Managing Editor at Charlton Neo Media, where he still manages to crank out a few stories…)

PROLOGUE

Sometimes I can remember my father. At least, I think I can. It's a warm fuzzy summer day, and I'm outside with my friends. In my mind, I know he's around. I can feel him. It's a dream-like memory, where so much is out of focus. The day is a dual tone of blue and green. My group of pre-school pals, a gawky troupe of shadows, is hopping around the periphery of my eyes. It's like I'm both there and somehow floating above it all, watching it take place. All the voices are mumbles, as if under water. We have our bicycles and our tricycles, and I have my red wagon.

I sit, wild hair and wide eyes in the rusty little re-painted wagon on top of a grassy hill. The pteranodons are doing lazy circles in the cloudless sky above me. I'm gripping the black metal handle of the wagon, while my friends egg me on. They chant some rhyme that doesn't even make sense and has nothing to do with anything. A knot forms in the pit of my stomach, yet I know this is something I want to do no matter how much my body tells me otherwise. At the bottom of the mountain of a yard, the grass ends and the driveway gives way to the parkway, way down the breezy breezeway. I want to fly. I want to know the feel of the thrill. In my brain, there is no fear. My tightly gripped knuckles beg to differ. There are obstacles in my way, bumps and holes, unexpected things that will pop up, and of course, the sudden stop at the end. Right at the road, right in my way, daring me to do it, is the family car. It's old and big and has an oil stain under it. It sits like a trophy, a brass ring waiting to be

1

grabbed.

Knowing there are no brakes, I have a plan instead. I will zoom down the hill, dodging all the problems along the way, and make a quick turn just a few feet from Dad's station wagon. Then, I will skid sideways like a stunt driver, kicking up dust, stopping mere inches before I touch the car. I won't even get any oil on me. It's a plan I'm growing less and less confident about as I rock back and forth, winding my nerve up, revving my engine, making the adventure larger and larger in my imagination. The old man next door is on a ladder, pruning his apple tree and yelling over at us. It's all just sound on the breeze. He might as well be a dog somewhere, yapping away in the forest, lost in the tangle and the tumble of all the other hills with all the other kids and all the other wagons on all the other summer days.

I remember looking around for my dad. This is panic time. I want his presence, his calm assurance. I look around and don't see him. I look around and know he's here somewhere. The air is full of moisture, making my breathing labored. All that is around me is the drop off of the land.

If this were a dream, then I would be floating in an anti-gravity space ship, tunnel vision, faster than light, headed for the stars, but this is a memory. I'm convinced it's a memory. It is too important not to be, because it's a memory of my dad, and I don't have any other memories of him left.

Someone laughs and pushes me, and the wind wraps around my face. The rusty bearings on the wagon squeak at first, and then jump up in pitch to a scream like a fork on teeth, clicking and squealing in an ever faster rhythm. The car at the bottom rushes even closer, as if the world is moving to me instead of me falling towards it. I wait for my perfect maneuver, and turn, and skid, and roll, and fly...

...but I never hit the ground. The hard, stern, loving arms of my father catch me and keep me from hitting the car. He comes from nowhere, like some hero in the powered age. He swoops in and pulls me from danger in perfect timing. Now I know I'm safe and sound. I would have hit the car for sure. I was careening unerringly towards it, like a bullet on a target.

Then, as I look up into his face, the sun blinds me. I see my father's outline. I see his halo. Nothing else matters. My friends are lost in the background. The neighbor's voice is carried into the wind. The wagon had continued into the station wagon. Then, the memory pulls away. Everything is gone. My friends are gone. The neighbor is gone. The wagon, the car, the world are all gone. I look to see my father's face...

I remember him that day. I think I remember him.

CHAPTER ONE

"It's been fifty years, ladies and gentlemen. Why, in that amount of time, nearly half a century has gone by," Alan spoke into the bus microphone and rolled his eyes at me. It was a joke he told several times a day, ever since he started driving the tour bus. He was running a little behind today. It was getting dark, and the tourists were antsy. He had told the joke three times already.

The tourists on the BB Tour were getting a little more than they paid for today. You see, Alan was a good friend of mine, even though he was somewhat older. He was a driver by choice, but he also was a full-time Trick. As a full-time Trick, it was Alan's job to help out certain crime fighting heroes no matter what got in the way. As a part-time Trick, it was my job to do the same thing, just on two weekends a month and two weeks in the summer. It was summer break now, and I had mostly been going on cases with Alan. The few times I went out on my own were pretty lame. Once I left a sack lunch for a hero, but he didn't even show up. This promised to be a little better.

"I know we were hoping to see the original battle sight, ladies and gentlemen, where all the superheroes and super villains just disappeared fifty years ago after Billy's Bargain, but there seems to be a slight road block."

Traffic had been slowing us and diverting our route for the last few turns. Alan had been deftly making detours to get to our destination. He was a good driver. At our last turn, we realized that the traffic jam had been intentional. In front of us, turned sideways in the street, was

4

a large black car. Two Roadies dressed in bright pink hoodies leaned up against the doors and chatted with a couple of rough-looking long-haired thugs from the Dead Millards motorcycle gang. The police were pretty busy with the crowds coming to town for the fiftieth anniversary memorial speech, so they hadn't gotten to the this scene yet. With roadblocks like this, it was no wonder.

Roadies were the opposite of Tricks. It was their job to help out the villains. Quite a community of brightly dressed heroes and villains had grown up in the last fifty years, since every single superhero and super villain had blinked off the face of the earth during a huge battle in New York City that threatened to destroy the world. Alan pointed at the Roadies and looked up at me. We both nodded. We knew what was going on. These Roadies were sent out to stop any help or police from getting in. I stood by the bus door, holding on to the pole. He was now driving with renewed purpose. He got a call from his girlfriend, Gina. She was one of the sidekicks for the popular Grade B hero, The Red Dart. Gina was a Dartette.

Alan turned the bus sharply down an alley. He knew the city better than most cab drivers. He once took a class from Ace, the cab driver to the heroes. It made a big impact on him.

"Lousy Roadies!" Alan spit.

Gina told him it was going down right now. The villain known as the Counterfeiter had been making a lot of money recently. The problem was, he was actually *making* the money. It was time he was stopped. Alan was supposed to have had plenty of time to drop off the tourists and meet with the hero known as The Red Dart, but someone, probably a guard or something, found out, and The Red Dart was in trouble. Alan now had to get supplies to the Counterfeiter's secret base immediately. We would have to slip on masks. I was never crazy about

5

masks. It never helped me too much anyway. Once somebody saw me close up, they would notice that I had one blue eye and one brown eye. There are just not a lot of people out there with two different colored eyes. Luckily, Tricks only wore masks when they had to work in public. We also had to collect cell phones and cameras. We didn't need our faces plastered all over the news and the Internet. That would make our jobs a lot harder. Tricks weren't in it for the fame, even though everyone in the chain of command was graded by a secret panel of judges who were not supposed to be affiliated with anyone. Even the heroes and villains were graded from Grade A to Grade D.

Grade B heroes were really the working heroes. Grade A heroes were mainly just stars and well-connected people. Everyone knew the Grade A heroes. The papers followed their "exploits," like which party they were attending, which celebrity they were dating, what new mansion they bought. They did endorsements and made millions of dollars. They could afford a small army for protection or to pull off their heroics. It was always a media event. Most of them didn't even have aliases. That went for the Grade A villains too. The top-grade good guys and bad guys seldom fought each other unless it was prearranged. The good guys always won, but the bad guys always escaped. It was a predictable outcome for the Grade A's. The fun came in how the adventure was done. They didn't want to lose their popularity or station, and they had to maintain their ranking. There was an awful lot of posturing and storytelling. Most people thought the Grade A stuff was all faked, but no one would ever want to say that to their face.

Heroes and villains alike now belonged to a secret organization called the SGHV, the Society for the Grading of Heroes and Villains. They paid an annual fee, the amount of which was based on their ranking, to be graded and judged. Lives and fortunes could change big-time by the rising or falling of a grade.

Grade B heroes didn't have as many connections or as much money. They had to go by works. They actually caught bad guys. Even though being a hero was just as illegal as being a villain, people pursued the vocation for reasons known only to them. In most cases, the law looked the other way. People remembered Billy's Bargain and the magic that used to exist in the world. It still held a special place in the collective psyche. Many people still believed it could come back. In some cases, the law actually used the vigilantes to help out. That was what was happening now.

The Feds didn't know who they could trust in their own organization, so they hired The Red Dart, a known Grade B, who could get the job done quietly. They couldn't hire a Grade A, because they didn't want it splashed all over the news and because they actually wanted the villain caught. The Red Dart did well finding the Counterfeiter and his secret base, but now the bad guys knew The Red Dart was in the building. Everything was blown, and this was no longer a quiet mission. Even as Alan swerved through the streets with a busload of scared tourists, a battle raged in a four-story brick building that was just too many blocks away at the moment.

"Well, I'll be..." Alan took his foot off the gas pedal.

A bulky taxi with flashing lights pulled up and around the bus. Even the crowded streets couldn't stop it. It swerved and ducked in and out of traffic. The driver was able to handle the vehicle in an almost superhuman way.

"It's Ace, Brand!" Alan smacked the wheel and hopped up and down in his seat. "He'll clear the way!"

"Don't say my name, dummy," I hissed. "*Masks*, remember?"

Alan made a face and hit the gas. Ace smashed into the black Roadie car in front of us and sent it spinning. Any other driver would have made a bigger mess than what was already there but somehow, Ace barely scratched his taxi. We pulled on through the opened street and headed in the right direction.

"What?" Alan put his hand to the phone in his ear and spoke to Gina. "Really? Okay..."

He pinched his lips and looked over to me. "We're not stopping at the building."

"Where are we going?" I looked out to see if Ace was turning away.

"Oh, we're going to the building," he said. "We're just not going to stop."

I looked out of the windshield and saw the building up ahead. We were coming up to it pretty fast.

"Hang on tight!" he yelled.

"Oh, my gosh," I said as the wall approached. "Hold on, everybody! Hold on!"

"I hope this is the right wall," Alan said.

Everyone started shouting and screaming as they realized what was happening. Ace slammed on his brakes, pulled up beside us, and shot a hook or an anchor or something that was attached to a chain out of the front of his car. It struck the brick wall just before we did. I think it was to help weaken the wall.

A bright light accompanied my head hitting the front of the bus. I thought of my little wagon crashing into the station wagon, but there was no one to save me this time. Then a blackness overtook me.

"...all right?" Alan asked as he dug himself out of the air bag.

Passengers were taking stock of each other, and initial reports were positive. I had a gash above my left eye that hadn't gotten around to hurting yet. Alan opened the front door at the same time that the back door came open.

"Everybody out back here," Ace ordered. "Head down the road and turn right. Is anyone injured? Watch your step." He wore a black leather hat and a worn brown jacket with zippers and snaps all over it. He looked just like I had seen him on the news. He didn't mind getting coverage, but never seemed to seek it out. He was ruggedly handsome, with just the right amount of stubble and muscles to melt the hearts of all the girls.

Three beautiful women jumped in through the front door. They were dressed in dark red costumes that accentuated their curves. They were the Dartettes, the sidekicks of The Red Dart. The oldest, a tall, thin woman with horn-rimmed glasses, which acted as a mask, and short-bobbed black hair, headed right past us to the passenger seats. She put her bow across her shoulder next to her quiver of arrows and pulled a cushion up to reveal strange-looking guns and some red arrows. She never even acknowledged our presence.

"Get the gas masks from here," she said to the second, younger Dartette.

I knew this younger girl. She was much curvier than the first woman and she liked to show it off. She was the same age as Alan. Her name was Gina, and she had been dating Alan for a few months. She wore a phone in her ear and she touched Alan on the knee. She looked at me and smiled.

"Do you need...?" Alan started to stand.

"Go with Ace." Gina grabbed the gas masks and ran.

We both started coughing. Once the doors opened, the steam from the front of the bus was mixing with gas from inside the building. Blood from my cut got in my eyes, making it even harder to see. My head throbbed as if I'd just bashed it into the front of a bus. Out of the haze, came two red velvet gloved hands.

"Put this on it." The youngest Dartette placed a cold

pack on my forehead. "And get to a doctor."

She slapped Alan's shoulder. "You're right," she said. "He is a cutie."

Alan swallowed a cough. "I didn't call you a cutie."

"I'm Darlene." She tossed a broken arrow shaft on my lap. "Give me a call sometime. Right now I've got stuff."

I could barely see her as she hopped off the bus and through the gaping hole in the brick wall, right into the melee. Her gold-lined red half-cape flapped in the dust and gas. Alan helped me up and out of the bus.

"Oh, man," I said, "Grandpa's gonna kill me."

"He'll understand." Alan guided me over some bricks. "He's been through this kind of stuff before."

"I didn't tell him," I said. "He doesn't even know I'm out here tonight."

"Yeah," Alan looked around, "he's gonna kill you. That's one of the Tricks' main rules, Brand. You gotta let somebody know where you are."

I shook my head and felt dizzy.

"I know you guys haven't been getting along lately..."

"It's just..." I said, "I don't know."

"Here, take this bag," Alan said. "We've got a job to do."

"I can't even hardly see." I opened the bag to the fuzzy contents. "Is this the, you know..."

"Bombs, yes," Alan said. "Hold on a minute."

I heard him cough in between my own coughs, as he jumped back up into the bus. Then, I heard him hit something in the bus. I crouched down and found that the air was a little clearer close to the ground.

"It's more smoke than gas," I said.

I could see his legs coming towards me.

"I had these on the bus," he said. "I keep a lot of survival stuff in my vehicles."

He squatted down beside me and handed me a black gas mask with goggles. He then put on a mask of his own that was black with a lighting bolt on it.

"No fair," I said.

"There's gotta be a better way." He pulled the mask around and situated it on his face. His voice got all muffled. "...better...something different...change to..."

"What?" I turned my head to hear.

He waved his hand and pointed at our bags. I pointed to the back of the building. He shook his head no and motioned in the direction of the hole in the wall.

"Swell," I said, but he didn't hear me through the mask.

It made no sense to me, but the air was actually a little clearer inside the building. All the smoke was being pulled out through the bus-shaped opening in the brick wall. I had to focus through the chaos. It was something we learned at Tricks camp. Thankfully, there was enough gas and smoke that I could only barely make out the body lying in the rubble just inside the building. The action was invisible to me. I heard gunshots and ricochets, which were scary enough. I heard Ace corralling people outside and the distant sounds of sirens. The popping electricity and flashing ceiling lights added to the confusion.

Alan held his phone up to his goggles so he could better see a map that The Red Dart had sent him earlier. He grabbed my shirt to make sure I was paying attention and pointed to the outline of a door. As we approached, I saw what was left of an arrow sticking out where the lock used to be. I touched the other arrow in my pocket that had the note in it just to remind myself that it was there.

The heavy metal door swung open, and Alan and I found ourselves in a semi-dark stairwell. Everything seemed gray. The smoke was much thinner in here, and Alan even took off his mask. The dim glow of the emergency lights barely lit up the concrete walls and steps. The smoke made an oval haze around the bulbs.

"Here we go," Alan said and started down the stairs. "The locks should all be open."

We made our way down to the basement where not only was the lock open, but so was the door. We could hear people scurrying around like rats.

"I didn't think anybody was supposed to be down here," I said.

"What?" Alan answered in a loud whisper.

"I didn't think anybody was supposed to be down here," I said again.

"What?" He motioned for me to take off my mask.

"I didn't think anybody was supposed to be down here," I said.

"Yeah, well, you know how people get in situations like this." He peered through the gray shadows and gray smoke and gray gloom. "Let's just try to do our thing and get back to the bus. I'll feel a lot safer when..."

"I don't want to hurt anybody," I said. "We're just supposed to weaken a foundation support. I don't want to hurt anybody."

"Gross!" Alan slapped me on the shoulder. "You got snot all over my bomb bag."

"My nose is all sticky and clogged," I said. "I'm worried that if we do this..."

"If we don't follow the plan, don't you think The Red Dart and the Dartettes could get hurt too?" Alan tucked his mask into his belt. "You're a Trick. You know how these things work."

"Still..."

"Try not to be seen," Alan said. "Maybe we can spook these guys out after we set up the timers. When I say *go*, we'll head to the right. The support is in the back right corner."

"*My* right?"

"Everybody's right, Brand."

"No, I mean, if I'm standing from the other side..."

"*YOUR* right, Brand."

"Right."

"Okay, ready...?"

Just as we were about to run into the room, someone came running right at the stairwell door.

"Outa' my way! Outa' my way!" he shouted.

His little rectangular glasses almost fell off the tip of his thin nose. His arms and pockets were full of electronics. He ran right between us and up the stairs. Even though he was weighed down with wires and boxes, he moved quickly, even taking two steps at a time.

"The bad guys even steal from themselves." Alan shook his head. "He won't get too far, though. These guys have a surprising lack of decent drivers."

"Let's go," I said. "I don't hear anybody else."

"Go!" Alan said and took off ahead of me.

We made a beeline to the back of the room, dodging boxes and pallets.

"Holy crap!" Alan said.

"What's going on?"

"They had the same idea," Alan spoke into his phone. "They've already set bombs on the pillar."

"Tell them," I said. "Is it timed?"

"I just did." Alan showed me his phone. "What do you think I..."

"I could defuse it," I stood over a box with a flashing light.

"No, leave it," Alan said. "The Red Dart said to leave it. Let's get out of here. We don't know how long we got. Go!"

Alan took off, and I was close behind. I was just to the door as he was bounding up the first flight of stairs.

"Help!" I heard the faint cry of a woman.

I skidded to a stop in the doorway and looked back. I wasn't really sure if I had heard anything or if it was even coming from the basement.

13

"Help!" I heard it again, coming from the opposite side of the room from where the bomb was. I saw a faint glow moving in the back, behind some wall dividers.

"Hello?" I called out.

"Let me go!" the voice cried. "Help!"

I gritted my teeth and ran across the room, hoping the bomb didn't decide to go off and blow me into pieces. I rounded a corner, and it was then that I saw the ghosts. I stood there bent over and huffing from the run and the smoke and the gas and the fear and watched two glowing ghosts attacking each other.

One ghost was like a clear green glowing woman. She had hair that was straight and long, like way long. It floated around in the air like she was under water. I couldn't make out her facial features. She was all blurry. She had her hands around the neck of the second ghost, like she was trying to strangle the life out of him. My nose was burning from the smoke and a kind of electric taste in the air. I could feel the hairs on my arm stand up. I nearly gagged.

"Help me, Brand," her voice just kind of came out of her like she was wearing a speaker in her long flowing green dress.

The other ghost was even more indistinct than the first. He—I think it was a he—was a white form with his arms around her neck. They both floated and bobbed in the air for a moment, until I remembered the bomb.

"Hey!" I said. "We need..."

Both ghosts immediately turned their blurry heads to me. They let go of each other and lunged in my direction. The woman screamed, and the man landed right on top of me. I closed my eyes and threw my hands up over my head.

"...the pedal to the metal!" Alan grabbed the back of my shirt.

I was standing in the doorway at the base of the

steps.

"Ghosts," I said as he dragged me up the stairs.

"Yeah, that's some crazy gas," he said. "I'm seeing swirly colors myself."

I couldn't hear any fighting when we got back up to the main room.

"They've moved to a different part of the building," Alan said.

I pulled myself up and out of his grip. "Then how is it going to help...?"

"I don't know," Alan said. "You know how you never know how things are going to go."

"I know," I said.

"This way," Ace called from the hole in the wall. "Let's go, Tricks."

The inside of his taxi was so comfortable. It seemed bigger than it was from the outside. Of course, that kind of thing was impossible now. I had heard stories of what it used to be like. Cars could fly. Stones had powers. People had their own pocket dimensions. All that was just fiction now, fiction and ancient history.

No hero or villain had super powers anymore. Physics just didn't work the way it was supposed to, or the way it used to. The world changed dramatically fifty years ago when the supers disappeared. Not one person was known to have gotten super powers since then. Now, if you got exposed to a massive dose of radiation, instead of developing incredible powers, you would probably just die. No one knew for sure what took place on that day, and there were thousands of stories, but it was widely accepted that the superhero Trick known as Billy, the Man Who Knows Everything, made a bargain with the bad guys to take the fight elsewhere. New York was being torn apart by a massive battle involving hundreds of super-powered individuals. There was no way the fight could continue without taking a terrible toll. There were

15

literal giants in those days. This stuff was not only taught in school, but recorded by the people at the time. There were god-like beings that could just blink us mortals out. The only thing that kept them in check were other god-like beings. Somehow, all the teams took up sides and took up arms and let it all fly.

"Your faces are bright green, and I don't like the look of that cut." Ace looked in the rearview mirror and maneuvered the crime zone at the same time. "Take off your masks and clean up. There's a first aid kit and some washcloths back there."

My favorite Tricks shirt was ruined with blood. It was a light blue button down shirt with a dark green collar and marbled green glassy buttons. I kind of considered it my costume. I didn't have a real costume, because Tricks don't wear costumes. I actually found it at a second hand store for three dollars. I figured maybe I could save the buttons, at least.

The green washed off our faces, and the gas didn't seem to be toxic, but for some reason, my cut was orange and pink, like florescent orange and pink. It started hurting, making up for lost time. Ace pulled up to the hospital a few minutes later. He was met at the door by a group of people who seemed to know him well. I got a few stitches and a large bandage. We got away free and clear with a wink and Ace's story that we were in with the tourists. Alan was pretty sure though, that BB tours was going to fire him. He was already in trouble for doing some hot rodding a few weeks before.

The police, of course, knew what had really happened back at the building, but they got the word from the Feds to cool it, and the investigation was immediately closed down. They had the Counterfeiter. I found out later that the Counterfeiter had hired a villain named the Gray Hand, who specialized in toxic and nontoxic gases. The Gray Hand was a protégé of the Counterfeiter and had stepped on a live electrical wire, electrocuting himself. All of his smoke traps and bombs went off at once. It was a crazy scene that was interrupted at the end by a tour bus crashing through the wall.

The Red Dart and the Dartettes made a clean getaway in the confusion. They always did. They were getting pretty popular. No one knew where they went or where to find them... no one but me. I had part of a red arrow with a note attached. The note had the name Darlene, followed by her phone number.

CHAPTER TWO

I never did hear the building blow up. By the time I was ready to leave the hospital, it was already all over. I hoped Ace would just drive me home and let me out while keeping his headlights off and then whisper away without saying anything to Grandpa. This hope didn't even have a chance of being achieved.

"Martin's on his way to pick you up," Ace said.

He slapped me on the back and put his hat on.

"You called him?" I said. "Why did you call him?"

"What are you talking about, kid?" Ace raised a thick dark eyebrow. "It's late. Somebody, you know, like your grandpa shouldn't have to worry about you. If you were my kid, I wouldn't let you anywhere near this business."

I wanted to say something smart-alecky, but you don't smart mouth somebody like Ace.

"He deserves a little peace and quiet," Ace said, "after all he's been through over the years."

"Where's Alan?" I sat down in a chair. My head swam each time I reached down to put my shoes on.

"I sent him home," Ace said.

I sighed.

"Looks like you're going to have to go home with Gramps," he said. "There's worse things."

I shrugged.

"Well, I got things to do." Ace turned. "The night is still young, my friend. Cheer up. Your gramps is going to need you. He's got a big day coming up."

"I know," I said.

Normally I would have been thrilled that someone like

Ace even talked to me. Right now though, I wasn't very thrilled with anything. He left before Grandpa got there. I couldn't blame him. He was known for being kind of a loner. I didn't even know if he had a family. I'm pretty sure he didn't want to get mixed up in the little squabbles of mine. He could have at least put in a good word for me, though.

I finally got my shoes on. I suppose it was a good thing that I couldn't drive yet, because if I could have driven, there was no way I could have driven right then. I closed my aching eyes and took a deep breath through my swollen nostrils. The cut on my head stung a little, and the bandage was uncomfortable. I leaned back in the cold metal chair and crossed my arms. The dizziness, when it wasn't making me sick to my stomach, was actually a little comforting. It was like I always imagined it would have been like out on a boat with my dad. He was a great sailor. I could just sit back and relax and let the waves rock me to sleep. He could tell me stories, and we could eat grilled cheese sandwiches. I must have been a little hungry. I smacked my lips together. A lemonade would taste really good right now…

I was sailing away with my dad, when we kind of entered a fog. The sun went away, and it got colder. I opened my eyes. The boat was tied up to an old wooden dock. I noticed that I was in the boat all alone, and it suddenly got colder still. I smelled a harsh odor, like hairspray or something. I tried a few times to get out of the boat, but the rocking wouldn't let me even stand up. I crawled in the wet boat to the front, where I took hold of the rope and pulled myself over to the dock. The boards were slimy and black, but I made it up onto the shore.

I saw a city in front of me: New York City, or a dream of it. It seemed like a cardboard backdrop. In front of it all was the war. It was the Super War. I saw flickering lights and heard the screams. I saw flying people amongst the dying people. I saw impossible acts but smelled nothing more than the ozone. I suddenly realized why. It was like I was watching it all on TV. I remembered seeing this very scene in school. Then all the players changed. There was the Hurricane and Kid Mist fighting some green-tentacled thing and some woman with a green-tentacled thing on her head, or in place of her head. They all seemed very far away.

"Come down here with me," a voice said.

I turned around and saw a little changing booth down by the water's edge. Darlene the Dartette was all dressed up in her red outfit. Her long curly red hair framed her pretty face. She was standing in the doorway with the curtain drawn. Her leg was sticking out, and she was waving me over.

"Come down here with me," she said again.

The original Tricks heroes joined the Hurricane and Kid Mist, and the tentacled things merged together into a single green woman with long flowing hair. They all attacked her, but she repelled each type of attack with her hair, or with some sort of a force field. She wrapped Kid Mist up in her hair and threw him away from the group. She seemed to throw him right at me. Then she looked at me. Darlene screamed, and when I turned, she and the changing station were gone.

"Bring him to me," the woman commanded in a voice like space.

Kid Mist got up and started marching towards me.

"No!" one of the heroes called out. "Bring him to me."

It was the Trick named Billy. He was the one who had made the bargain that ended the war and all the powers.

Kid Mist froze. He looked back over each shoulder in turn, and then he looked right into me and melted into the sand. Then I was watching him melt into the sand on TV. I was sitting in a cold metal hospital chair in a dark room.

20

The lights came back on.

"I'll bring him with me," Grandpa told some woman behind the counter.

I stood up. That had been some dream, but already parts of it were fading into the background. Luckily, my dizziness was gone or I would have face-planted on the tile floor. Grandpa turned to me.

"Go to the car," he said, like he was just reading it off a sign on the wall.

"I was just helping him with the set up," I said. "Alan said he needed some help."

Grandpa bit his upper lip. He took in a breath and looked at my bandaged forehead.

"Go to the car," he said again in a calm, level voice.

I went to the car.

"What were you thinking?" he began once we were safely on the road.

"I told you..."

"Yes, but to go out on your own without even telling me where you were and what you were up to." He shook his head. "It's not so much that..."

"Alan needed my help," I said.

"Oh, Alan needed my help," he said back. "Baloney! Did Alan tell you not to let anyone know that you would be putting your life in danger?"

I figured it was a rhetorical question.

"Huh?" Grandpa said. "Did he?"

"No."

"Of course he didn't," he said.

I knew it was a rhetorical question.

"What am I going to do with you?"

"I don't know."

"You can't just go wandering off," he said. "You think just because you're fifteen you can wander off?"

"I didn't wander off."

"No," Grandpa said, narrowing his eyes, "wandering

21

off would have actually been a better thing. You went and helped destroy city property and got gassed."

A little laugh popped out of my mouth. It was just a little one, and I had no idea where it came from, probably from the words *got gassed*.

"So, this is funny?" Grandpa looked over to me. "Do I need to ground you? Would that be funny?"

"No."

"I can still ground you," he said. "Just because you're... You listen... You're at an important age. When your father was fifteen..." He stopped suddenly and sat there quietly.

"What?" I said. "What did he do?"

"I don't mind that you're doing the Tricks thing, Brand. I really don't. I mean, I was jumping around the city in colored underwear when I was younger than you, so I can't really gripe about that too much. I just need to know, you know? There were powers back then, and in some ways it was more safe and in some ways it was less safe, less predictable and more predictable."

"I know," I said.

"The not knowing is what gets me now." He stared out the front windshield. "I have a responsibility. How can I keep my responsibility if I don't know what you're doing?"

"I don't know." I hung my head and shrugged.

"How are you feeling?" He put his right hand on my shoulder.

"I don't know," I said. "Fine."

"Fine."

"Did you guys ever fight a green woman?" I looked up.

"A green woman?" Grandpa said. "I don't remember, really. It was so long ago. I was just a kid."

"I was having a dream..."

"There was a dragon woman who was scaly and dark

22

green." Grandpa peered into the sky in front of us. "She smelled so bad. Oh my goodness, did she stink. It was like she rolled around on a dirty bathroom floor. She was quick but she smelled so bad, you always knew where she was. What was her name?"

"I was having a dream..."

"Boy, did she stink."

"And there was a floating green woman in it," I said.

"Did she stink?"

"It was a dream."

"Mmm." Grandpa chuckled at his memory. "Why did you want to know about stinky villains?"

"And all the old heroes were there," I said, "fighting her, like on TV. She was light green and like a ghost and her hair floated around. You know what? She did kind of smell."

"How so?"

"Like hairspray or electricity, kind of," I said, "maybe ozone."

"I don't know what that smells like," he said.

"Hair spray?"

"Ozone."

"Kind of like hair spray," I said. "To me, anyway."

"Well, I don't remember a green haired hair-spray woman," he said, "but it was a long time ago. Things are different now."

"Are they?" I said.

Grandpa took his foot off of the gas and looked over to me. He totally took his eyes off the road.

"What do you mean?" he said.

"I mean, people are still the same, really," I said. "Down deep, people are still the same."

"But no powers," Grandpa said. "That's still different."

I kind of nodded and looked out the window.

"Hey!" Grandpa slapped his hand down on my leg and startled me. "Right?"

23

"What?"

"No powers still," he nodded his head at me. "Right?"

"I haven't seen anything," I said. "Have you?"

"Not that I know about." Grandpa went back to driving. "Not that anyone's told me."

"I figure it would be on the news if those Blackout Prophets were right," I said. "Wouldn't you?"

He didn't answer. He didn't smile. He just looked down the road like he hadn't heard my question. Of course, he didn't really need to answer me. There were no more superpowers, and my fuzzy dream was just the remnants of the gas and the medicine and the night. There was no need at all to answer. It was a rhetorical question.

CHAPTER THREE

The thing about the heroes we had now was that too many people romanticized them. They compared them to the superheroes we had back before the battle. They expected them to still wow them. They expected magic, when all that was left was illusion. That's how the Tricks were born. The villains figured out real quick just how human the heroes were. Bullets didn't bounce off. There was no super hearing, no super sight. Dead meant dead. The heroes needed an edge. They needed some magic. They needed new tricks. For a while it worked. The bad guys were caught off guard. They were fooled for a while. It still worked sometimes, but now the villains expected it. They got their own edge. They hired Roadies, flunkies that would do anything for a price or a fix or a threat.

Heroes started specializing in Tricks. They had secrets that they didn't want out. It didn't take much to sway a fight, and the difference in who won the battle could mean life or death. The bad guys knew that, too. Many heroes started getting darker. It was the rare hero that still maintained the old positive values. Grandpa said there never were old positive values, that that was all romanticized too. I always thought that was too bad. There ought to be something that separated the way the bad guys thought from the way the good guys thought.

So everyone started distrusting everyone else. The whole thing threatened to fall apart, because the public didn't know what to think and they were scared. Then, the SGHV—the Society for the Grading of Heroes and Villains—stepped in. They started checking out the heroes and letting the public know the truth. The heroes went along with it because it brought prestige and trust back to what they did. Later the villains joined up too. Having a high rating on the villain scale might have meant a longer prison stint if they got caught, but it meant more street cred while they were out. Heroes still didn't totally trust each other, though. They still held their secrets close. So teamups were rare and hero teams went totally away after a while. Soon the hierarchy just kind of developed naturally.

Ace was a real leader in the Trick world. He was a driver, which was a subset of the Trick position. Most drivers were just considered background helpers. Some people became drivers as a way to be close to the action but never be in any real danger. They took outside jobs, never really getting into the middle of the chase. There was a need for that kind of driver. Ace was not that kind of driver. He was also the only Grade A Trick I had ever met and one of the few who actually worked. He got out there and got his hands dirty. Before Alan got his work with The Red Dart, he wanted to work for Ace. Ace though, took on very few apprentices and wasn't accepting trainees at the time. Being able to ride in his cab the previous night and be a part of a case with Ace had Alan beaming.

Alan was quite a bit older than me. He was nearly twenty-four, while I was only fifteen. He really took to the Tricks life, skulking around seedy places, slipping in and out of spots while remaining hidden, setting up trip wires and delivering supplies. He was driving and dating and adventuring all the time. I still lived with my grandpa.

Of course, I got into this whole business because of my grandpa. He was the legendary Mist. Back when he was my age, he was a sidekick to Hurricane, the Weather

Master. When all the supers disappeared all those years ago, Grandpa was one of the few that didn't suddenly vanish. He had no powers except for some guns that Hurricane gave him, but even so, many powerless heroes had vanished. It was a mystery to add to all the other mystery surrounding that day.

Grandpa and Ace knew each other from way back, so it was only slightly surprising when Ace rang our front doorbell the next morning after our little adventure. Ace's father, also named Ace, drove for a group that Grandpa was in called Left Behind. It didn't last long; I think it was more of a therapy group. They didn't solve very many crimes before they split up. It was made up of a half dozen non-super-powered individuals that were at the big battle but didn't vanish. There was a lot of infighting in the group, I guess. They didn't get along well after such a trauma. Grandpa didn't like talking about it. Ace's grand-father, also named Ace, beamed away with all the other supers fifty years ago almost to the day.

"Ace is at my freakin' front door," I said to my cell phone.

"What..." Alan's sleepy voice responded. "Wait, what?"

"Ace is at my house."

"Ace? *The* Ace?"

"*The* Ace," I said. "I'm looking at him out my window right now. Mr. Forest from next door is staring at him over the fence."

"Is his cab there?"

"You think he walked?"

"I hardly got to talk to him last night. I've gotta go," I heard him say to someone on his end, then to me, "I'll be right there."

Alan was kind of my best friend. There were a few kids in school I hung out with but now that summer was here, I didn't see them much. Alan was my mentor when I started the Tricks program. We had some bad stuff in common. My mom died when I was born, and I was real sickly for a few years. Alan's mom died when he was thirteen. She had cancer. My dad died when I was four. He was in the Navy and died in a terrible storm at sea. Alan's dad died too, but in some ways it was worse. Alan's dad committed suicide a couple of years after his mom died. Sometimes I feel like I'm luckier because I never got to know my parents, and sometimes I think Alan's luckier because I never got to know my parents. My grandpa raised me. Alan went to a foster home for a few years and moved out as soon as he was able. For him, the Tricks life wasn't a legacy thing like it was for me. It was a thrill thing. If he had been a better fighter, he might have tried to be a hero.

"Martin," Ace's voice had none of his regular edge to it, "it's good to see you."

I threw on my clothes and raced down the stairs. Grandpa and Ace were still standing by the doorway. A dozen pamphlets were scattered across the entrance floor from when Grandpa opened the door. This was getting more and more common. A religious group called the Blackout Prophets was gathering in town for the fiftieth anniversary of Billy's Bargain. They believed that the powers would return on or around the fiftieth anniversary, and since Grandpa was one of the most widely known retired heroes from the old days, he was also highly targeted. We mostly just tried to ignore the prophets.

"...look tired." Ace said.

"Yes, well, I..." Grandpa looked over to me, "*we* had a long night last night. You want some coffee?"

"I never touch the stuff." Ace raised his chin at me. "*You* recover fast."

I'd forgotten all about my head injury, and it didn't even hurt anymore. Grandpa was wearing his old robe. He hardly ever wore that thing, especially in the morning.

28

Also, his socks were pink.

"The Day of the Pink Socks," I said in my announcer voice.

"It's not going to work," Grandpa said. "There's no way I'm wearing that thing."

"Oh, come on." Ace closed the door behind him. "Let's take a look."

Grandpa looked at me and then at Ace. He rubbed his chin and looked around. Finally he sighed and opened up his robe. He was wearing a pink and blue skintight suit that showed way too much of everything.

"Wow." Ace looked away.

"What is that costume?" I said, suppressing a giggle.

"It's supposed to be my original Mist costume. The city had it made for my speech." Grandpa closed his robe. "I'm not wearing it."

"What happened to the later one," I covered a smile, "the one with the jacket and the pockets?"

"That's what I said." Grandpa pointed at Ace. "I'm going to wear the jacket and some nice slacks and some comfortable shoes."

"I'll back you up," Ace said. "We'll tell them you tried."

"I'm going to go change." Grandpa turned. "I'm not even going to the rehearsal like this. Brand, give Ace here some coffee."

"I really don't drink it." Ace examined my face. "No, I mean it. You had a heck of a bump last night. I thought you'd have a shiner for sure. Did you get stitches?"

"Yeah." I patted the bandage. "It doesn't even hurt."

"You guys have it out last night?" he said.

"I don't want to talk about it." I looked down. "Grandpa's been all weird lately. I think it's the speech."

"Yeah, I remember when I turned fifteen, and everybody else got weird," Ace said. "Still, it's pretty cool that Martin gets to speak at the ceremony."

Grandpa was best known as a Grade A sidekick.

Most everyone who was left behind got a grade raise, but he gave it up shortly after Billy's Bargain. For a while, he had a go at being a hero, but could only make it to Grade B. Even that, he thought, was charity based on his past. Since he was at the big fight fifty years ago though, he and a handful of others were to speak at a huge event downtown where the fight happened. The whole world would be watching, and Grandpa had been a wreck about it for months. He was on edge and not eating right. He was half sick and grumpy all the time. He snapped at me for every little thing and would question everything I did like I was on trial.

"Hey," I said, "do you remember Alan Severs? He took one of your trial courses a few years ago."

"We visited last night," Ace said. "He's a good kid."

"You mind if he comes over?"

"Sure, but we'll probably be gone," Ace said. "This may just be a rehearsal, but it's all timed out and televised. Why do you think they have me driving him in?"

"Oh."

"Say," Ace smiled, "I heard you got a date last night from one of those Dartette girls."

I blushed. "I don't think she was serious."

"Alan seemed to think she was." Ace shrugged. "Since you're feeling so much better, you ought to come to the rehearsal. I bet Martin would like that. Even though the city's not acknowledging that The Red Dart was even at the Counterfeiter smack down last night, he'll be there, too. I think he's going to be part of the show. I bet your little girlfriend is there too."

"She's not my girlfriend," I said and then realized how rude I sounded. "I mean..."

"Calm down, kid." Ace's edge crept back into his voice. "I didn't mean anything by it."

Grandpa came back out with his jacket and slacks and comfortable shoes on. He kicked some of the Blackout Prophet pamphlets over in the corner by the half bath.

"Is it too late to have this jacket taken out?" he said.

"It's fine," Ace said.

"You sure you're not coming?" Grandpa asked.

"I don't know," I said. "Alan's coming over. Maybe we'll come by."

"Suit yourself." Grandpa turned his back. "Don't forget your I.D. so you can get in."

"And slap on a little aftershave, Romeo." Ace pointed at me.

"What?" Grandpa looked at Ace.

"Oh, nothing." Ace smiled and walked out the door.

Grandpa half waved over his shoulder and walked off. Our neighbor, Mr. Forest, stood staring from his yard as the men walked down the sidewalk. It was strange though; he wasn't staring at them. He was staring at *me*. As the cab drove off, Mr. Forest dropped his rake and stepped up on his back porch. All the while, he was looking right at me, without blinking or smiling or waving or anything. He was a weird old tubby balding man who was never friendly. I wondered what I had done to make him mad this time.

I went on in the house to get cleaned up. I went into the bathroom and stood in front of the mirror, bracing myself for what I was about to see. Above my blue eye, I grabbed the edge of the bandage and slowly pulled the sticky cloth off. A sprinkling of stitches fell into the sink as I revealed a completely healed forehead. It was amazing. I looked out the bathroom window and saw Mr. Forest glaring at me from his own window. He raised one gray eyebrow and closed the curtain.

CHAPTER FOUR

Alan took me to the practice speeches, and it was a virtual zoo. There were people and press and police everywhere. The rooftops were covered in cops and a few out-of-town heroes. It's surprising what a danger snipers could be when no one had superpowers anymore. Grandpa said it was something they never even used to think about before. Nowadays, there are a lot of Grade B villains who are snipers.

I couldn't get close to the stage, but we saw some trainers with some second generation dinosaurs. One of the most amazing things that happened when the powers disappeared was the return of the dinosaurs. Suddenly, they were discovered in deserts, in forests, in oceans, in the sky, just about everywhere. To this day, no one understood the connection. The dinosaurs returned. Old growth forests sprung up in a matter of weeks, wrecking farms and homes and even cities. The skies and the water became clean again. It was amazing. It was like the earth was making up for all that the universe lost. People usually chalked it up to Billy's Bargain. It was just part of what he got, I guess. No one knew, really. Some people thought it was a good trade. A lot of people argued that it was not. In the end, the debate usually came down to figuring that Billy knew more than we did, and there was nothing that we could do about it anyway, except try not to mess up the second chance we got with our planet. There were really no clues. It was strange that fifty years had gone by and human beings were no closer to figuring out the biggest mystery of all time than they were when it happened. Hundreds of people and entities vanished from the planet. Great herds of formerly extinct animals popped back into existence. Mighty forests grew practically overnight. Trillions of nasty man-produced chemicals and particles that were infecting the air and water just poofed away, and no one knew why. That was five decades ago, and there were some people who claim it never even happened. People were forgetting. The older generation that had experienced it was dying off. The whole thing was barely mentioned in the press anymore until about a year ago when everyone remembered that it was coming up on the fiftieth anniversary. Now, for the last few months, it was almost all that was talked about. No wonder everyone had descended on the city in the last few days. The big fight, Billy's Bargain, and the re-born earth all made up the last miracle. Everyone was hoping or fearing, dreading or cheering for another one.

It took us forever to walk through the crowd of spectators and worshippers and protesters. The crowd was absolutely filled with policemen. Everyone was expecting some kind of mob fight to break out, but except for a few minor skirmishes here and there, the police kept things relatively calm. I got to see The Red Dart and Gina and Darlene. The girls waved at us from a distance and walked on. They were all in costume. Alan and I actually found an empty table outside at the Tricks Cafe. We had to stand and stare at the two men and a woman who were sitting there drinking coffee and trying to visit over the murmur of the crowd. Eventually, they got creeped out enough to leave. The cafe was named after the old superhero group that people like Billy and Millard and Sarah and Phil were in. These guys were such iconic heroes that they just used their real names. At least, I assumed they were their real names. The Tricks all disappeared with almost every other hero and villain, leaving us normal people, a cleaned up world, and all sizes and shapes of dinosaurs.

After a while, we actually snagged a waiter and found something on the menu that wasn't sold out. We had to pay for water. Alan had a pickle wedge sandwich on a single piece of toast that was sliced into two thin pieces. I had a glass of room temperature water and two crackers with a bit of tartar sauce smeared on them. The people were eating the restaurant supplies faster than the restaurants could supply them.

"You gonna call her?" Alan looked up over his sandwich and waggled a pickle wedge at me.

"No!" I guffawed. I didn't even know what a guffaw was until I did it. "She was just being flirty."

"I don't think so." Alan smiled. "I think she thinks you're cute."

"I didn't say she doesn't have good taste," I said.

"Just bad eyesight."

"Ha. Ha."

My phone bleeped. It was a text from Darlene.

"How did...?"

"I texted her and told her to text you," Alan said.

On Ptrol 2 nyt, the text read, *meet @ Johnnys Laundry @ 8?*

"I know that place." Alan read the text upside down. "It's the hideout."

"Ohmygosh!" I said. "She wants me to go on patrol with her. Ohmygosh! I've never been on patrol. I'm just a part-time Trick. She's a real sidekick. Ohmygosh! What do I do?"

"You should probably answer her text." Alan put some cash on the table and covered it with his glass. He unfolded his sunglasses and put them on.

"What should I text?"

"How about, 'Hey, Sexy Fox, I can't stop dreaming about your long legs and your bright red hair...'"

"I'm not going to text that!" I said, although I *had* been

dreaming about those things. "That's not her real hair, is it?"

"Ask her," Alan said.

"Thaaat's nooot..."

"No!" Alan reached across and stopped me. "Don't really ask her that, for God's sake. Just say that sounds great, and you'll see her then."

"Right, right." I typed.

"Now, send it."

"Um..."

"Go ahead." Alan swooshed his hand at me.

I pressed send.

"No turning back now." He smiled.

"You'll be there too, right?" I was suddenly very sweaty. "What if I..."

"Actually, I have my own thing going on tonight." He put his phone in his shirt pocket. "How did you *not* get a black eye? It'd go perfect with your brown eye and your blue eye."

"You think that's something." I peeled off the band-aid, revealing my completely healed forehead. "Look at this. I wonder what was in that gas?" I said.

"Well, we'll just call you the Healing Man, I guess." Alan kind of smiled. Then he shrugged and stood and smiled again. "What girl wouldn't be impressed by that?"

"You don't suppose..." I bit my lip.

"What?"

"What if the rumors are true?"

"What rumors?" Alan leaned on the table.

"What if the powers really are coming back?" I said and touched my forehead.

"You've been watching too much TV," Alan smirked.

"How do you explain this?" I said.

Alan's face grew stern. I don't think he was kidding. "And the power is going to pick you?"

I opened my mouth, but nothing came out.

35

"I'm just kidding you." Alan waved his hand and looked away. "Probably alla' that blood and gas made it look worse than it really was. Heck, who knows what was in that stuff. Maybe we imagined the whole thing."

That really hurt my feelings. Even if he was just kidding, why wouldn't I get powers if they returned? I had just as much right as anybody else. "I guess."

"But perfect timing." He socked me in the shoulder. "Wouldn't want to spoil how cute you are, right?"

We walked around a while. It seemed like the day went on forever. We saw a collection of antique cars that were owned by heroes and villains. At one time, some of them actually had, like, magic powers. That all went away too. I never did find Grandpa. The crowd was just too thick. There was one point before we left when I thought there might be a problem out in the crowd. There was one of those flowing murmurs rushing like the wind through the spectators, or more like when everybody does the wave at a football game. I'd never actually heard one of these murmurs before, so it was kind of a neat experience. People were talking, their lips were moving, I could hear voices, but I couldn't understand anybody. It was like doing a play at school when they told all of us background crowd people to just keep saying "watermelon."

Even though I couldn't understand anything, there was a shift in the feeling. I felt a dread in my chest all of a sudden. Then, like little popcorn kernels popping, I started hearing one word over and over.

"Sniper."

"Sni-sni-snip-ppp-sniper..."

A few people pushed us up against a table. People were pointing at buildings and looking up to roofs. There was a swell of the crowd that washed through and pushed people down. Other folks yelled at them. Helping hands pulled people up before anyone was seriously hurt. I stepped on some guy's foot and swung around apologizing and screwing myself deeper into the crowd.

"Brand!" I heard someone calling my name over the crowd. I turned again and again.

"Brand!"

I saw green smoke wisp up over some people across the street. Every inch of the area was packed with people, so I couldn't really see what was causing the smoke. Then I realized that it wasn't smoke at all. I could just make out, if I jumped up and down, the fuzzy head of the green ghost woman from the basement. I closed my eyes and shook my head.

"Enough!" I heard myself say, even though I didn't say anything.

People in the crowd started fainting. I looked back over, and the ghost woman with the long flowing hair was not there any more. I looked around until I stepped on somebody else's toes.

"Ow!" Alan said. "Watch where you step."

"Sorry, sir, I..." I said. "Oh, you watch where *you're* going."

"Let's scoot," Alan said. "It'll take us forever to get out of this place."

"What about the sniper?" I said.

"First of all," he cupped his ear and spoke over the crowd, "there is no sniper. Some guy fell from a building or something, and now they can't find him."

"How about at the bottom of the building?" I said.

"You would think," Alan said. "Some people were saying it was a Fist."

"What would one of the Fists be doing out in the daytime," I said, "falling off a building?"

"Anyway," Alan said and pulled me by my sleeve, "let's get away from all this. I've been working on some stuff I want to show you."

"Show me later, okay?" I put my hand to my forehead. "I think I'm still not feeling too cool from that gas or something."

"Oh?"

"Yeah, I saw that ghost again."

"The white one or the green one?"

"The green one," I said.

"Yeah, that's the one to see." Alan smiled. "Look, I'll drop you off at home and stop by later, okay? I got something I need to talk to you about."

Eventually, Alan took me home. He had to go on some minor Trick work, picking up supplies. Plus, he had to get his things from the BB Tours. They had fired him, like he figured. He thought he might get off because of all the new tourists in town, but it turned out that there were a lot more drivers too.

I took two showers and contemplated shaving. Alan was coming by to take me to Johnny's Laundry, but he was just dropping me off. I figured it would be better than riding my bike, and Grandpa was way too busy to help. This was really a perfect first date. I didn't have to worry about awkward alone time, because the whole group would be there. It was more like a working date. It would be easier to get to know each other that way. Most patrols were pretty quiet. It was almost a show thing, really. There wasn't much chance we would actually stumble upon a crime in progress. I guess we could hear something on the scanner and go there. I didn't know if The Red Dart did that, though.

Police radios were a popular tool among heroes. Sometimes they were able to get to a crime before the police. And sometimes they were able to help out. It was a mixed bag, though. Sometimes the heroes were in the way. Most policemen did not like having unknown and untrained heroes messing things up. Sometimes people even got hurt or the bad guy got away. The legal system did not turn a blind eye when something like that happened, so both heroes and policemen treated the scanner carefully. Smart heroes always gave deference to the police. Some heroes were well known and widely used in police cases. They often received training and were even unofficially part of the force. I had heard of The Red Dart working with the police before. He must have had a good relationship with them. Every few years, though, there were recurring problems with police radios. The bad guys weren't stupid. Well, many of them weren't stupid. They would jam the stations if they could get their hands on the equipment, or they would send out false information to get the heroes on the other side of town from where the real crime was taking place. All in all, it was a delicate situation.

When I finally got to talk to Grandpa later in the day, he seemed real concerned about my date, about me going out with a sidekick, and said we'd have to check her out. When I told him who she was though, he seemed relieved. He said that The Red Dart could help my career and send me in the right direction, and some more stuff about young people and discipline and things going to heck in a hand basket, and how The Red Dart was going to put things right, etc. I was too nervous to hear it all. I was even more nervous than the day before when I was on a bus getting ready to ram into a brick wall. I couldn't eat a thing all day. My stomach was too busy doing somersaults. I picked at my fingernails.

Finally, a knock came at the door. When I opened it, no one was there.

"Is Martin around?" a voice whispered.

"Alan?" I searched the porch. It was still daylight, but it was starting to get dark. "No, he's having dinner in the city."

"Good," Alan stepped out from behind a bush. He was wearing a black suit, a black costume.

"What in the world?"

"Whaddya think?" He posed.

"What's going on?" I looked him up and down.

"I'm going to be a driver," he said.

"No way!" I said. "You're a Trick. You can't be a driver. That's a step down."

"Are you kidding me?" Alan smoothed his leather jacket. "You tell that to Ace."

"We're supposed to be a team." We stepped into the house. "How am I supposed to be a Trick without you? I thought we were partners."

"Look, Brand," Alan put his hand on my shoulder, "you're like a little brother to me, but I have to run my own life. You'll understand when you get older."

"Bull!" I pulled away. "Is this about Ace?"

"No."

"We saw Ace last night, and now you want to be a driver."

"No."

"Bull."

"We've been planning this for a long time." Alan got right in front of me. "I thought you'd be happy for me. We've got a car and everything."

"Who, we?" I asked. "And since when could you afford a car?"

"We redid one of The Red Dart's..."

"You're driving for The Red Dart?"

"God, no." Alan rolled his eyes and flipped his straight black hair up under his driving cap. "Listen..."

"Oh, good grief!" I threw up my hands. "You're teaming up with Gina. Does The Red Dart know?"

"Listen!" he shouted.

I jerked back.

"I thought maybe you could help me," he said, pointing at himself.

"You want me to be your Trick?" I asked.

"Well..." Alan sucked in through clenched teeth, "I

40

don't really need a Trick, per se."

"Then what are you saying?"

"I'm saying I don't need a Trick," he looked at the floor and then up to me again, "but I could really use a good Roadie."

CHAPTER FIVE

"So you're just going to not talk to me?" Alan's eyebrows rose up under his bangs as we drove away from the house.

I crossed my arms and said nothing.

"It's not like I'm going to do anything bad."

I said nothing louder.

"Well, I can't tell you anything else if you're not going to be my Roadie."

"So, we're not even friends anymore?" I glared at him. My ears felt hot.

He started to say something.

"You idiot!" I interrupted. "You can't be a bad guy! And how could you figure I would ever be a Roadie?"

"I'm not gonna be a bad guy." Alan thumped the steering wheel of his old clunker. "Don't you get it? There's just too many rules. I need to get out there, Brand. I'm not a kid anymore. I need to make a name for myself."

"I think there are just as many rules on the other side." I squinted at the lights outside.

"No, man," Alan said. "You just got to be there and get away. That's it. I can do that. You make enough getaways, you move up quick. Once you move up, you can make your own rules."

"I don't even want to go tonight," I huffed. "Take me back home."

"Aw, man, I'm not trying to ruin your first date." Alan went to sock me in the shoulder, but I moved. "C'mon, just forget about it tonight. We'll talk about it later, if you want to."

"Just take me home."

"No, I'm not gonna do that." he looked straight ahead. "Darlene has been looking forward to this, and Gina would kill me. Look, just don't say anything, okay? Let's talk about this later."

I said nothing again.

"Darlene's a cute girl," Alan said. "Don't let her outgoing appearance fool you. She was real nervous about giving you her number and texting you. Gina had to talk her into it."

"Swell."

"No, dummy." I could tell he rolled his eyes, even in the dark. "I mean, she was interested, but kind of shy about it. She just puts on a brave face when she's a Dartette. I don't think she's done much dating either."

"I haven't done ANY dating."

"Well, who knows," Alan puffed his cheeks, "maybe she hasn't either. I don't know."

"Whatever."

"Listen," Alan said as he pulled into the parking lot, "don't talk to Gina about this driver thing, okay? I thought you would be in. I didn't know you were gonna get all... well, whatever. Just... It's important, okay?"

I started to open the door, but Alan grabbed my arm really hard.

"OKAY?" he leaned over.

"Geez, OW!" I pulled my arm away. "Fine, Geez. What's the deal?"

"I'm serious."

"Fine, whatever." I slammed the door behind me.

I didn't see any lights on in the building or any cars in the parking lot and was just turning around to get back in the car, when Alan drove right off. He stopped at the road like he was coming back, but when I took a couple of steps towards him, he took off.

Now the parking lot was getting pretty dark. Johnny's was obviously closed, and probably not even a real laundry. It was a one story little rectangle with a red roof and bars on the windows. There was a sign in the front window that read *Johnny's Laundry* with a giant J and a giant L together on the top and the other letters going down the sign at a diagonal. The sign itself was crooked, though, and the diagonal letters looked almost straight. The dim yellow street light in the parking lot was filled with dead bugs and would flicker occasionally. I could hear faint voices around the building, like arguing, and figured that's where I was supposed to go. I kicked a brown paper bag out of my way and an empty plastic cup that was behind it. I should have realized that a secret headquarters wouldn't be very obvious. As I approached the building, the voices stopped.

"Hello?" I called out in a voice that was much more quiet than I had intended, "I, uh..."

I looked back at the road again and when I turned back around to the laundry, I was grabbed by a large black man in a gold sparkly costume and high heels.

45

CHAPTER SIX

"It's just the kid," The Red Dart said as he pulled his red dart gun away from my head. "You can let him down."

"I wanna see for myself." The man in gold lifted me right up over his head and examined me in the yellow light. "Yeah, I guess."

He dropped me, and I fell flat on my butt. I actually said *oof*!

"Sydnafly?" I looked up.

"Yeah." He nearly struck a pose. His muscles had muscles.

"Wow." I got up and brushed off the seat of my pants.

"Sure," the Red Dart holstered his gun, "*he* gets a wow."

"I...I..."

"DD's inside." The Red Dart pointed. "Go on around back and stay out of things."

I jogged towards the building, and they started talking again. When I looked back over to them, they stopped talking and looked at me. Sydnafly put his hands on his hips. The Red Dart gave me a backhanded wave. I made my way around to the back door.

Sydnafly was big news right now. If people weren't talking about the fiftieth anniversary, they were talking about Sydnafly. He had quite an online following. His real name was Sidney Feldspar and he was an actual legacy hero. He struggled for years as a Grade D and Grade C hero. He was mostly flash, riding on his forefathers' name. His grandfather, the second Sydnafly, disappeared with Billy's Bargain. His great-grandfather, or great-uncle, or something, was the first Sydnafly. He changed his name from Sidney Feldstein to Sidney Feldspar. He had these magic accordion-like wings under his arms that actually let him fly. He was killed, though, by a villain named the Red Rat.

Of course, *this* Sydnafly couldn't actually fly. No one could these days, except a few gliding heroes and villains and some with jet packs. This Sydnafly had been on all the talk shows recently for being promoted to Grade B. It was a rare thing to be promoted. In most cases, it was generally accepted that a hero or villain needed three super human-like acts to be promoted to Grade B. They had to make an actual difference. In some ways, that was the hardest promotion. To be Grade D, you just had to say you were Grade D. To be Grade C, you had to dedicate a serious amount of time and effort as your alter ego. For Grade B, though, you had to dedicate your life to your alter ego. A high percentage of active Grade B heroes and villains were at least a little crazy, or eccentric, as many said, but mostly just crazy. Grade B was a full-time career. At this level, you had to demonstrate a personal hierarchy.

Sydnafly had been searching for several months for some full-time Tricks. He and some others had a camp up in the north part of the state. For a while they even held open tryouts. First, there was a background check, then the person had to demonstrate some kind of helpful skill or background. They were looking for professionals, Tricks, and even Hangers-On. I had even considered trying out, but Grandpa said I was too young, and it would mess with my school work, and maybe next year or something. That was why I knew so much about Sydnafly—that and the fact that he was all over all media.

Another sign that he was getting popular was his

catch phrase. Most heroes associated having a catch phrase with Grade A status. It wasn't something they really used in a real fight, but all the really famous Grade A heroes and villains had one for a while—until it got tiresome. Lately, Sydnafly's catch phrase had been seen in all the graffiti and T-shirt shops. It wouldn't be long until they were using it on the news. It was "You got DAT right!"

I never learned what his third super human act was. His first was to calm a riot at a discotheque. A new giant disco ball blinded some dancers who fell into other partiers. One thing led to another and a brawl broke out. Sydnafly used his agility and cunning to calm the mob down. He grabbed the microphone and shut down the music. I guess it was pretty awesome. There were some important people at that particular party. His timing was right, and he caught the notice of the SGHV. Not long after that, he stopped an armed robbery of a convenience store. There were two guys with guns, and he stopped them without anyone getting hurt. Well, he DID throw one gunman through a plate glass window, but even the cops said it was self defense. A lot of people said he finally grew up, and that excellence was in his blood. Now, here he was teaming up with The Red Dart.

"Um, Brand?"

I had walked right past the open door with Darlene standing in it. She was so beautiful, I couldn't even say anything. She wore a crimson suit that had a small half-cape in the back like the other Dartettes. Her outfit didn't have the plunging neckline of Gina's or the pleated slacks and padded shoulders of—whatever the oldest one was named—but she didn't need them.

"Your hair..."

"You like it?" She smiled and twisted her long hair between her fingers.

"It's brown," I said.

"Of course it's brown." She touched my arm and pulled me inside.

"No, yes," I said. My arm felt warm where her hand was. "I mean, no, yes."

"I wear a wig in the field," she said.

I stood quietly.

"I like your eyes." She smiled at me. "I never noticed, you know...before..."

I think I smiled. Sometimes I liked having different colored eyes, one brown and one blue. It was a good talking point when I couldn't think of anything else to talk about. Sometimes, I felt too conscious about it. Right now, I blushed.

"I'm sorry. Did I...? I mean, the light is better than..." She cleared her throat. "This is our hideout," she waved her arm and looked away, "our headquarters, or as Dart calls it, the workshop. We get all our stuff ready here, and we have rooms in the side."

She tilted her head and looked around. There were several laptop computers, a long row of benches with parts on them, piles of unfinished arrow shafts, lots of red paint, two vans, a cool car and a couple of motorcycles. Tools and stuff hung on the walls everywhere. All in all, it was clean but a little cluttered and well lit. It was kind of what I expected, actually.

"Hey, kiddo," Gina turned around from a computer and put her hand over a telephone microphone in front of her mouth.

I completely and actively ignored her.

"So, do you make your own arrows?" I pointed at the stack on a bench.

"Oh, I wish," Darlene said. "I've been trying, and I'm getting better, but Wilma makes most of those. I even hope to make my own bow some day. You should see the lab in the basement, though."

49

"What kind of a lab?"

"Well," Darlene looked over to a door on the opposite side of the room, "Dart makes all the chemicals he puts in his darts. I even help him. He's taught me everything."

"And you wouldn't brag about it, would you?" Gina smiled and said.

"Hey, I'm really good at it." Darlene shook her head at me. "I get straight A's in chemistry."

"That's because you're home schooled," Gina said.

"A's are A's, Gina," she said then turned back to me. "The Red Dart doesn't just give out A grades. You have to earn them. I could take the orange out of your finger-nails. That's probably from the Austrenaline gas at the Counterfeiter's base. It's mostly just a stain."

That was embarrassing. I forgot that the color wouldn't come off my fingernails. Good thing I was able to get the green off of my face. I'm glad she didn't just think I was eating Cheezee Cheeze Chips. "Is there going to be a team-up tonight?" I asked, purposely changing the subject.

"What do you mean?" She smiled ever so slightly. The curve of her lips were accentuated by her light pink lipstick.

"The Red Dart and Sydnafly." I pointed. "They're out in the parking lot."

Darlene looked over to Gina, who tapped a switch on a keyboard. Their faces got serious. A gray picture of the parking lot popped up on the screen, but the heroes were not there.

"There." Gina pointed to a some blurry movement on the screen.

"Wonder why he was here?" Darlene leaned into the screen to look and nearly brushed my arm. "They're not exactly buddies," she said to me.

"What did they say?" Gina asked me.

I paused. I was still in no hurry to talk to her. I didn't

agree with what she and Alan were planning.

"Well?" Darlene said.

"What's going on here?" Gina spun her chair around.

"Got the police band turned down again, girls?" The Red Dart burst into the room.

The girls immediately jumped. Gina tapped away on the keyboard, calling up the city map. Darlene leapt for the radio and turned it up.

"DD, get your wig on." The Red Dart looked at the computer. "We're heading out as soon as possible."

"Where?" Gina asked.

"Are we having a team-up?" I asked.

The Red Dart looked at me. He put his hands on his hips.

"You're a Trick," he said to me as he examined the darts in his gun. "Load those bags in the van."

I wanted to remind him that Tricks didn't do loading. Tricks delivered things and set traps. Sure, there was loading involved, but Grade B heroes were supposed to have regular people for that. Instead, I picked up the bags and put them in the van.

"Wilma back yet?" The Red Dart looked around.

"No, but she..." Gina put her mask on.

"We go without her, then." The Red Dart waved his red gloved hand in a circle and looked at his red watch. "You stay here, kid."

"Huh!" Darlene huffed and crossed her arms. "He's supposed to go with us tonight."

"He was going on PATROL with us," The Red Dart said. "This is different."

"We have a fire?" Gina zipped up her long red boots.

"Sydnafly is already on his way." The Red Dart turned Darlene towards the van. "We have to get there quick."

"I'm not going without Brand." Darlene grabbed the edge of a bench.

"Fine," he pushed us both towards the van, "he can

51

stay in the Dartmobile."

We both ran up to the side door. Darlene stopped and looked at me.

"After you," I said.

She giggled and hopped in.

"Hold on, RD." Gina held her bow in front of The Red Dart. "What's going on?"

"We need to get to the new hospital," he said. "The Montbloom one."

"What's the big hurry to get to an unbuilt hospital?"

"There has been a report." He turned his back on us and lowered his voice. "There has been a report of powers. Someone is using actual superpowers."

CHAPTER SEVEN

I think she did it on purpose. When Darlene (who says I should call her DD) got into the van, she sat right in the middle of the seat. So, I got into the back seat.

"Sit here," she said and patted the seat next to her. So, I climbed up in the middle seat next to her. After that, I don't remember anything The Red Dart said for most of the trip.

Darlene wore a very slight perfume. "I like your smell," I said. "I mean, you know, you smell good."

The Red Dart looked in the rear view mirror at me.

"I can't wear anything stronger than this," she said. "It lets the bad guys know where we are."

"Well, I like it."

"Thanks."

I sat so close to Darlene that the edges of our feet touched. I noticed it when we took a sharp turn, and I had to strain every muscle in my body to keep my foot in place. I was kind of embarrassed at first, until I realized that her foot never moved either, and she was working on the feathers on an arrow at the time. When she finished, she slowly slid her hand down to her leg and let it slide over to the side where the back of her hand was actually touching the side of my thigh. I took a deep breath and looked out the window and put my own hand up against the back of her hand. We hardly said two words to each other for quite some time. The lights outside whizzed by, but I mainly just looked at her boot. Occasionally, I would glance up to her face. She was usually looking out the window.

"Put your gloves on," Gina called back to Darlene. "You got your trip arrows lined up?

"Yeah," Darlene reached into a pouch in her quiver at her feet, "I know what to do, Gina."

I gave Gina a look. She rolled her eyes. She'd been spending too much time with Alan.

"Get your head in the game, girls," The Red Dart said. I wondered if he was their father. Did they call him Dad when they weren't in costume? I don't know why I never thought of it before. It would be kind of neat to go on patrol with your dad. Was this a family business? I'd have to ask Darlene later.

"Now, listen." The Red Dart adjusted his rearview mirror to see us better and he straightened his red domino mask. He didn't look like the girls, that was for sure. His nose was chubby and pushed up. He had freckles all over his face and neck. Unless he dyed his eyebrows to match, his hair and eyebrows were naturally almost cartoon red. "This is uncharted territory," he said and took a drink of bottled water. "One of the Fists—they're saying Gold Fist because of the pair of painted gold sunglasses found at the scene—is halfway up the unfinished Montbloom Memorial Hospital. He's supposedly controlling machines with his mind. He's got giant cranes and spotlights and microphones and maybe even a hostage. There are so many people in town tonight that a crowd is already gathering. He's demanding news crews, which always makes things harder. I figure Sydnafly will be glad to grandstand for them. This will allow us some 'quiet time'."

Quiet time was what a lot of heroes called the time before the fight, when they could prepare or set traps, or bring in reinforcements. It was much needed and appreciated. Without quiet time, many heroes would get killed. Tricks were often called in during quiet time. Plans were

54

discussed, if there was enough time. Supplies were distributed. I was surprised that he didn't call anyone in. This could have been a huge deal. The timing was certainly perfect, right before the big memorial. Why would he want to take chances? Maybe he figured that he and Sydnafly could handle things.

The Red Dart had a variety of tools to work with. The Dartettes were well trained in many aspects, especially shooting. He would communicate to them with sign language or tapping or code. He had lights and some smoke and ropes and knives. He had different kinds of darts for different kinds of jobs. His favorites by far, though, were his knock out darts. He couldn't carry everything everywhere—that was what we Tricks were for—but having sidekicks was a way to use less external help.

"Brand," he startled me, "you know your directions?"

"You mean, like..."

"We are heading north now." He pointed forward.

"Look where the moon is." Darlene tapped a gloved finger on the window.

"I'm not sure what we're going to get into," he continued. "I'll leave this radio on in the van. Gina, give him the flashlight from the glove box."

"The red one?" Gina smiled.

The Red Dart looked at her.

"Right," she said.

"We studied this kind of stuff at Tricks camp," I said as I took the red flashlight from Gina, "our directions and stuff."

"Brand, you are Quark," he said. "If I call for Quark, you know it's you. Got it?"

I nodded.

"Got it?" he said again.

"Got it.' I snapped to attention. I got the feeling he was used to giving orders. Successful heroes were entrepreneurs, after all. They had to know how to run the

55

business.

"Then I'll say the floor number and what side of the building I'm on. Yes?"

"Yes."

"4N means, what?" he asked.

"Fourth floor on the north side." I looked at the girls. "Why don't you just say a room number?"

Gina looked out the front window.

"It's an unfinished building." The Red Dart actually sounded very patient. I felt like an idiot. "There may not be numbers. Also, if someone is listening in, we don't want them to know right where we are. It's not exactly a genius code to begin with."

"Okay."

"Gina is G-Girl. DD is Crimson..."

"I picked that one," Darlene smiled.

"And I'm RD." He studied the road up ahead as we approached. "You bring the bags if I or either of the girls call."

DD took some long breaths in through her nose and out through her mouth. Gina tested some radio gear on her head and in the van.

There were already cars and cops and lights and media everywhere. People were carrying signs. Where did they get signs already? It was like they came to the city just to protest. That was probably true for some of them. Just like there was a whole industry built up around heroes and villains, there was also a whole industry built around fighting the entire concept.

"I could really use a driver," The Red Dart said, under his breath.

Gina and I both snapped our eyes on him.

"I'm going to have to park out here in this alley." He turned the van. "It's not ideal, but it will do. Open this door for no one, Brand. I don't care if it is your own mother. No one gets in, and you come only if I or one of the girls call for you. What's your code name?"

My mind went blank.

"Quark," Darlene said.

"Right," I said.

"That is the password for tonight, ladies and gent." The Red Dart smiled and pulled the key back. "Let's go check out this guy's powers."

CHAPTER EIGHT

There was an explosion, and I was thirsty for lemonade. That's what I was thinking. Then I thought, "What's the deal with lemonade?" Then I smelled the electric ozone high up in my sinuses and then I remembered my earlier dream.

In the dream, I sat on the asphalt in the middle of the highway as the sun was either going down or coming up. It seemed important to know if it was going to be morning or night. I must have been dreaming again, because it was just night a minute ago, and I was with Darlene at the hospital. It was hard to breathe. My shirt was wet, and there was a long translucent green tentacle of hair protruding all the way through my body and out through my chest. I really hoped I was dreaming, because otherwise this would be a bad thing.

I stood up on the road and turned in a circle. I felt somebody behind me no matter which way I turned, but I didn't see anything but road and grass. I took a step forward, and there she was, the green woman. She was just there suddenly, right in my face, nose to blurry nose.

"Brand," she said like it was a weird word to say, "Wah-wah, wah. Wah-wah..."

It sounded like she was talking through a balloon, all muffled. My ears rang.

"Wah!" she said and threw me down the road.

I fell and screamed in pain as her hair pulled out of my chest.

"Now do you hear me?" She floated about a foot off of the ground.

"Ah... ah..." I huffed. That was all I could say at the time.

"I need to know if you are quiet or if you are making noise," she said in her strange accent. It didn't seem like she was from around here. Of course, there were more obvious signs other than the accent.

"Quiet or making noise?" she demanded. "Hmmm... quiet, I think."

"Who?" My mouth watered, and I spit on the road.

"See?" She floated closer to me. "You do not even recognize me. Say my name, little boy."

"Who are you?" I rolled over on my back. "I've never seen you before except in my dreams."

"Yes!" she said and raised a blurry finger. "That is how I am usually only seen."

I thought she might have smiled.

"I am the Dream Based Aspect of..." she paused as if she wanted me to fill in the blank. "You do not know my name, little boy?"

I did not know her name.

"This is the best you could imagine?" she said. "You are far from your roots, from your home. You must stay quiet."

The darkness at the edge of the grass throbbed like it was trying to press in.

"Speak!" she said. "Say the words that you will be quiet. Tell yourself. Convince yourself. Command your-self."

"I don't know..." I scooted myself back to the edge of the grass and sat up, "I don't know what's going on."

"Yes, you are the little boy," she said. "You must keep quiet so you do not know."

"I already do not know," I said.

"Yes."

"...yes."

"Good."

59

"Good?"

"Yes."

"I don't know," I said. "Can I wake up now?"

A big truck drove past me. Well, the *space* of an eighteen wheel semi truck and trailer zoomed past me, and plowed right into the green woman. I say the space of an eighteen wheeler because the vehicle wasn't actually there until it was suddenly there, and because it honked as it roared past. It must have been one of those dream things that happen in the subconscious. I never even really saw a truck, as such, as it went by, just a white space where a truck should be. It didn't seem like a real truck.

The green woman sure felt the realness of it, though. She was thrown way past all the grass and into the darkness beyond.

"Need a hand?" a voice said.

A kind of pear shaped man with greasy hair reached down for me. I recognized him immediately.

"Billy?" I said and stood up.

"No," Billy said, "and you would do well to remember that. I'm just a visualization of who you want me to be."

"'Cause it's a dream, right?" I said. "You're just a figment of my imagination."

"No and yes." He smiled. He looked more familiar than just a figure I had seen on TV. "Although, it's funny you should say that."

"Dad?" I said.

The sun was behind him now, and he sort of seemed to shimmer and change shape.

"You'd do better with Billy," he said.

The green woman shot out of the shadows as if she was fired. She slammed into Billy, and he evaporated into a puff of smoke. She turned in mid flight and hovered above me. Her fists were clenched.

"Who was that?" she said.

60

"Billy?" I said. "Just a dream, maybe?"

She landed in the road and ducked down slightly. She looked around wildly in all directions.

"He is being quiet!" she screamed to the skies. "Barring that being," she looked me straight in the eyes, "I must find other ways."

"Is there, like, a secret you want me to keep?" I said. "Is that what all this is about?"

"I can kill you." She glided towards me. "I can kill you, and you won't even know you are being dead. To save those you love, I can be killing you, and you may be wanting me to."

She wrapped a tentacle of hair around my wrist, and I pulled away. I backed into the grass a couple of steps. From nowhere, there was a deep ravine behind me that led off into the dark.

"I can be making your loves so dark," she said. "They will be loud and bad, and they will hate the light. Oh, so villainous, they will be. They will gnash at you and slay you. I will wither their souls. I could blind them from light. Old loves, new, many or few, I can tame them to me. They will not hear your loudness."

"You know, if you want him to be quiet," the Billy dream reformed in the road, "you should keep your own mouth shut."

"He is being quiet," she said to him.

"He is in that state, yes," Billy said.

"I can make him dead," she hissed.

"You will shut up," he said.

I wanted to interrupt, but I really didn't want to draw any attention to myself.

"I made his father dead," she smiled.

"What?" I grabbed a strand of her floating hair. "You did what?"

"She's lying," Billy walked up to us. "Don't listen to her. She did nothing of the sort."

"I made him DEAD!" She pushed me backwards into the ravine.

I fell into the darkness, felt it clutching at my throat.

"No, wait!" I clawed at the air. "You answer me!"

I could see them falling up away from me.

"I'll find you," I said as the darkness won over me.

I landed hard on my back, and the dream was knocked clear out of my head.

CHAPTER NINE

I was cold. I was laying on wet rocks and rubble and sand. It was pitch black, my head pounded, and I had dropped my flashlight.

"Darlene?" I called out.

Earlier that night, after The Red Dart and the Dartettes left the van, I moved up to the front seat. After a few minutes, the radio crackled to life.

"Testing, testing," The Red Dart's voice whispered, "RD to Quark, you copy? Over."

"Quark copies," I said. "I mean, over. I copy, over."

"At BS," he said. "over."

BS? Oh, yes, basement, south.

"Okay," I replied, and added, "over."

Right now, it was later in the night. I had no way of knowing how much later because I had been knocked unconscious. My ears were full of sand. I crawled through broken glass and iron rods. I missed the soft van seat I had maybe a few minutes ago—I decided to assume it was a few minutes ago. I didn't dare stand up. I just knew I would fall head first into something pointy if I did: broken glass, torn metal, busted concrete blocks. I bumped something with the side of my hand, and like a miracle, a flashlight popped on right next to me. It was the red one I had dropped. I shined it to where I had been laying. There was dark liquid spattered all over where my body had been. Was that oil? Was it blood? I felt all over myself, and found no injuries, only the pliers that Darlene had shoved into my pocket when the floor collapsed. There was liquid all over my back, and it was blood, but it couldn't have been mine. I was all right.

"Darlene?" I called out again. "Crimson? DD?"

Earlier, about thirty minutes after The Red Dart left the van, I heard booming noises outside. I even thought I felt the van shake. I wanted to get out of the alley to see what was going on, but I knew I was supposed to stay put. A group of scared people rushed by. I wondered what this guy's power was. The very thought was incredible.

"Quark!" Gina's voice came over the van radio. "Bring supplies. 3SE, 3SE, come through BSE..."

"Only one bag," The Red Dart's voice interrupted, "the one with the blue stripe. It's lighter, and you need to hurry."

I grabbed the bag with the blue stripe, flung open the door, and headed out of the alley with my flashlight and my anxieties..

That was then. Now, stuff was falling or dripping on me. The flashlight barely helped. I called out once more, and heard DD from behind. She seemed to be far away. That made no sense. We were together when things fell apart.

"Brand?" her voice carried over a slight rumbling sound, "I mean, Quark?"

My light searched across the rubble. Either the ceiling was gone, or it was way above me. I thought I was getting quick glimpses of the moon, but it could have been anything in this dust. Large girders were thrown everywhere like a pile of straws that was hit by a tornado. Aways away, sticking her arm out and waving from behind columns of upright girders, I barely made out DD's hand, swinging around in the dust of my light.

"I'm coming." I rushed and stumbled and climbed to reach her. "Are you okay?"

Earlier in the evening, when I had first gotten out of the alley, I was surprised to see so many people and

64

lights. There must have been dozens of Blackout Prophet fanatics waving signs and screaming at the scene in front of them. I raced around the outside of the crowd. All eyes were fixed on the action happening up on the skeleton of a building up ahead. All around there were upside down cars on fire, and metal debris. Two giant cranes on the roof were swinging wildly. They were smashing into each other and the beams of the building. They were knocking debris down on the crowd. Firemen were up on ladders trying to get to the action and save people. The police were attempting, in vain, to corral the crowd and get them to leave.

I saw Sydnafly up on the building. He was fighting someone. It looked like he was fighting two people. It was hard to see. He glittered in the light. The other person or people were harder to see. Something made Sydnafly lose his balance, and he fell off the front of the building. You could hear almost everyone call out at once. Then it was the quietest I had heard it. When he caught himself on a rope, all the craziness broke out again.

Sydnafly was hanging from a beam by his arms just below two men in light brown suits that covered their whole body except for their head. Each had dark boots on and a big fist painted on his chest. One fist was reddish, and the other was gold. The gold-fisted one was also wearing gold sunglasses and had a belt with other gold sunglasses hanging from it. He seemed to be a little bulkier than the other one. The two men fought while they balanced on a girder that jutted out into the sky several stories up. I wasn't sure who was who. I mean, I didn't know who was the bad guy here. Was Sydnafly fighting both of them? If so, why were they fighting each other now?

My mind reeled even now as I climbed up the remains of the broken building.

"I'm stuck," DD said through the girders. "They fell

65

like a teepee. Every one of them missed me. It was like I had a force field protecting me. I just have a cut on my shoulder. Have you seen, Gina?"

"Hnnng!" I pushed on a beam that wouldn't budge.

"No, I just found my flashlight.

"Dartette!" DD called. "G-Girl, are you there?"

"G-Girl!" I hollered and looked around. "How are we going to get out of here?"

"How am I going to get in here?" I had thought earlier, as I made my way through the throng.

"Quark!" I had heard Darlene call to me. She was at the side of the building in the drainage for the basement. "Down here. It's quicker."

I half stumbled down the slick clay embankment until I got to her.

"RD sent me to get you," she grabbed my arm. "I'll lead you, or I can just take the bag myself."

"I can take it." I clutched the bag. "It's a Trick's job."

"Follow me," she said, and a large smile came over her whole face. I could even see it under her mask.

We made our way up on dew damp metal stairs with no railing. Darlene's voice was drowned out by the chanting crowd, the police sirens and P.A system, and of course the violent banging and swaying of the entire building.

When we reached the third floor, we saw a flashlight running at us from across the building. The whole place was really banging at this point. Darlene and I both shone our lights on the figure. It was Gina. She was yelling something, but we couldn't hear.

"...OUT!" she screamed as she got closer. "Get out! Get out, now!"

Darlene reached into my bag and pulled out some electrical pliers.

"What about..." was all she could say before there was a bright electrical explosion and a feeling of swaying

66

on a huge swing.

Darlene put her arms around me, and dropped the pliers. Then, the floor was gone. We didn't see what happened to Gina.

"I don't see G-Girl." I held DD's hand through her cage. "I don't know where..."

My light came across something, and I took a step away.

"Brand?" DD's grip tightened. "Brand, what's going on?"

"Hold on a minute," I said and let go.

I saw something swinging in the distance. I had to concentrate to see.

"Hold on." I stumbled closer.

"Don't leave me." DD flailed her arm around in the dark.

"Oh, my." Things became clearer. "Oh, my. Oh, my."

Hanging by one leg, well above my head, was Gina. She was unconscious. At least I hoped she was just unconscious. A metal cable had wrapped around her knee, and her bow that was over her shoulder, had caught a concrete outcropping. She was just hanging there, but I didn't know for how much longer. Her head was pointed down about forty-five degrees, and blood ran down her back and dripped off of her shoulder.

"G-Girl!" I shouted at her.

I thought I saw her move. I thought I saw her breathe, but she didn't say anything.

"You must be Brand," I heard a pained voice say from the dark.

I swung my light to the sound and saw the figure of Gold Fist coming out of the rubble just a few feet away from me. He was holding his left elbow, and his left wrist was bent out wrong. White padding tufted out of cuts in his costume. He had rubber or leather sticking out and dangling from his outfit. One lone pair of broken, gold colored sunglasses dangled from his belt.

"Who are..." I backed up a step as he tried to back-hand me. "How do you know me?"

Gold Fist walked right up to me. "Grim kept asking about you." He grabbed my hand that was holding the flashlight. The light shone on his face. He gritted his teeth. Sweat and blood and filth covered him.

"Grim..."

"What's the deal, kid?" He held me up as tall as I could stand and jerked me around like a doll. "How'd you know about this? How'd you find Grim Fist?"

An arrow hit a stone block next to us and ricochetted away. Gold Fist looked up towards DD and threw me aside.

"Leave him alone!" DD shouted.

"Where are ya', Dart?" he growled. "I thought we had a deal. You got your babies shooting at me like snipers?"

I got up and ran towards him. I was going to say something heroic and brave, but I tripped on a pipe in the dark and banged my knee.

"Aaaah!" I rolled around. "Sssssss..."

I jumped up through the pain to see Gold Fist walking off with my flashlight. I took the pliers from my pocket and threw them at Gold Fist's head. I had to stop him some-how. A moment later and he would be out of sight and out of range. He roared in agony and flailed around madly. I totally missed his head, but instead, must have hit his broken elbow or wrist. He turned around and headed back towards me. He held the flashlight up over his head like he was going to smash me with it. I couldn't run. There was no place to go and no way to get there.

Right as he towered over me, his face so contorted with pain and anger that I could see it in the darkness, he stopped. His shoulders slumped. He brought the light down and fell to his knees. He looked up, but not at me, not at anything, really, and he sort of almost handed the light to me. As he fell forward, face down, I could just make out a red feathery dart sticking out of his neck.

"That was an incredible shot," I said.

"I wish I could agree," The Red Dart stepped out of the shadows and into the edge of the flashlight's beam. "I had to shoot six other times before I hit anything. It was more of a lucky shot."

"Aah!" DD yelled. "Who's there?"

"It's okay," The Red Dart waved his own light, "it's me."

"Is he...?" I said.

"He'll be fine." The Red Dart reloaded his gun. "Did he say anything to you?"

"I don't know." I shone my light on Gold Fist's body. "Not really."

"You know, you can't believe anything they say." The Red Dart cocked his gun and shone his light right in my face. "Right?"

We were both breathing hard. Our faces were covered with dirt.

"Did he have powers?" I squinted. "Did he really have powers?"

"Naw, he didn't have no powers," a voice from up by DD rang out. "Did he, Mr. The Red Dart?"

The Red Dart and I both swung our lights up the jumbled pile to a man holding a rope. It was Grim Fist. I recognized the shiny red rope from the Dartmobile. It must have been how The Red Dart got down to us.

Grim Fist jumped out of our light while still holding the rope. He didn't seem to be slowed down by the rubble or the shadows. The Red Dart fired four times, but I don't think he hit anyone. I heard Grim Fist let out a low grunt as he landed somewhere near us. From out of the darkness, he grabbed The Red Dart and they began to wrestle around. The dust they kicked up made everything kind of blurry, even the objects in the light. It was even worse than before.

"Not so much up close, huh?" Grim Fist mocked. "You do alla' your fighting from a distance. Me, I like to get in close."

The Red Dart said nothing.

"What kinda' deal you got going on here?" Grim Fist talked through the punches.

"You know nothing," The Red Dart said.

I could never figure out how heroes and villains could carry on whole conversations while they were fighting. Even in this situation, even while they hit each other in the face, they seemed to be able to talk.

"You need to go back to your clubhouse and leave the hero work to the professionals." The Red Dart swung his coat in an attempt to flummox Grim Fist and maybe get a shot in, but Grim Fist avoided the cloth.

After a few more punches from both sides, The Red Dart's flashlight went out.

"My gun!" he shouted a moment later.

I saw another light coming down from where DD and the rope were, but that was all I could see. It might have been the firemen. Just a few passes of my light off of a reflective gold outfit as he got closer left little doubt who it was, though.

"Sydnafly!" I yelled. "Grim Fist is attacking The Red Dart!"

"Like hell!" Sydnafly dove into the fray.

The Red Dart found his light, turned it back on and stumbled away. He was coughing heavily in the thick dust.

"My gun," he said to me, "have you seen it?"

I shook my head, no.

"Have you seen it?" he demanded.

"No, no, I..." I looked around. "I'll look."

I searched through the rubble until I heard Gina scream. She had woken up and moved, and was now

70

dangling only by her right knee. She swung back and forth, completely upside down.

"Go on!" Sydnafly held both of Grim Fist's wrists, and looked at The Red Dart. "I'll take care a' this."

"I don't think so," Grim Fist butted Sydnafly with his head, and they fell back into the darkness.

Sydnafly was a loud fighter. He grunted and growled and puffed and spit and shouted. I couldn't tell if he was getting some really good licks in or if he was getting the stuffing beat right out of him.

I took a step and almost stepped on The Red Dart's flashlight. "Here!" I turned on the light and tossed it to The Red Dart.

"Grab some pipes," The Red Dart ordered as he caught his light, "and lean them up against the wall."

Most of the long pipes and bars were hooked to something, or under something, or too heavy for me to lift. Gina seemed kind of out of it, and couldn't get ahold of the steel line that was wrapped around her leg. She dropped her bow and started crying. The Red Dart had a pipe against the wall, but it was too short for Gina to reach. She was way up there against a partial wall. I got ahold of a long pipe that led off into the dark. I pulled as hard as I could, and felt a slight movement.

"Come on..." I said to myself. "Come on, come on, come ON!"

As I screamed orders at myself, the most horrible scraping noise I had ever heard came from the other side of the room, over by where DD was. One of the giant girders was falling away from her steel prison. It was scraping along walls and beams. Great sparks and chunks of concrete rained down as it fell... as it fell right towards Gina and The Red Dart and me.

The fighting stopped. A huge section of this destroyed structure seemed to be defying gravity and pulling itself up out of the wreckage.

"No!" DD screamed above the pandemonium.

The Red Dart just stood there, and I fell to the floor and covered my head. Sydnafly pushed Grim Fist away and actually started running towards us as the giant beam picked up steam. About a foot before it struck Gina, it stopped dead, wedged in a nest of smaller girders. For a moment, all sound turned off. The moon now shone behind the beam in some of the only light around except for our paltry flashlights. The pelting of masonry and glass and wires rained down like hail on top of us. Gina reached out like she was part of a flying trapeze act, and held to the beam. Sydnafly climbed up it, not seeming to care if it was safe or not, and took Gina in one of his muscle-bound arms, and lifted her up to untie her. He struggled with the cable for a minute and finally just pulled it out of the wall instead of continuing to try to get it off of her leg. Then, he put her over his shoulder and climbed back down.

Gina was unconscious again. The wire had cut her leg pretty bad. It was starting to swell. DD was now free, and practically jumped down to us and over to Gina. Sydnafly was puffing and sweaty. The Red Dart started applying emergency first aid. I was able to find the electrical pliers, and we used them to get some of the cable off of Gina. DD and I helped each other stand by putting our arm around each other's shoulders, temporarily forgetting about any injuries we may or may not have. I searched the moonlight for any movement of Grim Fist, but he had climbed the rope and was gone.

CHAPTER TEN

The lights in the hospital waiting room seemed harsher and bluer than any lights I ever remembered. The air conditioner ran constantly, and everything was cold to the touch. The flickering TV played events from the previous night over and over. Sydnafly was on every channel, talking up his part in taking down Gold Fist. The talking heads were speculating on the possibility of him and The Red Dart possibly being candidates for Grade A promotion. This was a pretty big deal. Many people in the crowd were injured when the building fell. The Red Dart had me sneak back to the van and grab some plain clothes for DD and Gina. Then they "rescued" the girls, who then just became part of the crowd and the many people "rescued" by the heroes. There was no word from Gold Fist. It turned out that he didn't have any powers. He just had a remote control hidden in his costume. Once the fighting got intense, the remote messed up and flung the cranes around like drunken boxers.

No one knew what part the Mysterious Grim Fist played in all of this latest hoax, or where he disappeared to after the fight. That seemed to be his new name, the MYSTERIOUS Grim Fist. I couldn't remember if Grim Fist was Grade C or Grade B, but I didn't think he was Grade A. Being tagged with an adjective, however, meant that he was at least Grade B, or soon would be. "Mysterious" was also a highly coveted adjective. He would have made a few other heroes mad about that. Few heroes or villains shared adjectives and often failed at marketing their own. Adjectives had to just evolve through the media or the grass roots. The public didn't usually like two or more people sharing an adjective. For now though, the Mysterious Grim Fist was just that, mysterious. Tomorrow, someone might come along even more mysterious and claim the title. Of course, it was hard to be well known and mysterious at the same time, and it was hard to get the adjective unless you were well known enough for the public to find you mysterious.

All the people from the crowd or the mob that had been brought to the hospital had to stay over night. The police took statements about who saw what and got a list of people who were there. The part of the hospital I was waiting in was packed a few hours before, but the police started in this area and slowly worked their way around. Once I was able to prove (off the record) that I was a Trick helping The Red Dart and that my grandfather was the Mist, they were fine with my reason to be there. On the record, they just wrote spectator and said I could go.

DD got stitches in her left shoulder, and Gina was pretty banged up. She would have to be there for a couple of days to have tests run. Her leg was in pretty bad shape. Everything was taking forever because of the sheer number of people.

Sitting here in the waiting room the next morning, going over all this in my head, was actually not what bothered me the most, though. The night before, Grandpa came to vouch for me and brought me over a change of clothes since mine were ripped and covered with blood. He was acting all weird again and for some reason, he was carrying his old water guns. He was dressed in his old jacket, too, and if I was handing out adjectives, I would have called him, the Enigmatic Mist, even though that adjective was currently being used by a woman in Arkansas calling herself the Enigmatic Electrode.

"Just what were you up to?" he said as he held out a white trash bag.

"I told you," I said, "it was just supposed to be a patrol, and then everything went crazy."

"But a building fell on you." He looked in the bag. "Your clothes are rags."

"I was just lucky." I buttoned my shirt. "DD just got a single cut and some bruises."

"But you didn't." Grandpa put his face right up to my face and opened my eye with his fingers. "You didn't even get a bruise."

I pulled his hand away. "The doctors already did that," I said.

"Are you sure you..." he licked his lips, "look... I'm your grandfather. You can tell me things, right?"

"Grandpa..."

"Your father told me, when..." he swallowed hard and wiped the corners of his mouth, "your father told me things."

"I don't..."

He grew very serious. He dropped the trash bag and put his hands on my shoulders.

"Listen, you... Listen, Brand," he nearly shook and was sweating, "if things are happening... If you... notice... I'm who you tell, who you trust."

"Is this about me and DD?" I asked. "Because I hardly know her. I mean, last night was our first date, and as far as dates go..."

"No!" Grandpa studied my face like he was looking at a bug crawling on it. He tightened his lips like he was going to spit, or something. Then all at once, he relaxed. His eyes became Grandpa's again, and he almost smiled. "No."

He patted my shoulder and seemed satisfied. He pulled out a well-used handkerchief from his jacket, wiped his face and eyes, and asked if I was coming. I told him I wanted to wait until DD was awake or ready to go. He shook his head and picked up the bag of clothes.

75

Sometimes I just didn't know what he was talking about. I remember him getting severe bouts of depression when I was growing up. He would shut himself off for days, barely eating, not wanting to talk to anyone. After a while, he would come back out of his shell and take a really long shower. Then, it was like nothing had ever happened. I tried to talk to him about it a few times, but he just got mad. It finally became a way of life. A couple of times a year, Grandpa would go hide from the world.

This seemed different, though. He wasn't trying to get away from things, he was trying to find out stuff from me. I used to think it was about how he was left behind when everyone else was taken, and I think those other times probably were. It could be that now I'm getting older and he's worried about me. He could be concerned that I'm going to fall in with the wrong crowd.

"Is this about Alan?" I asked. "'Cause I don't think he's gone bad. I just think he likes the car and the outfit. I don't think..."

"What?" Grandpa raised an eyebrow. "No, this is... I'll have to talk to that boy. No. Everything is..." he looked me deep in the eye and sighed, "everything is fine. Call me if you need a ride."

He walked out into the hallway and put his arms behind his back. He stood at the big window and looked out at the lights. "Some crazy stuff is going on out there," he said. He looked over his shoulder at me waiting in the waiting room. Then, he walked off down the hall to the elevators.

I went and visited with DD for a while. She was going to stay all night with Gina. We talked until she got real sleepy. They had given her some stuff, and it kind of wiped her out. We talked about family and our lives and things we liked and didn't like. We talked about movies and music and little stuff. We talked about bad things that happened to us. Her shoulder hurt. The hospital let her

76

sleep in a cot in Gina's room along with a few other people. Once the room filled up, we had to be more careful
about what we talked about. She apologized for such a
crappy first date, and I wished I would have said something cool about it, maybe how the next one would be a
lot better. Instead, I just shrugged and shook my head.
Pretty soon she fell asleep. I came back down to the waiting room and fell asleep on the cold couch.

It was a tough night. I figured that Grandpa was just
worried. I was all he had. Plus, he had that speech coming up at the memorial. That had to be weighing on him. I
had caught him looking at some old news clippings a few
nights before. I figured he was working on his speech and
was checking out some of his old adventures. Instead, he
was reading old clippings about Dad. He didn't want to
talk about it, and we both went to our own bedrooms. I
cried a little, and I bet he did too.

I kept seeing Grandpa's guns in my dreams, and
then I was drowning. Obviously, being attacked recently
was not something my subconscious liked. My skin kept
peeling off and regrowing. Rocks fell on me. People
came out of the dark—Gold Fist, the Mysterious Grim
Fist—and I kept getting hurt. A giant waterspout came out
of the ocean and attacked me. I started spinning too, like
I'd turned into a tornado. Sparks flew from my eyes, like
when electric lines explode in a hurricane or in a collapsed hospital.

Thankfully, no one else was in the waiting room, because I woke up on the floor, covered in sweat. The
vending machines were the only lights in the room.
Someone had drawn the blinds, shut off the lights and
given me a blanket. The darkness reminded me of being
back in that pit. I must have been wiped, because I
crawled back onto the hard smelly slab of a couch and
went right back to sleep. I dreamed that a woman who

was see-through, like a ghost, was standing in the doorway of the room, turning the crowd away. Her hair danced like she was in the wind or under water. It flowed through the air across the room to me. It wrapped around my face and pushed on my eyes. Something was pushing her back, though, and she never spoke. I twisted and jerked awake.

When I woke up, the lights were on, the TV was on, and Alan was sitting in the chair next to the couch I was on.

"Where's your costume?" I sat up and wiped a bunch of building out of my eyes. "Your VILLAIN costume?"

"Quiet, you moron." He slapped my leg. "I'm here to visit Gina. Man, this is all over the news. I'm gonna go tell Darlene you're awake."

"DD," I said.

"Huh?"

"She wants to be called DD." I rolled the little blanket up.

"She wants YOU to call her DD." Alan stood.

"She's awake?"

He gave me that *Duh!* look. Then he left, and I let my mind glaze a little while the TV droned on.

Was it possible that Grandpa had been talking about powers? Was he thinking that just because my cut healed so fast, or because I was so lucky under the building, that I had some kind of power? Wouldn't I know? Did he think I was lying to him? There ARE no powers. Everyone knows that there are no powers. So, why did he have his guns? They must have just been part of his costume.

Before I realized it, I was flicking my fingers in front of me. Then, I aimed my hands at the TV like I could shoot lasers.

"Shoot!" I shouted and felt instantly dumb.

I stood and walked to the door. No one was around. I spun around like a gunslinger, and shot at the window with my finger.

"ZAP!"

Nothing happened. A pigeon stood on the stoop out-side and hopped away at my sudden movement. I sat back down and shook my head. Sydnafly was holding a press conference and letting everyone know that New York was safe. Neither villains nor Blackout Prophet ter-rorists would stop the memorial celebration. Gold Fist had turned out to be a fraud, but even if the powers DID re-turn, heroes like him and The Red Dart would never let anyone get hurt. I flicked my fingers at him.

"Got something on your fingers, there?" Alan poked his head in the door. "I told you to keep those out of your nose."

"Shut up."

"Come with me." he motioned. "I want to show you something."

"Where's DD?" I got up.

"She's gonna meet us downstairs," he said. "She's getting dressed. You want to watch her getting dressed?"

"Don't be stupid." I blushed.

"Yeah, well, I wanna show you something before she gets here."

As we got into the elevator, Alan ran his fingers through his hair. He pulled a black leather hat out of his back pocket and arranged it just right on his head. It looked like a hat that Ace wore.

"You know that was a setup last night, right?" The elevator stopped. "With Gold Fist, right?"

"What was?"

"The whole thing." Alan stepped out into the parking garage. "Dart and Fly set the whole thing up to get them-selves a pay raise."

"Who told you that?" I scrunched up my nose.

"I don't know where Grim Fist came in, but he messed things up good," Alan laughed.

79

"How do you know this?" I said. "Does DD know?"

"I've got my ways," he said. "I'm not just some Trick anymore."

"Hey!"

"You know what I mean," he said. "I mean, I know people who know, that's all."

"I'll ask him," I said. "The Red Dart, I'll ask him."

"I wouldn't." Alan stopped and looked around. "I'm just warning you, that's all. You need to come work for me and get away from him."

"I told you..."

"Yeah, yeah. Wait'll you see this."

We rounded a couple of corners in the parking garage, until we came upon an incredible sports car that had recently been painted black. I recognized it immediately.

"That's The Red Dart's DeLorean," I said. "You just stole it?"

"Black hat," Alan grabbed the front of his cap, "I can do that kind of thing now. The Red Dart just has the keys laying around in his hideout, in a drawer with a combination lock. Anybody could get it. Seven-seven-three, by the way, if you ever want to steal one of his cars."

I couldn't believe it.

"Seriously, though." He beeped a remote and the gull wing door started sliding up. "It's not really stealing. Wilma's name is on it too. We have every right to take it."

There, sitting in the passenger seat, in a black skin-tight leather outfit, red tear-shaped sunglasses, and a black beehive hairdo, sat Wilma. She had one of those long black cigarette holders with a bright pink cigarette sticking out of the end. Smoke rose up around her hairdo and out of the car, as she placed one long leg out and then the other. Her thin black heels were sharpened to a point.

"Aren't we done here, yet?" she said to Alan in a

80

voice dripping with boredom. "How's your little sweetheart?"

"She's doing okay," Alan said. "They want to..."

"Why don't YOU go see her?" I said to her.

She looked up over her glasses at me.

"We had a falling out." Her lip twitched, and for the first time, I noticed a pronounced gap between her two front teeth.

"Now I understand why," I said. "I thought you were striking out on a life of villainy with your girlfriend. Now, I see it's with old Mrs. The Red Dart.

"How dare you!" Wilma flicked her ashes.

I wasn't sure if she was upset because I called her a villain or because I insinuated that she was involved with The Red Dart or because I called her old. She was using her cigarette to good effect, anyway.

"How do we know we can trust this child?" She dropped her cigarette on the ground and crushed it under her high heeled boots.

"He'll keep quiet." Alan raised his hand. "He's gonna be our first Roadie."

"I am NOT." I crossed my arms.

"Alan..." Wilma reached into the car and pulled out her bow and quiver. She stroked the black feathers on the arrow with her long thin fingers.

"Now, this is what..." he said to me.

"Alan, I don't like the looks of things." She tapped her finger on the sharp tip of the arrow head. "He seems suspicious to me."

"Hold on." He turned to her. "This is Brand. He'll be quiet."

"It's too late." She looked at me. "You've told someone, haven't you? It's that little brat, Darlene."

She must have seen something in my expression. I guess I didn't have that good of a poker face.

"Look, I..." I put my hands in front of me and looked at

81

Alan, "I might have accidentally told my grandpa."

"Brand!" Alan slapped his forehead. "I told you to keep it quiet!"

"I thought he knew." I backed up a few steps. "I didn't mean anything."

"Put that down." Alan pushed Wilma's bow away. "It'll be fine."

"It will be ruined before it is started," Wilma spit through the gap between her two front teeth.

"What, are you going to shoot me?" I looked back and forth between the two of them. "Alan?"

"No." He pushed her again, and she jerked out of his way.

"The Black Dart can find another driver, Alan," she sneered and loaded another arrow in her bow.

"Who is...?" I looked around.

"I'M the Black Dart!" She took aim on me.

"No, now stop!" Alan said. "You've scared him enough. Everything is fine. Just hold on."

"Is this, good cop, bad cop?" I asked. "'Cause right now, I don't like either one of you."

"You need a good smack down, old lady," DD's voice echoed as she jogged down around the curved road. Her shoes clacked on the concrete. She was in her street clothes, but she was every bit as pretty as she was in her costume. "So, back off."

"Oh, Please." Wilma lowered her arm, but kept the line drawn. "Little Miss, 'I Cant Shoot the Deer'. Missed any barns lately?"

"Alan, you'd better leave this B-Witch," DD said. "Gina and I have known for a long time that she was going bad. I mean, look, she's smoking cigarettes and everything."

"You don't know anything, girl," Wilma sniffed. "The world's a lot darker than you think. Some of us just know how to keep secrets better than others."

"Tough talk." DD cocked her head. "I'm telling The Red Dart on you. Your days of being as spoiled as old milk are through. If you'd been there last night, Gina might not be up in that hospital bed. Instead you're out partying with her boyfriend. You've got a lot to answer for."

"I've known you since you were too little to pick up a bow, little girl," Wilma raised her bow, "and that's long enough."

DD kept walking towards us. She had none of her weapons.

"You're done." she pointed her finger at Wilma. "Gina and I are..."

The only way I can explain what happened in the next fraction of a second is to slow it way down, because it was actually faster than I could even see. Wilma shot. The Black Dart actually shot her shiny black arrow right at DD. In what I can only remember as a blur, like something out of a cartoon, DD's arms whirled around and grabbed an arrow out of her quiver, put it in her bow and fired. I know she didn't even have a bow and arrow, but that's what she did. They were just suddenly there, and they were shimmering.

This silver spark of light shot from her body and hit Wilma's arrow in mid flight. The black arrow exploded. The silver spark then hit the floor and bounced up right at Wilma. It hit her bow and smashed it to pieces. Then, it just disappeared. DD stood there with another arrow of light and fire and electricity, drawn back in a bow of energy and aimed at Wilma's rose-tinted glasses.

We all looked at each other, totally dumbstruck. Wilma nearly tripped all over herself and fell into the car.

"Alan! Drive!" she screamed as she jerked off her glasses.

Alan stared at DD. Then, he looked me in the eye.

"I'm..." he said with his mouth gaping.

83

His door opened and the engine started as he jumped the hood and climbed in. In another second, they were gone with the echoing roar of the engine and the smell of the burning rubber of the car tires. I looked back to DD, who was now standing there looking at her own empty hands. The shiny bow and arrow had vanished. Her shoulder had started to bleed again through her shirt.

"What just happened?" she said to herself.

"What just happened?" I said.

"What just happened?" she said.

"I have no idea," I said, but I thought I really did.

CHAPTER ELEVEN

"The powers are back." DD looked at her hands. "Oh, my God, the Prophets were right. I'm going to be responsible for the world being destroyed." She began to cry. "I wonder how many other people this has happened to. Who else has powers? How long has this been going on?"

"That's not true." I put my hands on her shoulders, careful not to touch her injury. "You've only used your powers for good."

"I almost killed Wilma!"

"But, you healed me." I wished I hadn't said it but continued anyway. "At least twice."

"What?" She stopped crying and cocked her head to the side.

"And you pushed that giant beam!" I didn't know if I sounded encouraging or was digging a deeper hole. "Like antigravity or super strength or something."

"What? No way!"

"We've got to tell someone." I took her by the elbow. "Someone we can trust."

"Wait, no." She pulled her arm away. "That's not how it works, is it?"

I had no idea how it worked.

"You can't tell anyone. The hero can't tell anyone." She paced in circles and pretended to grab at invisible arrows. Nothing happened. She wiped her eyes with the bottom of her T-shirt and sniffed. "Because family could be hurt, or you could be blackmailed or killed in your sleep or shot by a sniper when you go to the grocery store."

"We could tell Grandpa," I said, "although he's never had anything nice to say about the Blackout Prophets. He wouldn't even let me watch the news about them."

"What do you mean, I healed you?" She placed her fingers above my eye. "Your cut?"

"You handed me ice, and it healed in hours."

"That can't be." She ran her thumb across my eyebrow. "When else?"

"When the building fell," I said. "I was covered in blood. My clothes were cut and torn, but I was fine. You were holding me right before, searching for me, reaching for me as the floor collapsed."

"But," she touched the wet bandage on her shoulder and winced, "why didn't I heal myself? Why is Gina still up there in a hospital bed?"

"I don't know." I watched her begin to pace again. "I'm just saying."

"I suppose..." she took a deep breath, "I suppose I could see if The Red Dart has heard anything."

I suddenly felt flush and a little sick to my stomach. I wondered if she had heard the rumor that Alan had told me. I didn't want to say anything.

"Wait, um," I clenched my teeth, "I need to know... I mean, you can hate me, or whatever... I mean, I won't say anything, but..."

"What?" DD stopped short. "What?"

"Alan said," I took a deep breath and puffed it out, "Alan said that stuff was all a setup."

"What stuff?"

"The building stuff," I said, "with Gold Fist."

"What do you mean?" She stepped closer.

"*Alan* said," I stepped back, "that Sydnafly and The Red Dart set it all up with Gold Fist to make them look good and get upgraded."

"No way!"

86

"So you didn't know about that?"

"I'm saying, no way," she said. "It's not true."

"Well, I think we should talk to my grandpa about it."

"It's not true."

"I'm not saying..."

"It's not true," she said.

"I'm not saying it's true. It, look..." I said, "we should just..."

"Brand," DD placed her strong but somehow soft bowfinger up to my lips, "I have to tell you something, and here's why we can't tell your grandpa."

"Why?"

"He's crazy."

"Stop it."

"No, I'm not even kidding," she nearly whispered. "I'm serious."

"He's not crazy." I scrunched my brow. "You're just mad."

"They made him retire."

"He's... Who made him retire?"

"SGHV and some heroes," she said. "The Red Dart, Ace maybe."

"They did..." I said, "he's just old. He wanted to retire."

"Not what I heard."

"When?"

"What do you mean, when?" She put her hands on her hips. "Oh, maybe after the Place-Mart thing."

"What Place-Mart thing?"

"What do you..." She cocked her head. "What do you... You don't remember?"

"What are you talking about?"

"You don't know?" Her eyes got big. "You don't know."

"I don't..."

"He almost killed that guy, that shoplifter guy," she

said, "the one who said he could turn invisible, Invisible Fist or something."

I hadn't heard anything about this. There was no way something like this could have happened without me knowing.

"He attacked the security guard?" She raised her hand, trying to prompt my memory. "Ace had to come get him?"

"Grandpa never said..."

"You must have been in school." DD looked off. "I can't believe he didn't... that *nobody* ever..."

I felt on fire with shame and embarrassment. How could anybody, how could *she* of all people know this personal private thing that even I didn't know? This just couldn't be true. I could remember a couple of years ago, Grandpa moping around after he officially retired. I could understand that. He even snuck out at nights for a while on some secret patrols. As his Trick, I brought him a sandwich once.

"You don't know," I said. "I bet I know what is going on."

"Don't say it," DD smirked, "I'm jealous? The Red Dart is jealous? Everybody is jealous?"

I wasn't going to say..."

"What, then?"

"Everybody *could* be jealous..."

"He's CRA...!" she stopped and put her hand over her mouth. "Man, am I a B-Witch," she said. "He's not crazy. Forget that."

I turned away. Darned if I was going to let her see my eyes well up.

"No, I mean, he's not crazy, Brand." She put her hand on my shoulder. "That was just dumb. You're right. He's not. He's just getting up there, that's all. Man, that was stupid. I didn't mean it."

"At least he's not a secret villain like The Red Dart," I

said with my back still turned.

She dropped her hand and backed up. I could feel her looking at me.

"Huh!" She said and we stood there in silence. "I'm going." She turned and started to walk away. "I'll see you later," she said over her shoulder.

I just stood there.

"Call me," she said as she walked off, "or don't... whatever."

I realized as she walked off down the curved pavement that I needed to walk that direction too if I was going to get to the bus stop. The last thing I wanted to do right now was walk with her. It was also the only thing I wanted to do. Even I was smart enough to realize though, that I was not stupid enough to try that.

I was still simmering about Grandpa. Should I say something to him about that, or about DD, or about the powers? How would he react? Maybe I could get him talking about the good old days. That was a gamble. He could just as easily end up sad as glad, sappy rather than happy.

DD disappeared down at the exit. I kept myself occupied long enough to stop myself from calling out to her. Yay, me. I don't know if I'm my own best friend or my own worst enemy. Since when do I ever listen to myself? I didn't even get to see if she paused and turned around to look back at me. I was too busy feeling the heat in my eyeballs and staring at the scorch mark in the concrete. Sounds like she was just feeling sorry for me anyway. Good thing we didn't get to know each other better, or I might have started getting feelings for her. I had other things to worry about, like Grandpa, and The Red Dart, and the Alan craziness. Of course, it wasn't like I could do anything about any of this stuff. I'm no policeman. I'm no hero. I'm just a Trick, a kid that gets to have little adventures, not somebody important, not somebody that anybody would care about. Maybe I would be better off spending my summer vacations playing video games like the other kids. I bet none of them were threatened with an arrow. I bet none of them had a friend turn into a villain, and a girlfriend who dumped them after she suddenly developed superpowers. Maybe I should just go take tuba lessons or something.

Then, I thought about what DD had just gone through, and how I would feel right about now, and I really wished I would have stopped her from walking away from me.

CHAPTER TWELVE

When I went to talk to Grandpa, I got home to a flooded, darkened house. I ran to the living room to find Grandpa on the couch. Everything was soaked.

"You lied to me," he said. "The powers are back."

"What in the world is…"

"Powers change people, Brand." Grandpa pointed his antique Kid Mist pistol at me. He was shaking.

Things became a little more clear in the house. The water on the floor was running up the walls and windows. The ceiling was like gelatin, all wiggly and dark.

"What's going on?" I turned around in a circle and looked at the room.

"They do something to your brain." He was crying, but the tears were floating up. "You need to stop it."

"Stop what?" I said. "I don't even know what's going on. Grandpa, what the heck's going on here?"

"Stop!" He straightened his arm and raised his gun as I stepped towards him. "Do you remember it all?"

"Grandpa, this is really freaking me out," I said. "I really, really don't know what you're talking about."

"They get all up in your brain." He put his hand up to his temple and pressed. "They don't just change your body. They change your mind."

"What do?"

"Powers!" he said. "Look!"

He lifted his gun and pulled the trigger. A round rope of dark green water snaked around in mid air and crossed the room. It grew in length, but stayed hooked to his gun, until it knocked the heavy front door closed.

Then, it broke up and splashed down into the water that was still slowly climbing the walls.

"You got your gun to work?" I said. "How?"

"I didn't." He set the gun down on the couch beside him and put his head in his hands. "I'm not the one who did."

My head was swimming. It was like I was inside of some video game. It didn't even seem real, even though there was water over my shoes.

"There was a reason," he said into his hands, "that all the powers went away. There was a reason that I..."

I sat down beside him and put my arm around his shoulders. He was cold and wet. "We need to get you dried off," I said, "and what's with all the water? I'll turn off..."

"No," he reached up and grabbed my wrist. "You have to leave. You have to run."

"Why?" I said. "What's going on?"

"Maybe if I look away," Grandpa said to himself. "Maybe if I close my eyes..." Grandpa's grip tightened. "I know about your powers."

"Hey!" I pried myself loose and jerked my hand back. "I don't have any powers, Grandpa. I don't know what you are talking about. You're going to catch pneumonia in here." I stood up.

"Yes. You. DO!" He pounded the cushion. "You healed in the building. I know you have powers."

"That was just luck," I said. "That wasn't MY power. That was..."

"It was you," Grandpa said. "I know because... You think this is the first time? You just don't remember."

"I think you're sick, Grandpa." I sloshed across the room towards the small half bath, past the front door.

I heard Grandpa stumbling around behind me as I walked into the little room and shut off the lavatory faucets.

93

"You're such a liar!" he screamed. "You know! You remember!"

"I honestly..."

"I know," Grandpa ran up to me by the front door, "because I got *my* powers back."

With that, the water on the floor started climbing up my legs and body, holding me in place. It was like it was plastic; it had a mind of its own.

"And the last time that happened..." he waved his hand, and the water snapped around my chest and rose to my neck.

"Stop! Stop!" I yelled.

"The last time that happened was the last time you got your powers back," Grandpa swayed. "The last time," his voice was low, "when I had to kill you."

I was struggling and twisting. My head felt like it was going to pop off. The water seemed to have a mind of its own. It could do things that water shouldn't be able to do, impossible things like grab onto me and hold me in a liquid straight jacket.

"I never! I never had powers!"

"It's my job." He turned his back to me and raised his arms. The water by the couch rose up, and the water on the ceiling stretched down, and it formed a wall, a wall with a watery face, the distorted mad face of the Mist, my grandfather.

"That's why I was saved from the big battle," the face said. "That's why I'm still here. I have to stop you from destroying the world."

He turned his head to me. "I love you, Brand, just like before, but I have to stop you. That's why I helped form the Blackout Prophets. That's why I have to do this."

"Grandpa, please!" I screamed as the water rose up above my mouth.

Grandpa turned ninety degrees and waved at the far wall. The waters came together and formed a second rolling water wall with another version of Grandpa's face. The two walls started snarling and biting at each other.

"I never wanted this," he said. "I thought you were going to be different this time, that the prophecies were wrong. I raised you as my grandson. I loved you like my son, even when you *were* my son."

My eyes opened wide. I struggled to pull free, but the water around me moved with me. I could barely breathe through my nose. Grandpa was talking nonsense. He seemed to think I was Dad. Those Blackout Prophet nuts had done something to him. He had gone crazy with power, and he was flat going to kill me if I couldn't get out of here.

"I killed..." Grandpa bent over in what seemed like pain, "I... did it once. I can do it again... but no more!"

He turned an angry face to me. "You rose from the mud, and I couldn't... a little baby... not again! You won't rise again."

He waved behind me, and another wall rose up. The three walls started moving inwards towards us. Grandpa's face either mimicked the pained expressions on the three angry walls, or the walls mirrored his. They started forming words as they approached. At first, it was just a babble, then a scream, then I could actually hear what they were saying. I understood the water.

"Liar...liar...," the waters shouted, "killer...killer..."

"Mmmm! MMMM!" I was struggling but couldn't move.

"I am the Grand Prophet," he said. "It is my duty. I know what went wrong last time. I had no real sacrifice, no blood sacrifice. My adopted son wasn't enough."

I could barely hear him over the pounding of the waters and my own heart. He raised a fourth wall by the outside window. Everything was dark. The waters crashed and pulled in.

"Destroyer of the world...!" the waters chanted.

"I must die too!" he wailed. "I will sacrifice my life to save the earth. It's the grand bargain. It's the true bargain!"

Then the water rose up over my head, and I couldn't breathe at all. The water walls pounded into me, and I was swirling around, hitting the ceiling and walls. All I could hear was the thumping. I started spinning, and suddenly realized that I was somehow making myself spin like in my dream. There seemed to be a light all around me. I could make out shapes in the water, but I couldn't breathe. My chest was burning. I was trapped and dying in my own living room. My chest ached so bad that I thought it would burst, and then it seemed to. A yellow spark shot out from me in all directions, and the whole world exploded. It felt like a car hit me from behind, and I screamed out what little air I had left in my lungs.

The next thing I knew, I was lying on my back in the mud in the front yard. The front door was off the house and over by the bushes, and the water had dispersed. I could barely see in the bright sunlight, but I thought I heard Grandpa moaning. I turned on my side. It hurt everywhere to move, like my skin was broken glass. I choked and spit up water. My head was pounding, and my ears were ringing.

Through some miracle, my phone was vibrating. I pulled it from my shirt. It was from DD. *Dead Millards*, it read, *Don't go home.*

A large walking stick knocked the phone out of my hands and into the mud. Mr. Forest from next door took a step over and smashed it with the heel of his shoe.

"Get up, boy," he said in his whiny old man voice. "Come with me right now. You won't have a second chance to live."

And as I stumbled out of the yard, I heard the water in the yard whisper one last time, "Murderer..."

CHAPTER THIRTEEN

Mr. Forest was just an old man in the sidelines of my life. I don't think I ever had a real conversation with him. When I was little, I was scared to death of him. I never really got over that feeling. I didn't know anything about him, and I never had any desire to learn. He was never nice to me, or anybody. Grandpa never said much more about him than to stay out of his yard. He would call our house every once in a while to complain about something like noise or grass or snow removal or some silly thing. Now, here I was was in his house. Orchestra music was coming from the other room. I think he was playing actual vinyl records.

Mr. Forest's kitchen looked like some kind of old black and white TV show kitchen. First of all, it was black and white, from the floor tile squares to the old strange pictures on the wall of the old strange people. Secondly, it was full of big clunky metal appliances with rounded edges and chipped paint. They must have been antiques, and I must have been in shock. I sat on a metal stool, and leaned my elbow against a cracked black and white countertop. I kept belching from taking in all that water.

"Good and bad," Mr. Forest said as he walked into the room. "It is always never so easy to tell the two apart. Things, like people, are never as they seem. There are times when even those closest to you are not who you think they are."

His voice sounded weird until I realized that it was because he wasn't shouting at me. In one hand, he held a gnarled tree limb, which he used as a well worn walking stick. Over his other arm was an identical outfit to the one I was wearing, only it wasn't soaking wet. That was creepy.

"You've some mud behind your left ear," he set the clothes on the counter next to me, "and scales over your eyes."

I wiped my ears and eyes. I found mud, but no scales.

"I've got to..." I said.

"No you do not." He clicked his stick on the floor. "Your grandfather is fine, well, physically fine, just shocked and winded. He has already recovered and phoned the police."

"The police?"

"Yes." Mr. Forest looked down his nose at me. "On you, for attacking him."

Attacking him?" I sat up straight and flipped my still wet hair.

"Yes," Mr. Forest said again, like he was talking on the telephone to a salesman. He half closed his eyes and reached over beside me and moved some old chrome shiny thing. I think it was a toaster. He slid it back on the counter.

"Apparently, you have been taken in with a group of thugs called the Dead Millards." he seemed to almost smile. "Your degenerate friend, Mr. Severs, convinced you to go bad and rob your own grandfather, probably for liquor or narcotics or prostitution. Tsk, tsk, tsk... and on the eve of his big day."

"That's not true!" I jumped up but forgot about my wet socks. I slipped and caught myself on the counter. Good thing Mr. Forest had moved the toaster-bot, or I would have hit it. "That's not true."

"Well, you know it and I know it," he said, "but Martin's good friend, Police Chief Marx, believes everything that Martin Meeks says."

98

"Why would Grandpa do this?" I pulled off my wet socks. "Why would he say this?"

"Throw them in the box." Mr. Forest pointed his stick towards a cardboard box in the corner of the kitchen next to a potted tree. The tree was black and white too, with white bark and shiny black leaves. I'd never seen anything like it. His record skipped twice, and that annoyed him.

"I think I ought to go." I held my wet socks tight against my wet shirt.

"Suit yourself." Mr. Forest gave his stick a little tap. "Keep in mind that if you go out the front door, your grandfather will see you, and if you go out the back exit, you will be spotted by the Dead Millards."

I looked out of the window in the kitchen door. In the street in back, I saw a few Dead Millards slowly driving around on their bikes. Were they looking for me?

"You should eat something." Mr. Forest took down the giant toaster. "Have some homemade bread. It's good for you. It will help you clear your mind... eventually."

"I need my phone." I patted my pockets. "Why did you break my phone?"

"Here," he pulled my phone out of his jacket pocket.

"How did you... When did you fix it?" I asked. "How did you fix it?"

"I didn't," he said. "This is another cellular telephone similar to your own, but with no easy way to trace it to you."

I stared at the phone. It looked just like mine. I checked it out. It had my contacts and information.

"Now no one can use your device against you as a tracking beacon."

I looked out the window again.

"Excuse me," Mr. Forest walked over to a white phone hanging on the kitchen wall, "I have to answer the telephone."

The phone rang.

"Hello?" Mr. Forest said. His voice had that cranky edge to it. "Yes, I saw him crawling around in the mud in your front yard. He ran off down the road, the dirty little boy. You really should keep a closer eye on that child, before he falls in with the wrong crowd. No. I don't know. How would I know? I must warn you, Martin... yes, of course. I must warn you... I will. Mr. Meeks! I must warn you to keep your plumbing hijinx under control. If anything should happen to my marvelous Petreculus Apple tree due to you or your grandchild's exploits, then I would be most annoyed. I don't threaten legal action lightly, Mr. Meeks. I should have to report further excesses to the neighborhood committee..."

He made a locking-my-lips motion to me.

"Yes. Very well. Good-day, sir."

I felt like I really needed to just talk to Grandpa. Something terrible was happening, and I needed to figure it out. In my mind, I was still rolling circles in the animated waves in my living room.

Thunk! The toast popped up.

I was so confused. I was too afraid to go home. I needed to talk to someone, but I didn't have anyone to talk to.

Mr. Forest pulled a chrome lever on his refrigerator, and the door opened. He brought out a small crystal tray with a crystal lid. Inside was a rectangle of butter. I hardly knew Mr. Forest, and he was just creepy. Grandpa had gone crazy, but I was afraid no one would believe me. Alan had gone over to the villains. I didn't know if I could trust him, and DD... well, I was pretty sure she didn't want to talk to me ever again. She did send me the message, though.

Mr. Forest leaned his stick against the wall. He held a silver butter knife over the toaster for a few seconds.

Then he sliced easily into the cold butter and melted the pat on the hot fresh bread. It smelled incredible. All at once, I remembered bits and pieces of something that happened with Mr. Forest. I was really young, and Grandpa had gone into one of his deep bouts of depression. He hadn't been out of the bedroom in days. I must have been a real mess. The doorbell rang, but I was too scared to open the door. Whatever grownup was on the other side would want to speak to Grandpa, and he wasn't seeing anyone at the moment. Then I smelled the bread. I must have been pretty hungry. Goodness knows what I had been eating. I remember that I had a stash of jerky in my room for emergencies. I must have been living on jerky at that point. I peeked out my bedroom window and saw Mr. Forest walking away from the house. He had left a box with fresh bread and pies and other foods, but I especially remember the fresh bread and pies. He must have known what was going on. He never mentioned it, and I never thanked him. I must have put the whole event out of my mind.

"I'm truly not trying to tempt you." He handed me a saucer with the bread on it. "That is not my job, but you should eat something."

The saucer seemed heavy and cold and really old. I took it from his wrinkled spotty hands and sat back down on the stool. The bread was soft with a hard crust, and had a slightly bitter taste that was offset by the smooth creamy butter.

"You need to know a few things," he said, "and so do I."

Thirty minutes later, I felt better, a bit calmer, a bit dryer. Mr. Forest went in to his living room and turned off his record player. I had some toast and apple juice, and changed clothes in the bathroom into an identical outfit to the one I was already wearing. This was too weird. Had he been spying on me through the window? There was even a pair of shoes in the bathroom on the hamper that matched mine perfectly, down to a picture I had drawn on them in magic marker. I walked out of the room with a pile of wet clothes in my arms and a pile of questions in my brain.

"Just throw them in the box," he said, pointing.

"What's going on here, Mr. Forest?" I said. "Why do you have clothes like mine? How do you now about Grandpa?"

"I know about a lot of things," he said.

I looked out the kitchen door window. At the moment, I saw nothing. What was the deal with the Dead Millards? Why had DD warned me about them? I wondered if I could get away from them if I ran right now.

"Mr. Forest, when I was little..."

"Do you know me?" he asked.

"You're Mr. Forest," I said.

"Do you know me," he stepped closer, "from before?"

"Before what?"

He frowned and mumbled.

"You sound like Grandpa." I got a tight feeling in my chest. "You're not going to attack me, are you?"

"No," he raised an eyebrow, "but I *do* know about what your grandfather was speaking. I also know, for example, why the Dead Millards are looking for you. I know, as well, that the powers are back."

"No, that's... I don't know..." I put my hand on the doorknob. "What you're... talking..."

"I believe you." He sat down in a metal kitchen chair with a black and white plastic cushion. "Unfortunately, I believe you, but you don't understand. You should understand."

"I don't understand," I said.

"I'm not going to tell you." He shook his head. "I can not be responsible again. You should know on your own, blast you."

102

"Responsible for what?" I took my hand off the door.

"Responsible for... Well, *that* particular incident has naught to do with you," he smiled a slight crinkly smile, "but let me explain some things to you."

"Really?"

"Obviously, I have powers." He tapped his stick on the floor. "This branch helps me to retrieve certain information. It is maddeningly fickle, but it helps me focus, to get through the fog of this... atmosphere."

He looked me in the eye. "Remember anything yet?"

"What should I be remembering?"

He stood up with the help of his stick and walked to a drawer under the counter.

"*You* have powers?" I said. "For how long?"

"For a while," he said.

"Who else?" I said. "Who else has powers? Does everybody? Do you know about..."

"DD?" He pulled a hose nozzle out of a junk drawer. "And Martin, and you, of course."

"I don't have powers."

"Of course you do." He set the black and white plastic nozzle on the counter next to me. "That is why you are able... Well, I need you to remember this part on your own."

"Why are the powers back?" I looked at the spray nozzle. "How? Who else?"

"You need to save her," he said.

"Who?" I said. "DD?"

"She is at The Red Dart's base." He stepped over to the window above the sink and pulled the shade aside with his stick. "She asked too many questions. She gave too many answers. She got caught texting you after The Red Dart called on the Dead Millards to come get you. Then your grandfather called."

"How do you..."

"Magic stick, boy." He held his walking stick up.

"Right," I said, "right."

"You are no doubt wondering how to get there," he said.

I had, in fact, been wondering how to get there.

"I made some calls while you were changing." He walked into the living room and locked the front door. I could hear motorcycles coming by. It sounded like the Dead Millards had gotten around to this block now. "I got you a driver, the best in town."

"You know Ace?" I perked up.

"I do." He pulled the living room shade. "I know Ace *and* I know his number. I know a lot of things."

The sound of motorcycles got very loud. They were pulling up on Mr. Forest's lawn.

"Watch the flowers," he mumbled, "and the tree, you morons."

"They found me!" I said and looked around the room.

"Yes." Mr. Forest came back into the kitchen. "As I said, The Red Dart hired them to capture you. You, who know too little, seem to also know too much."

"Gold Fist," I said. "It's true?"

"It was all a setup," Mr. Forest said, "but they never would have found you in time. So, I had to call them."

"You had to what?"

A loud knock came on the front door.

"Open up!" a voice commanded.

"I had to let the Dead Millards know you were here," he said, clearly enjoying my annoyance.

"How could you..." I grabbed his shirt with one hand and his stick with the other. Suddenly my anger was gone, and I understood. There was so much information in that branch, but it seemed alien and powerful. He yanked his stick away.

"You had to..." I put my hand to my forehead, "to let me escape out the back, you had to get them all in the

105

front yard."

"You will have to hurry," he said. "They may be idiots but in thirty-seven seconds, they are going to figure out that there is a glass window right next to the door, and that there is also a back door to this house."

They started pounding on the door. I could hear more of them on the porch.

"What about you?" I stopped at the back door.

"I know places to hide." He clicked his magic stick on the floor. He tossed the black and white plastic hose nozzle to me. "Put this in your pocket. I will call and explain in a few minutes. Right now we are out of..."

"Bust the window!" a voice shouted from the porch.

A horn honked out back. I opened the door to see a slick black car driven by Alan. He waved.

"I thought you said..."

"Best driver in town." He smiled. "Now, go! You are already a Trick. Now you need to be a Hero."

CHAPTER FOURTEEN

So what massive change happened to Grandpa, The Red Dart, to Alan? Is their core corrupted? Did they have some kind of jolt that messed up their brain? If the powers are coming back, I have to assume that anything is possible. Maybe this is some kind of melodramatic, soap opera mind control. From the look on Alan's face, it appeared he might have gotten jolted back onto the right side of the road.

"So," I said.

"I don't want to talk about it," he said.

"I was just wondering..."

"Let's change the subject," he said. "I believe we are being chased by a motorcycle gang."

"Who all dress like they are the mutant zombie offspring of the thirteenth president of the United States," I said.

"MZO is a great band," Alan said, "but I'm not convinced that Fillmore ever really dressed up in leather chaps."

"Can you see out of that?" I looked over at Alan's swollen and blackened left eye.

"I'm fine." He adjusted his rearview mirror. "How many do you suppose there are?"

"Do you know Mr. Forest?" I said.

"Creepy old guy that lives next door to you?" Alan said. "Likes to yell at anybody who accidentally guns their engine a few times at three in the morning?"

"Yeah."

"Never had the pleasure," he said. "But somehow he

had my number."

"I think he has everyone's number," I said. "Do these guys have guns?"

"I don't see any yet." Alan studied his mirrors. "Good thing, too. I doubt this car has the armor that Ace's cars have."

A pack of wild Dead Millard thugs chased us down neighborhood streets and through red lights. Children and residents and visitors in town for the big day jumped and dove for cover. I figured it was only a matter of time before the police and the helicopters showed up. If we could just get to Johnny's Laundry, maybe the craziness and noise could help DD be found. Maybe I could use this to my advantage to help her. The cops might catch me, but the Dead Millards wouldn't, and I could point them in the direction of The Red Dart's hideout.

"I still prefer a high speed chase to dealing with Wilma." Alan touched his cheek. "Man, that woman is hard."

"So, you left her, huh?" I said.

"More like, escaped with my life." He smiled and put his "cool" shades back on.

"She seemed pretty shocked at DD's little trick," I said.

"I think we were all pretty shocked." Alan adjusted his glasses lower on his face.

"I'm *still* pretty shocked," I said.

"So, what, she can make things out of energy?" he asked. "Can she make anything? Could she make a motorcycle? Man, that would be incredible."

"I don't have any idea," I said. "I don't think she does either. It freaked all of us out."

"Yeah, once we got a block or two away, Black Dart started screeching like worn out brakes." Alan checked out my side mirror, pushed a button and the mirror moved out a little. "That woman has some issues."

"I heard."

"She does not in the least like Darlene," Alan said. "I guess they fight all the time. She puts up with Gina okay, but they have some stuff in common."

"Their ex-heroes?" I said.

"Yeah, DD tell you about that?"

"We talked at the hospital last night," I said.

"Makes a girl have intimacy issues, I tell you what." Alan took a quick corner. "You see them anymore?"

"Dead Millards?"

"Yeah."

"Not right now," I said. "Did we lose them?"

"Maybe..." Alan squinted his good eye, "but I'm not convinced."

"What's your next step," I said, "assuming we get out of this alive?"

"I tried to talk to her about it," Alan said, "about what we saw, just *talk* about it, and she blew a gasket. She was all, 'Black Dart this, and Black Dart that'. She destroyed all of our targets with her arrows. Then, she busted up a bunch of her arrows. I stayed cool for a while, but man, after a while, I had to stop her. She was just nuts and a half! I tried to calm her down and that harpy shot freakin' arrows into my old car. So I took her arrows."

"And she socked you in the eye," I said.

"No, she plastered me in the back with her bow," Alan ducked down a little, "so, I took away her bow. Well, I tried to take away her bow."

"And she socked you in the eye," I said.

"She's surprisingly strong and bendy," he said.

"Did you guys ever, you know," I said, "were you guys... Did you..."

"Good Lord, no," Alan said. "She was strung tighter than a... Let's just say, she's not into guys."

"Ah."

109

"And besides, she's a little too old for me," he said. "Hey! I think I see a Dead Millard."

"And besides," I said, "you have Gina, right?"

"Dog Rabbit!" Alan swore. "They're back onto us."

"So the villain life isn't for you then?"

He just kind of shrugged and turned another sharp corner.

"*This* is for me," he said. "This must be what the original superheroes had to deal with."

"How so?"

"Well, lookit," he said. "We're racing to save a damsel in distress. We're being chased by rabid insane bad guys. We can't call the police because we'll be arrested by the good guys. Our personal lives are a mess and all tied up with our hero lives. Man, it just doesn't get any better than this."

One of the Dead Millards pulled up alongside the car and swung a mace into the back driver's side window. Glass exploded everywhere. Alan swerved and drove him off the road.

"If it got any better, I'd have to shoot myself." I picked glass out of my hair.

"Yeah, about that," Alan flicked glass off of his leather jacket, "I can't tell you... I had no idea that woman was so cold."

"And scary," I said.

"I mean, she tried to shoot Darlene," Alan said. "I had no idea."

"That's what bad guys do," I said.

"Yeah, yeah, I know." Alan frowned. "Scary and cold. I was so glad Forest called. It was perfect timing, but I hope you can forgive me."

"Whatever," I said and shrugged. "Just get us away from the biker thugs in one piece. *Then* I'll forgive you."

"I think I'm gonna have to do some rethinking about this driver thing," Alan said. "I just don't want to be tied down, you know? I just want to be able to drive."

"You can do that for the heroes," I said. "Who knows? Now that we saw somebody with powers, maybe there will be a bunch of superheroes popping up who need drivers." I looked him in the eye. "You think there are going to be other super types popping up?"

"I don't know." Alan frowned. "No, I'm not driving for any superhero."

"Why?"

"Well, first off, they can fly and stuff," Alan said. "Who needs a driver when you can fly and stuff? Second, I'd be scared outa' my wits around those guys. I mean, the guy with bulletproof skin ain't gonna be the target. The skinny guy hiding in the car makes a perfect hostage."

"I looked at all the broken pieces of glass in the floor. "What about DD?" I said.

"Hey," Alan said, "put your mask on."

"I don't have my mask with me."

"Dang," he said. "That'd be cool."

"I'm serious," I said. "You saw what happened. What are we going to do about DD?"

"What's it for us to do anything about DD?" Alan said. "It ain't our business."

"She's my.. friend," I said.

"I think maybe we should get her outa' this jam," he said, "and think about finding a place to drop her off."

"I don't think so!" I pounded the door. "We're here to rescue her and save her."

"And then what?" Alan said. "She could be, like, a bomb or something. She could be leaking radioactivity. I've heard alla' the old stories, too, you know."

"If I can't trust you, then I don't want you around," I said.

"Oh, come on."

"Can I trust you?" I said. "Can DD trust you?"

"Come *on*," he said, "I was just... You just gotta

think."

My phone rang. It was an old fashioned ring tone, like an actual antique telephone. The ID read *Wm Forest*.

"Hello?"

"Does the word Tulsi mean anything to you?" Mr. Forest asked.

"No, what... wait," I paused. "Is that a city in Oklahoma?"

"Never mind," Mr. Forest said. "Do you have your nozzle?"

"Yes." I pulled it out of my pocket.

"Tell Mr. Severs to take Third Street Road," Mr. Forest said.

"Take Third Street Road," I said.

"Why?" Alan looked over to me. "Woop!" He turned sharp on Third Street Road.

"There is a correlation between an object and a power," Mr. Forest said as if he were talking to a child. "Do you understand?"

I really wanted to but I had to admit that I didn't. Mr. Forest had a way of talking down to people like he knew everything and they knew nothing. When he wasn't yelling at someone for letting the paper blow over into his yard, he was talking down to that same someone like they were an amoeba and he was God Himself.

"Martin has his guns. I have my branch," he said. "Even your little girlfriend made her own item through which to focus."

I looked at my hose nozzle.

"So what, I just," I rolled down the window, "point and click?"

"Possibly."

"What's going to happen?"

"That is one of those tricky questions that I told you about," Mr. Forest sighed. "It all depends on the forces inside of you."

112

I leaned out the window, nearly dropped the nozzle, and aimed at one of the Dead Millards that were now gathering behind us in greater numbers. I concentrated and pulled the trigger. Nothing happened.

"Nothing happened." I got back into the car.

"Yes, I know," Mr. Forest droned.

"Holy crap!" Alan shouted. "How'd they get ahead of us?"

A line of bikes blocked us off on almost all sides. Alan did some kind of crazy maneuver like I'd only seen in the movies, and before I knew it, we were heading down some alley.

"No ramming buildings," I said.

"Now, the leader of the Dead Millards is called Prez," Mr. Forest said. "I had to tell them where to find you."

"WHAT?" I screamed into the phone, but he had already hung up. "Is this guy for real?"

"Crapcakes!" Alan hit the steering wheel. "We've been tricked."

"What's going on?"

"You know what this alley opens up into?" He gestured in front of us.

"What?"

"Nothing," he said. "It doesn't open at all."

He slammed on the brakes so hard that the back driver's side slid into the brick wall beside us. We stopped in front of another brick wall. The Dead Millards drove in behind us.

"I'm gonna have to ram them," Alan said.

"No, you could kill them," I said.

"They'll move." Alan looked back.

"What if they don't?"

Just then, a bus pulled into the alley behind the Dead Millards, effectively blocking our way out.

"No way," I said.

"Really." Alan nodded.

113

"Okay," I held up my nozzle, "we're going to have to fight our way out."

"Are you crazy?" Alan rolled his eyes and winced at the pain.

"We have to save DD." I opened the car door, and it slowly slid up. "It's what heroes do."

"Since when are we heroes?" Alan opened his own door.

"Since now," I said. "Grade D and ready to party!"

"I like our battle cry," Alan smirked. "Too bad we won't ever be able to use it again."

The bikers parked their bikes and got off. They each had weapons: clubs, knives, hatchets, and that one guy with the mace. They never said anything but slowly walked towards us. A few of them kept looking over their shoulder at the bus. Alan stepped back and put one foot back in the car. I held my black and white plastic hose nozzle in both hands and pointed it at the thugs. I closed my eyes and concentrated.

"Hey, wait." Alan stood back up. "That's my old bus number, see?"

The BB tour bus that had pulled in behind the motorcycles was loaded with people. The door opened, and the bus started to empty. Each passenger was another Dead Millard, and they were all dressed the same. Their dark overcoats blended in with the shadows in the alleyway and with the other Dead Millards. Now, the alley was filled with twice as many Dead Millards as before. To me, that was twice as many too many.

"You don't suppose they'd give me my job back," Alan stammered.

All the Dead Millards stopped moving. They began looking at one another and murmuring. Some of them seemed to purposely bump into the others. Tempers flared, and pushing turned into shoving. Before the biker Dead Millards could jump us, the bus Dead Millards jumped THEM. It was crazy, Dead Millard versus Dead Millard. They shouted and cursed and rolled around. The minute that Alan saw the bus pulling out of the alley, he jumped in the car. One big guy at the front of the crowd looked over and shouted at me.

"GO!" he said. "We can't hold 'em all night!"

"Are you Prez?" I started backing into the car.

"Yeah, now GIT!" He punched a guy in the throat.

Alan burned rubber and shot out of the alley backwards. Some of the bikers tried to come after us, but the Dead Millards left on the bus jumped out and grabbed them. Before we knew it, we were headed once again for Johnny's Laundry. Behind us, the fighting spilled out into the streets as the bikers tried to get away from the bussers.

"So," I said, "those *other* Dead Millards..."

"Called by Forest, I guess," Alan said.

After a few blocks, Alan did a double take out his window. "Crap!" he said and pushed the gas. "I saw some more bikers a block over."

"Did they see us?" I asked.

"You heard me say 'crap', right?"

"How many of these guys are there?" I looked out my own window but didn't see anything yet. I didn't know if these new bikers were actually new people, or if they had escaped from the fight. They should have to wear numbers or colors or something to tell them apart.

"Oh, they're quite a large group," Alan said in a professor voice, like it was something he read online.

Just as we turned a corner, I saw a few Dead Millards round a corner a couple of blocks back.

"Crap," I said.

"I know," Alan said. "That's what I said."

"Look," Alan tapped the steering wheel, "I'm gonna have to drop you off and hope they follow me."

I didn't see many scenarios where that worked out,

not the least of which involved me jumping from a moving car.

"I need to get up speed to put some distance between us and them," he said. "This may get tricky."

Alan practically used the sidewalks as another lane in the road. I don't know how he missed the other cars and the people. I had no idea that he had this level of talent. He did put several dents and scrapes in his own car. It was not very pretty, and I kept expecting to see the police show up, but they never did. When we got to the street where we were headed, he flung it into neutral and killed the motor.

"Gotta be quiet," he said. "Jump when I tell you."

"You're going to have to slow down about a thousand miles per hour first," I said and opened the door.

"It'll work," he said. "I'll call you later, or you call me."

"Well..."

"Brand," he said, "you can trust me... about everything, you can trust me."

"...Okay," I said.

"NOW!" he shouted and pushed me out of the car.

CHAPTER FIFTEEN

I had had some Trick training that actually involved jumping out of a moving vehicle, but we jumped into ditches and onto grassy shoulders, not laundry parking lots. At camp, I remembered a few grass stains and skinned elbows. This time, I remembered a lot more rolling and a narrowly missed light pole. There were more rocks than I would have liked and possibly a broken beer bottle or three. There was also a sticky bush filled with trash and discarded soft drink cups at the end of my tumble.

I didn't even hear Alan restart the car, but as I dug myself out of the shrubbery at the far end of the lot, I heard the distinct growling of motorcycles. Still disoriented, I buried myself deeper into the greenery and hoped I was headed in the right direction. When the sounds were gone, and no one had hit me in the face with a mace, I crawled out of the opposite side of the shrubs and dug something slimy out of the back of my collar. The Red Dart either hadn't seen me or he wasn't home. I really hoped he wasn't home, because it looked like my brilliant plan to just get caught by the police at the right time was going nowhere.

I snuck around to the side of the laundromat and poked my head around the back. It was starting to get later in the day, and I could see a light from the doorway. The door was open. This was very bad. The only thing worse than a locked door was a wide open door. I looked around the surrounding area. If I was able to get out of here with DD, I would have to know which way to run. On the far side of the building was a small wooded area. It would be hard to follow with a car, and there would be stuff in the way of any darts fired from a gun.

I wondered if I could get in through the front door, and poked my head around that side. The sign said *Open* and the camera was pointed out towards the parking lot. With my back up against the wall, I made my way to the front door and hoped no one picked this moment to stop by and have their costume dry cleaned.

The door was unlocked, so I slid inside. Other than looking like someone who was sneaking around, I looked very cool and innocent. I almost started whistling, but there was no one inside. The machines were off and hadn't been used by anything other than spiders in a long time. It looked like no one ever did their laundry here. If I had a hideout that was a laundromat, I would at least do my laundry there. There was a faded red curtain leading to a back room, and I found myself walking towards it. I actually looked at my feet and wondered what in the world they were thinking. Why were they so brave all of a sudden? I saw footprints in the dust where someone had recently come out of the back room and walked over to the window sign. Other than the footprints I was leaving, those were the only ones. I could see most of the next room around each side of the curtain, so I went in.

The back room was small and empty and dark. It smelled like moth balls. A light shone under a door that I was just sure would be unlocked. I turned the doorknob and confirmed that I was right. I let go of the doorknob and took a deep breath. I watched the yellow line under the door. My palms were sweating. I wiped some stickers from the bushes off of my leg, and pulled a beer cap out of my hair. I grasped the knob again and got right up to the edge of the door to look in. I held my breath and opened it a crack.

As my eyes adjusted to the light, I could see The Red Dart's hideout just like it was the other day. I could see completely through the room to the open back door. I could *not* see The Red Dart. The sight I saw, though, made my heart go to my throat. It was unbelievable, truly unbelievable.

Sitting in a chair in the middle of the room was DD. She was tied with her hands behind her back, and her ankles to the legs of the chair. She had on her full outfit, quiver and bow, and she was blindfolded and gagged. This couldn't have been a more obvious trap if there had been a big electric arrow that said *Trap here* in flashing neon letters.

Was DD involved in this? Was she helping The Red Dart? Did she know about this all along? If she did, I would quit. I would be done. I'd just go to jail or run away or die. This would defeat me right then and there. That's when I realized how much I cared for DD. If losing her made me lose all reason for trying, then I was in some kind of love. There was no way I wasn't going in there. Now I just had to convince my feet, who were so gung ho a few minutes ago, to move again.

"Fine," I said out loud in my head, but apparently really quietly out loud.

I didn't even try to sneak. I just took a deep breath through my nose and stuck out my chest and started walking. I blocked out everything else in the room, which is, like, the opposite of what you're suppose to do, and focused on the girl in red tied to a chair in the middle of the room.

"It's me," I whispered in DD's ear.

She started squirming and making quiet muffled noises. I took her gag and blindfold off and tried to take one of the arrows out of her quiver to cut the red scarves that had her tied up, but it was stuck.

"Push and twist to get it out," she whispered. "We have to leave here quick. It's a trap. You're..."

"I know it's a trap," I said. "I'm a Trick. I know traps."

119

I got an arrow out and started cutting her hands free. As soon as she could, she grabbed another arrow and started cutting the straps on her ankles.

"That was really quite amazing," The Red Dart said from the other side of the room. He was leaning up against a filing cabinet that was painted red. His arms were crossed. Wilma stood next to him. An arrow was in her bow. She placed one boot up on a bench in front of her.

I just about jumped through the ceiling. I mean, I was expecting it and everything, and it still just about gave me a heart attack.

"I mean, you jumped from a speeding car and you don't have a scratch on you," he said. "Don't you think that's amazing?"

Wilma gave a single quick nod.

I hadn't even thought of it before he mentioned it.

Wilma was still dressed as the Black Dart, so I figured they hadn't quite made up yet.

"Come on," DD said to the last strap that she was cutting.

"Let me tell you what we are going to do." The Red Dart stood up straight and took a casual step towards us.

"I want my car back!" Wilma snarled and kept her arrow trained on DD.

"Hush, Dartette." The Red Dart waved his red gloved hand. "I wouldn't worry about that. Once we're Grade A, we'll buy you another car."

"Okay!" DD jumped up. "Let's go."

"There are a hundred ways I could have stopped you. You know that." He patted his holstered gun. "Don't you want to know why I didn't?"

"Come on." DD grabbed my arm. "Don't listen to him."

"DD's been awfully keen on making grown up decisions lately, judging people, taking sides," he glared at her. "Are you going to let her make your decisions too? Hers got her tied to a chair."

"Why?" I said. "Why'd you set a trap, but not stop me?"

"I needed to get you in the room. Your Grandpa called," he took another few steps towards the middle of the room. "He thinks the powers really are back. He thinks you have powers. He's crazy, of course. The powers aren't back."

DD looked over to Wilma, who quickly looked away. She hadn't told him.

"If they *were* back," he said, "Martin thinks they should be stopped. Now, I don't necessarily agree. I think maybe they should be controlled. IF they were back. What do you think?"

"The powers aren't back," I said.

"You see? Now, that is what I said," he said, "but your dear old beloved and insane grandfather has gone completely off the deep end, and that's a problem."

"What do you mean?"

"Let's just go," DD said.

"Well, when he cries wolf, and nobody shows up with powers, then people aren't going to believe him. They might start thinking that the powers will never come back, that we don't even need heroes to protect us. Sure, he might be able to convince a few gullible people, people with mental problems, children, and the desperate, but sane rational people will figure it out. The SGHV will figure it out," The Red Dart looked around and pulled some keys out of his pocket. "How can I convince the SGHV that I can control the supers if there ARE no supers? My pending Grade A might be in jeopardy. Of course, if there really are powers, then it is a whole different ball game."

"What do you want?" I said. "Just say it."

"You young people," he shook his head, "so blatant, no finesse. DD made her choice. What's yours?"

122

I looked at DD. She dropped my arm and took a step towards the door.

"Come on," she pleaded, "please."

"It's simple, really," he said "You want to be an adult? I'll treat you like an adult. Whether you have powers or not, it doesn't matter. I've been compromised. I can't even trust my own daughter."

DD turned away.

"I'll make you a deal," he sat down on a bench and tossed the keys up and caught them again. "You work with me and I'll take you to the top with me."

Wilma dropped her bow and arrow right in the middle of the floor, turned and stormed out of the room. "Good luck with that," she said.

"Don't mind her," he said. "Sour grapes. I'll protect you from your grandpa, and we will even get him the professional help he needs. You join me and you will be rich and famous. You can continue your little affair with DD, here. Everything will work out. Nobody gets hurt. In fact, with a higher SGHV grade, and better resources, I can help even more people. You will be literally saving lives. You will be a hero, a hero like your dad, like your grandpa was."

"And if I don't?" I said.

The Red Dart tossed the keys over to me. They slid on the floor and hit me in the shoe. I felt like an idiot for jumping back. The Red Dart smiled.

"You think this is where I threaten you? He stood up. "I'm not a villain, Brand."

I picked up the keys.

"Who hired the Dead Millards to beat Brand up, then?" DD crossed her arms.

"That was Sydney's idea." He frowned. "I just wanted them to catch you and bring you here. I never wanted them to hurt you."

"I was already coming here," I said. "So, that makes

123

no sense."

"It was Sydney's idea." He gave a backhanded wave. "Look, you're a grownup. It's up to you. Stay and make everything right. Stay and help people like your dad did. Stay and be a hero... or leave. It's up to you."

I held up the keys.

"They go to the van," he said. "If you leave, I won't stop you. Of course, you will still have to deal with the police, and your grandpa, and maybe even the Dead Millards."

"Take them," DD said. "Can you drive?"

"Of course he can drive," The Red Dart said. "He's a man."

"I, uh, sure," I said, even though almost all of my driving had been at the arcade.

"I'm not going to stop you," he said. "I still want to make a deal. If you want me, you know where to find me, but you'd better decide fast. After the memorial starts tomorrow, all bets are off. Then, I'll bring you in myself. I'll bring you in. I'll bring her in, and I'll get my stolen van back."

I looked at the keys and was about to throw them back to him, when DD grabbed them.

"Enough," she said. "He'll talk you to death. Let's go"

"Where?" I said.

"Oh, that's right," The Red Dart said. "You have nowhere to go and no money. Perhaps you should stay. In fact, I would highly recommend it."

"Brand," DD pulled up to me and whispered in my ear, "you can't trust him. I can't trust him anymore. He tied me to a chair. Please, I'm not just some little girl having a tantrum. I need to know if...," she took a deep breath, "I just need to know if you're a hero or a villain, okay? I just need to know. Whatever you decide, I just need to know what I need to do next. I know I can't stay here."

"Let's go talk about it," I said and walked to the van.

"Wait." The Red Dart held out his hands and then stood back up straight.

I looked at him over my shoulder as DD pulled me to the van.

"That's unfortunate," The Red Dart brought out his phone. "It looks like I can't wait until tomorrow, after all. I need to have your decision right now. Hello, police? Yes, I need to report a stolen vehicle. Yes, I know who took it..."

"What are you...?"

"Don't even try." DD jumped in. "Let's get out of here. I know a place."

"Well?" The Red Dart raised his red eyebrows at me.

I got in the passenger side and closed the door. DD hit a button and raised the garage door. The van jerked a few times, but she pulled out and drove away.

"I've driven this old bucket a hundred times," she said. "Well, at least a few with Gina, when Dart wasn't around."

"Now the police are after us," I said.

"Weren't they already after you?" she said. "Besides, I know a place."

It was getting dark, and there was a fine mist in the air. I got a chill when the mist made me think about Grandpa.

"So what happened with you and him?" I said.

She turned on the van lights and pulled over to the side of the road.

"This is your place?" I said. "Along side the highway?"

"No." She opened a hatch between our seats and pulled out a screwdriver. She dove under the steering wheel and started pulling wires.

"What are you doing?"

"Here." She handed me a white square plastic piece

125

with several wires coming out of the sides.

"What is this?"

"Tracking device," she said. "I'm not some dumb kid who doesn't pay attention."

"I never said..."

"Throw it out the window." She pointed. "We're on a bridge."

She climbed back up in the seat and started the engine. She did a U turn in the middle of the road and headed in the other direction. Now that we were alone again, I started thinking about our argument. We just sat there in the silence, looking for flashing lights, saying nothing. The night seemed to be colder than it should have been and very vast. After a while I got up the courage to speak.

"I'm, you know, sorry about the hospital," I said. "I don't know."

"Yeah, well, you were right and I was mean," she said and took off her mask and tossed it in the back seat.

"What happened when you got back to the hideout?"

"You hungry?" she asked. "There's a little refrigerator under the back seat."

"Yeah, I kind of am." I took off my seat belt and climbed in back over her bow and arrows to the very back seat. "You want something?"

"Is there a peach in there?"

"Yeah."

"I'll have an apple," she said.

I noticed that we were heading down into a bad part of town. We hadn't seen a single policeman.

"I'm pooped," I said.

"He was so mad." DD took the apple from me. "He said he felt betrayed."

"You were the one betrayed." I climbed back up front with some beef jerky.

"He turns everything around," she said. "He's trying...

126

Well, you heard. He's trying to make this a good thing."

"People were hurt," I said.

"People were hurt," she said, "*and* Gina was hurt. He didn't even seem to care."

"Did you show him?"

She didn't say anything.

"Did you show him," I repeated, "you know, your power?"

"It wouldn't go," she said. "It wouldn't work."

"It wouldn't work?"

"It's all like a dream," she said, "like it didn't really happen."

"Oh, it happened," I said. "I was there."

"Your grandpa told Dart that you have powers." She looked over to me. "I thought you thought I had the powers."

"You do," I said. "I saw it, but people keep saying that I have powers."

"What do you do?" she asked. "Heal yourself?"

"I don't even know." I shook my head and pulled my plastic nozzle out of my pocket. "Mr. Forest gave me this thing."

"That hose thingy?" she said. "What do you do with that?"

"Look ridiculous," I said, "mostly."

"You could water the flowers." She smiled.

I smiled back and put the nozzle back into my pocket.

"Who's, Mr. Forest?" she asked. "Your mentor?"

"Grandpa is, was, my mentor, I guess," I said. "Mr. Forest is my neighbor."

"Did you tell him what was happening?"

"No, he's weird," I said. "He just seemed to know."

"He just knew."

"He's weird," I said, "but he helped me get away when Grandpa... you know."

"What?"

"The Red Dart didn't tell you?"

"Tell me what?"

"He could, like control water," I said, "like nothing I've ever seen, like powers, like massive powers."

"How did you... Did he attack you?" she said. "How did you get away?"

"Yeah." I looked down into the dark. "I don't know what happened. I don't remember. I was drowning. It was... I don't know. I think maybe the water hit an electric line and shorted us out. If the powers are back, though, what would it be like? How could the world survive with people that can control the elements?"

"I can't even think," DD said. "It's like a book."

"Or a video game," I said.

"Give me your hand." She pulled her glove off with her teeth and reached out.

I reached out and took her hand. It was warm.

"Promise me," she said.

"What?"

"Promise me if we have powers," she said, "you promise me you will be good, that you'll be a hero."

"I promise," I said, "but you..."

"No, you promise," she said and squeezed my hand. "You *really* promise. Never be bad. Never abandon your principles. Never betray or abandon people."

"I promise, I promise," I said and took a breath and looked her in the eye. "I really promise."

She gave my hand an extra squeeze.

"We're here," she said.

She drove around some holes in the street and broke through some construction tape.

"Is this safe?" I looked around at the vacant buildings.

"It never has been," she said, "but it beats the alternative."

She stopped the van and turned off all the lights.

"Grab the flashlight from the glove box," she said.

"The red one?" I said.

"Yeah, the.. yeah." She smiled and took her wig off. She tossed it in the back seat, reached over and picked up her archery gear. She tucked her hair behind her ears, put her glove back on, and slipped her quiver and bow over her shoulder.

"Follow me," she said.

"What about the van?" I locked my door behind me.

"I'm a little worried that Dart can still find it," she said. "Plus, the police won't have much trouble spotting a bright red Dartmobile in broad daylight. We'll have to find some way out of the city tomorrow."

"Tomorrow?"

"Maybe in all the confusion with the memorial."

"Alan," I stopped walking, "I should call Alan."

"Alan?" she said. "Are you sure? Can we trust him?"

"He drove me to you," I said. "He let the Dead Millards follow him. I have to know if he's all right."

I pulled out my phone.

"Wait," DD said. "They could trace your phone."

"No, it's not mine," I held it up. "Mr. Forest gave it to me."

"Can we trust HIM?" she said. "Maybe he's not as much weird as he is evil. How does he know so much?"

"I don't know," I looked at the phone. "If he was working with Grandpa or The Red Dart, he wouldn't have helped me."

"I suppose," she said. "But, can't they trace Alan's phone?"

"Who, they?"

"The police." DD looked up and around. "It's how they catch everybody."

"He was supposed to call me," I said, "to tell me he was okay."

"Here we are." DD stepped into an abandoned brick building. "Here's my building."

129

"Your building?"

"Where The Red Dart rescued me from a fire," she said. "Where my parents used to live. I've been here several times. GIna and I even spent some nights here. We found a room that's still in good shape."

I couldn't understand why she wanted to come here, or why she thought it would be safe. It was ready to fall down. It was wet and stinky and had rats.

"It's always been here," she said, "but its time is done. It's not going to last much longer."

We tripped our way through the garbage until we found one door that was still closed. It reminded me of when we were trapped under the hospital. She had a key and unlocked the door.

"It doesn't look like anybody's been here lately," she said. "Maybe my stuff is still here."

She locked the door behind us and turned over some boxes. She pulled out two sleeping bags and a battery powered lantern.

"I hope you don't mind pink," she said. "It's Gina's."

"You know," I said, "I don't want to sound... I mean, should we stay here? Shouldn't we get out of town or something?"

"You have a better place to go?" She turned on the light. Seeing the room didn't make me feel better.

She kicked a few cans and spread out her sleeping bag. The window was broken and had a black trash bag taped over it. I unrolled my sleeping bag next to hers.

"You kind of have to roll up the top to use as a pillow," she said. "It works better that way."

We both laid down and listened to the sounds of the city and the building. I was so tired, but I couldn't even start to sleep.

"Brand?" She reached over to me.

My phone went off and nearly scared me out of my skin. I jumped up and shouted. My heart pounded. I looked at my phone. It was a text from Alan.

U OK? it read. *Trashed car but lost DM.*

I showed DD.

"Thank goodness," she said. "You think maybe he should come get us?"

I'm OK 2, I texted back. *Talk 2 U soon.*

"Maybe tomorrow," I said. I climbed back into my sleeping bag and sat up against the wall.

DD got back in hers and sat next to me. "I was thinking," she said, "about my powers."

"Yeah?"

"You know how, and this may sound stupid, but I was doing some work, trying to get up the nerve to talk to Dart," she said, "but you know how when you pour all of the oil out of the quart, there's still a little bit left in there?"

"Okay…"

"You know, it dribbles forever until you get all fed up and just throw the container away?" She propped herself up on her elbow. "What if the powers are like that?"

"Like oil?" I said. "What do you mean?"

"No," she said. "I mean, like, what if the world was emptied of all the powers, but there's still a little bit just dribbling around that never seems to pour out."

"Okay…"

"And maybe people just slip in it sometimes and get themselves a little oily," she said. "And then it just slips right back off."

"You think your power slipped back off?" I said. "You think it's gone?"

"It seems like it," she said. "I don't feel all powery."

"Did you feel powery before?"

"Only right at the time," she said. "At the time, I felt twelve feet tall. It was amazing and scary. Then, when it wore off, it was just scary."

"Oil wouldn't slip off," I said. "Oil leaves a stain."

131

We talked quietly for quite some time about Grandpa and The Red Dart and Tricks summer camp and school and the powers and the new world, and not once about what we would do tomorrow.

The battery lantern got dimmer and so did we, and before we knew it, it was tomorrow.

CHAPTER SIXTEEN

I was battling the green woman thing from my dreams. We were in a desert.

"You can't fight me with little boy power," the green woman said. "You can't fight me with imagination."

"I won't stop," I said and stood.

"I know," she smiled. "That be the whole entire. The more you call me, the more I come. The more I come, the more I infect and spread and take over."

"Not if I stop you first," I said and pulled the water nozzle out of my pocket.

"Too late for powers now," she said. "You need to just keep fighting, keep mad. Keep wanting me and I keep growing. I was not able to keep you quiet, so now I must control you, envelope you, smother you."

Grandpa was there. He motioned and a giant bubble of water flew through the air at me. It sent me flying. The dry sand soaked up most of it. I wondered if that was why I picked the desert.

"You don't have to win. You don't have to lose," the woman said. "You just have to keep wanting me, inviting me in."

"Then, go away!" I shouted.

"Your anger keeps me here," she said, "and then you forget it all but your anger. Finally, I control all of little boy, and he doesn't even know. I control all in the sleep. I control all in the wake. I control all of everything, and he even thinks I help him."

"You can't control me," I said and wiped the gritty wet sand off of my arms.

"Oh, no?" she said and snapped her fingers.

Then I woke up.

I had slept hard. My dreams were rolling and twisting shapes like a dark ocean fighting a hurricane wind. They seemed so vivid, even disorienting, but I couldn't remember them later. When I woke up I had, like, motion sickness, and I was sweating. It was mostly dark, but I could see through holes in the trash bag on the window that it was daylight. I smelled at least as bad as the room I was in. DD was asleep halfway in and out of her sleeping bag next to me. Her bow was in her hand.

In the dim light, I could see her sleeping there. Her hair was in her face, but she was lovely. I don't think I had actually ever used that word before and meant it. I realized then that it had a different meaning than pretty or even beautiful. It was one of those things that can't really be defined by other words. It was something that had to be experienced to understand.

I got up and kicked the sleeping bag away, trying not to make much noise. I straightened my clothes and smacked my lips. I needed a shower and a toothbrush and something to eat and a change of clothes and a bathroom. I was sure that if I turned myself in I'd get all of those things. Life on the run wasn't much like in the movies. Sometimes it would be heaven to have clean underwear. I hadn't done anything wrong. Maybe Grandpa had calmed down and would get help. Maybe I should just go home.

A match lit on the other side of the room, and the grim face of the Mysterious Grim Fist lit up as he puffed on a cigar.

"'Bout time you woke up, sleepyhead," he said in a low and quiet voice. He put his fingers to his lips.

For some reason I stayed quiet. Maybe it was because he was just standing there. I turned to DD.

"Let her sleep fer a minute," Grim Fist whispered.

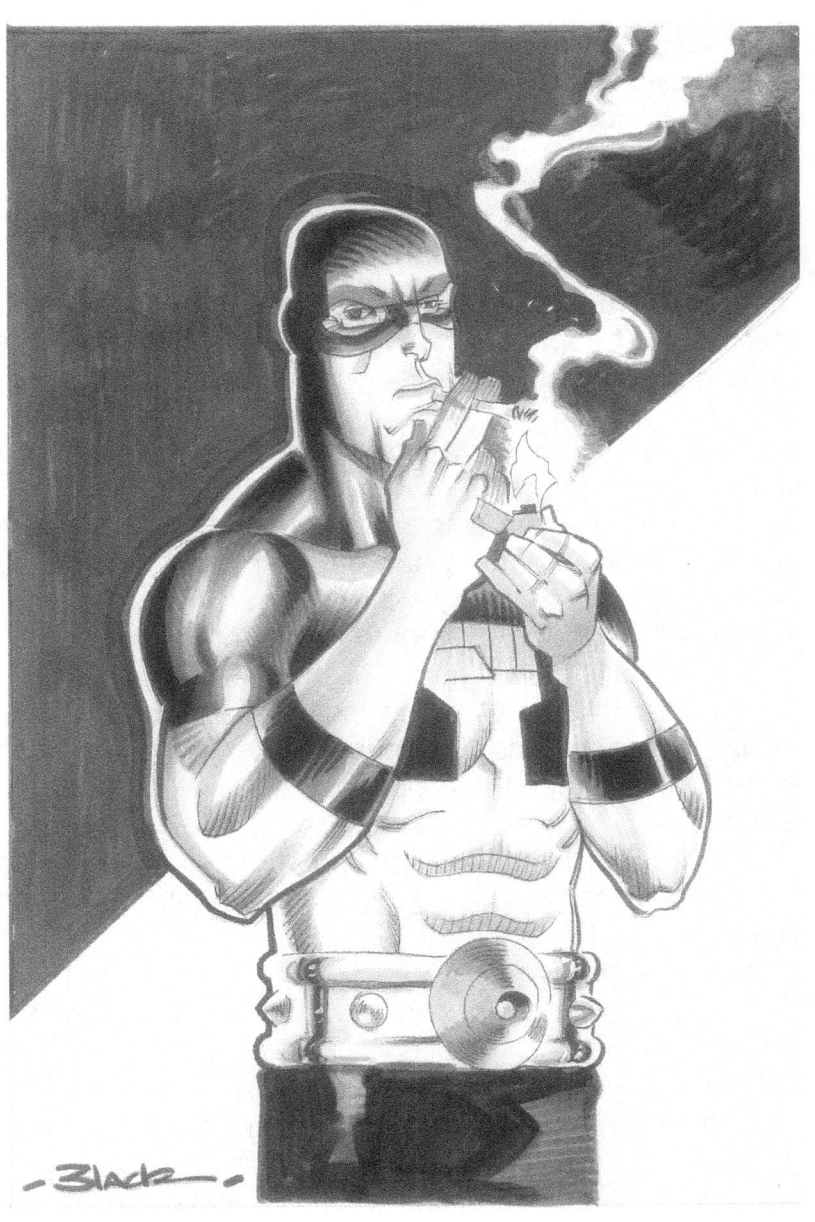

135

"C'mere, I need to talk to you."

I took a slow hesitant step towards him. He puffed on his cigar and gritted his teeth in what I supposed was a smile of sorts. A smoky low chuckle came out of his mouth.

"I won't bite, kid," he snapped his teeth. "I'm on your side. Forest sent me."

"How did he...?"

"Yeah, I don't know how he does it," he said. "He tipped me off about the hospital deal too. Said you'd be there, but that you had nothing to do with it. Told me to find you."

"Why are you here?" I stood close enough that I got a whiff of his nasty cigar.

"I gotta haul yer butt outa' here," he puffed away. "Makes no sense to me, what with your problems, but the old man knows so many weird things, things he can't possibly know, that I've learnt to trust him."

The room lit up in a burst of light.

"Like what?" DD stood on the other side of the room holding an arrow made of energy in her bow. The shaft crackled and popped and hummed like one of those in-sect zappers. All three of us squinted.

"How did you find us?" she demanded.

Grim Fist calmly put his cigar out in a large-mouthed beer bottle next to him.

"Now, now, little missy..."

"I have powers," she warned. "Don't come near me. Nobody's taking us in."

"So much for your oil theory," I said.

"Little busy here, Brand." She glanced at me out of the corner of her eye.

"I'm on your side," Grim Fist smiled again. There was something about a guy named Grim smiling that didn't seem natural. "Mr. Forest sent me. You know Forest, right?"

"Yeah," she sighted him, "creepy old guy that lives next to Brand. I'd probably point this thing at him, too."

"Look, I'm here to get you outa' here," he said in a calm voice that he probably didn't use very often. "Red Dart already knows where ya' are. If he wanted you bad enough to send me, you'd be his already. I'da just nabbed you while you slept. Me and him ain't exactly friends, if you remember."

I remembered. "Let's try it," I said. "Let's give him a shot."

DD pointed the arrow.

"You know what I mean," I said.

"Really, kid." Grim Fist took a step forward and looked at the crackling weapon. "Go on and put that thing away."

"I..." DD said.

"I c'n getcha' anywhere you want," he said. "Like I said, if I was after you to catch you or hurt you, I'da done done it already."

"I suppose." I looked at DD.

"I... can't," she said.

"Look, I know yer scared." He held out his hand. "This stuff is some scary sh... stuff. I'd wanna run, too. I'd be peeing my pants with this end of the world kinda' stuff."

"No, I can't," she said again. "I can't shut it off. I don't know how." Her arm trembled a little. "What do I do with it?"

"Uh..." Grim Fist looked around.

"Up," I said. "Stick it into the ceiling."

She pointed it up. "What if it catches the building on fire. What if it burns the building down?"

"Out the window?" I pointed.

"You could hit somebody," Grim Fist said. "Just think it gone. You thought it here."

"I can't!" DD said. "It won't go away. I don't want to

137

touch it."

She pointed it back up and shot it into the ceiling. Instead of embedding itself in the old plaster, it smashed clear through the ceiling, where it evaporated into the sky. A hail of plaster, wood, and rat poop rained down on us. Grim Fist had some descriptive language about it.

"Oh, my God." DD looked at her hands. They were glowing, but getting dimmer. "What is this stuff? Am I going to get cancer?"

"We need to get the hell outa' here." Grim Fist spit out plaster. "Anybody that saw that's gonna wanna check it out, especially today when every cop's on the lookout for suspicious behavior."

"The speech," I said, "the memorial."

"Yeah," he went to the door. "Why do you think the cops haven't been all over you? Every one of 'em's on duty, but none a' them's here."

DD picked up her quiver and put it on. She kept looking at her hands. I started rolling up my sleeping bag. Grim Fist checked out his vibrating phone.

"Leave it," he said. "The natives are getting restless. We gotta move."

"Where are we going?" I said.

"Wish I knew," Grim Fist put away his phone. "You're supposed to tell *me*."

"I don't know," I said, and just then, my phone rang that familiar old fashioned ring.

"Mr. Meeks," Mr. Forest's voice droned, "I need you to go with Mr. Fist."

"I was just..."

"Take Miss Deville with you."

"Where are we going?" I asked.

"To the car," he said.

"Where we going?" Grim Fist said.

"To the car," I said.

"I know *that*," Grim Fist said.

138

"We know that."

"Then, do it now," Mr. Forest said. "I will call you right back."

"Well, at least we know he knows Mr. Forest," I said.

"Look, you ain't gotta be scared a' me." Grim Fist led us out into the hall. "I don't care if you got powers. Frankly, I could use the help."

"Doing what?" DD said.

"If you guys got powers," he said, "there's gonna be a whole bunch of bad guys out there that do, too. I can hit a guy in the face, but electric arrows are a little beyond me. It's hard to come back from an arrow that could do *that* to ya'."

We came out a back door from where we had come in. There must have been a dozen alive Dead Millards laying around on the ground, tied up to one another and to a post and to concrete pieces. Some were knocked out. Some were angry and cursing. Ace, the cab driver, was polishing the chrome on one of their bikes. His cab sat in the road, running.

"It's about time," he said and hung a soft towel over his shoulder. "Some of these thugs we took out were starting to wake up."

"Yeah, well the kids needed some persuading," Grim Fist said.

"Did you...?" Ace looked us over. "You didn't..."

"Naw, a'course not." Grim Fist shook his head. "Like I'm gonna wail on a couple a' kids." He stepped over one of the Dead Millards. "Lookee here, kids. See what I said? Told ya' Red Dart knew where you were."

"Come on, Brand, Darlene." Ace opened the door. "I just couldn't destroy those bikes, Fist."

"Hope that don't come back to bite us in the a... rear end," Grim Fist got in the front seat.

I looked over at DD. She nodded. We climbed into the back seat and closed the door behind us.

"First of all, I have to know the truth," Ace said. "Martin called me. He was furious and convinced that you had powers. He said you attacked him. He sent me out to find you. Mr. Forest and Grim Fist here persuaded me otherwise. Now, I should at least give you the opportunity to tell me what is going on. I've never seen Martin like this. He's unhinged. Is there something I need to know? Tell me what I need to know."

"They got powers," Grim Fist chomped on a half smoked cigar, but didn't light it.

"Now, hold on," DD said.

"Is Grandpa all right?" I leaned forward.

"I want to hear it from them." Ace looked over to Grim Fist, then, back to me. "Brand?"

"I, uh…" I looked at DD.

"I don't know what I have," DD said. "I just have these... Sometimes I... "

"Energy arrows," Grim Fist said.

We all looked at him. He chomped his cigar.

"She makes energy arrows," he said, "arrows, but outa' energy."

"We need to get out of town," Ace said. "I have a cabin where I work on my cars."

"Have you heard from Alan?" I put my hand on the back of Ace's seat. "He's not answering my texts."

"I'm just sayin'," Grim Fist said, "if I had powers, everybody'd know about 'em. The bad guys would be filling their pants, boy."

"What do you do, Brand?" Ace said. "What are your powers?"

"I'm not even for sure that I have powers," I said. "Maybe self-healing or something. Even that is just a guess."

"Yeah now, *healing*." Grim Fist slapped the dashboard in front of him. "That's what I'd like. Imagine what you could do with that. You wouldn't have to worry about bullets or electric arrows or getting hurt or beat up. Heck, I bet you wouldn't age or get sick, even."

"People keep telling me I have powers," I felt in my pocket for my nozzle, "but I've never seen anything yet, not like DD, not like Grandpa."

"Wait," Ace said, "Martin has powers? Since when? What does he have?"

"Since when, I don't really know," I said. "Yesterday, I..."

Mr. Forest called me back.

"He is with me," Mr. Forest said. "Mr. Severs is with me."

"Hey, Bro," Alan said in the background.

"I may need a ride from him," Mr. Forest said.

"Ace said we should go to..." I said.

"Don't!" Ace said. "Don't say anything. I'm still not entirely sure we can trust him."

"What the...?" Grim Fist said. "Sure, we c'n trust him. He's helped me out fer years."

"Really?" I said. For some reason this really surprised me. I just couldn't see this old man worrying over his shrubs in the daytime and being a hero helper in the nighttime. Was he a Trick? An informant? Some sort of professional? Also, Mr. Forest has had his powers for years? Just how long have the powers been back?

"Yeah," Grim Fist said. "He's on the level."

"Where should we go then?" I asked.

"Let me tell you a little of how the universe works," Mr. Forest said. "The future, for one such as me, is generally set to just a few choice determinations. Sometimes, and most especially if I, or one with powers, is involved, the actual outcome of what will happen with certainty depends on a choice that has not yet been made."

"Okay," I said.

Mr. Forest paused. "Mr. Meeks," he said at last, "Do you have anything to tell me?"

"I'm getting really tired of..." I heard Alan say.

"Brand," he said, "tell me... what was your father's name?"

"I thought you... It was... " I looked around the car. "What does that matter?"

"You mean you don't remember your father's name?"

I remembered rolling down a hill in a wagon. I remembered him saving me. "Of course I remember," I said.

"Tell me," he said.

"It was..."

His name was Dad. Of course I knew it. Why was he asking me such a stupid question? What difference did my father's name make? What business was it of his?

"Trevor," I said, "Trevor Meeks."

"Fine," Mr. Forest said. "If that is the way you want it to be."

"What does that mean?" I said. "It was Trevor. Trevor!"

"Yes," Mr. Forest said. "You will need to turn around. Mr. Cannon's cabin will have to wait."

"How did you...?" I stopped myself.

"There is now a bomb," Mr. Forest said with a matter of fact tone, "at the memorial, right in the middle of thousands of people."

"A bomb?" I said.

Ace stomped on the brakes and threw us forward.

"Where?" Ace turned back to me.

"At the speech," I said, "at the memorial, right in the middle."

"We gotta get there," Grim Fist said. "We gotta stop it."

"Who put a bomb at the memorial?" Ace spun the cab around.

"Who set the bomb?" I asked Mr. Forest.

"You did, Brand," Mr. Forest said. "You set the

bomb."

CHAPTER SEVENTEEN

He seemed to know just about everything. Why did he keep asking me questions? Now he was accusing me of setting a bomb in the middle of thousands of people. Why was he doing this? Why did he insist that I knew more than I was saying?

"It's gotta be those Blackout Prophet nuts." Grim Fist spat a chunk of his cigar out of the window.

More and more people clogged the streets the closer we got to the memorial site. It slowed Ace down to a near crawl.

"I think the power of flight would be the best power right now," he said.

"Yeah, well, we don't stop that bomb, we'll all be flyin'," Grim Fist said.

"I don't know what he's trying to pull." DD put her mask on. "There's no way you set a bomb in the middle of the memorial."

"I don't even know *how* to set a bomb," I said.

It got somewhat darker as Ace pushed a button and tinted the windows.

"Maybe Mr. Forest set the bomb," DD said.

"Maybe," I said. " I've been wondering about him. Why is he acting all mysterious? And why would he set the bomb and then warn us about it?"

"Maybe he wants to kill alla' us with one go." Grim Fist moved his arm off the back of the seat as a glass partition rose up between the front and the back. Then it tinted too. "Maybe he wants the 'Mysterious' adjective."

"What's going on?" DD asked Ace. "Why are you rolling up and tinting the windows?"

"The crowd's getting curious," Ace turned on a speaker between the two halves of the car, "and not wanting to move. Cars aren't supposed to be here right now. I'm turning on the lights."

There was a thump on the roof as Ace switched from his cab lights to police lights.

"This is technically not at all legal. Let's hope that Mr. Forest is on the level about all of this." Ace's voice got that steely edge to it. "I'm about to blow all of my clout if he is lying."

"He ain't lyin'," Grim Fist mumbled.

"How in the world would you even get a bomb in here?" DD looked out at the crowd. "How could anyone?"

"Yer grandpa could," Grim Fist said.

I looked up at him.

"Just sayin'," he said.

Some policemen up ahead were not very happy to see us. They held up their hands for us to stop. They were already being shoved around by the crowd. Now here came a vehicle that was obviously not supposed to be there, and it was flashing lights to boot. Grim Fist grabbed the door handle.

"Stop," Ace told him. "Don't get out. You'll cause a riot. Let me handle this."

"Just what are you trying to pull here?" the first, somewhat tall policeman said as he walked up to the window. "Let me see your license and..."

"Whoa, whoa," the second equally tall policeman said, jogging up behind him. "I know this car."

"Thank goodness," Ace said. "Come up here." He motioned for the men to pull in close.

"You have got to quietly and quickly clear this area."

"Yeah, right," the first policeman said.

"You know me," Ace looked at the second policeman, "you know I'm serious. There's a..." he lowered his voice.

145

"I have a credible source who informs me that there is a bomb here at the memorial, set to go off at any time. We need to save these people and stop that bomb."

"There's no way to do it," the first policeman said.

"Four-Eight-Nine-Nine," the second policeman spoke into his radio. "This is NOT a drill. I repeat, Four-Eight-Nine-Nine."

He turned back to Ace. "If you're wrong..."

"I'm not," Ace said.

"My uncle wouldn't be alive if it weren't for you," the second policeman put his hand on the window opening, "and there's at least two other people I know personally who wouldn't either. You can always count on me."

"I know, Jim," Ace said. "It's the only way I can do my job."

Ace had a secret network of helpers throughout the city. It was one of the only perks of being Grade A that he liked.

"We gotta go now," Grim Fist said.

"Clear the way" the first policeman shouted.

"Four-Eight-Nine-Nine," police radios started repeating.

The policemen wandered off, directing people away in an impossible task. As we snaked our way through the solid mound of people, Ace kind of kept a low banter going. Most of the time I think he was talking to us. Some of the time, I think he was just using the sound of his voice as kind of a mantra to help him with this balancing act of driving through people without actually driving through a person. He talked about the day and the weather and different people that he saw. He told us about how he kept up his network of helpers with a woman back home who acted as a secretary. He told us a little about his father and his grandfather and his great-grandfather, all named Ace, all drivers for the Tricks.

"A trick," I said, "what if this is some kind of trick?"

146

"Then it's a good one," Grim Fist said.

"Then we've already fallen for it," Ace said.

He honked and blew air and puffs of smoke from the sides of his car to get people to move. Eventually, we got to the block with the large stage on it. Pandemonium was already starting to ensue. As we got closer, I saw Grandpa and a few old men and politicians being shuffled off the stage. The Red Dart and Wilma stood on the steps on the right side of the stage, and Sydnafly stood on the ground on the left side. When he saw the cab, Grandpa went back up on the stage alone. He was waving his arms and pointing.

"We can't go any farther," Ace said. "We'll run over somebody."

The cab was rocking from people bumping into it. Ace put on the brakes.

"Everyone please step away from the stage," he announced over his P.A. system.

"The stage, eh?" Grim Fist started to open the door. "You reckon that's where the bomb is at?"

"As close as I can figure," Ace said. "It's as much in the middle as anything."

I couldn't open my door for the people, and neither could DD. Then, I heard the screaming start. A manhole cover shot into the air because of a massive gush of water from the sewers. The cover landed safely in a small tree, but the water sprayed all over the place. It just kept gurgling up like an active geyser. Alongside the street, about halfway to the stage, a fire hydrant burst straight up with a torrent of water. Ace rolled down the windows, and we all climbed out and headed for the stage. Water poured out of the doors from the buildings on either side of the street. Grim Fist was like a train, pushing and practically running against the flow of the crowd. DD made some progress by squeezing through the people. I felt like a human pinball, being knocked around. Water under

147

my feet was running up the road towards the stage. I made some headway, but lost Ace in the crowd. Then I couldn't find DD either. It was like I was swimming up-stream.

Wilma had an arrow drawn and was trying to aim through the crowd. The Red Dart put his hand on her shoulder, but she pulled away and jumped up on stage, then down onto the steps. She couldn't seem to find a clear shot. Grandpa jumped off the front of the stage like he was a young man and went over to the drier side of the street. Every time he took a step, little rainbows shot up from his feet. The crowd around the stage thinned, and I could see Sydnafly duking it out with Grim Fist. The stage was empty. DD had snuck up on Wilma from be-hind and had her bow around Wilma's neck. Wilma was trying to smack DD with her own bow.

"Stop! Stop!" I screamed, but no one in the chaos could hear me.

Why were we fighting? We had to find the bomb. We had to stop it. I saw Grandpa over on the side of the street with his hand on another hydrant. I started walking towards him when I saw a man on the stage. It was Mr. Forest. He stood there tapping his stick, staring right at me. He tapped until he was sure I saw him. Then he pointed at his feet and walked off the stage.

There under the edge of the stage, was a circular trash can-like sphere about three feet tall. It was bright orange and had a small flashing light on top. How could I have not seen this before? In capital letters on the side it read *BOMB* and there was a digital display below it. Why didn't anyone see this? Why didn't EVERYONE see it?

Wilma flipped DD over her shoulder. DD rolled away and jumped back up, but Wilma grabbed her by the neck.

"Bomb!" I pointed and screamed.

"5... 4... 3..." the readout counted.

Grim Fist heard me. He broke away from Sydnafly

and ran to the now obvious bomb.

"2... 1..." the display read.

He leapt at the bomb as it exploded, and was caught in the blast of enough energy to level half of New York City.

CHAPTER EIGHTEEN

Time froze—literally—and I seemed to freeze with it. I saw the bomb countdown. I saw the blast... and then—time froze. I examined myself. I was leaning in towards the bomb. My arms were straight out in front of me, and my palms faced forward like I was warming them on a campfire, a nuclear campfire. I put my arms down and stood up straight. Absolute quiet engulfed the area. The water was frozen in giant spouts, but not ice. Even the water at my feet seemed as hard as the asphalt below it. I had a time pulling my feet out of it, like it was clay or putty.

For as far as I could see, the crowd was still. People on the rooftops, policemen and helicopters didn't move. Dogs were stopped. Flashing lights paused in mid flash. Grim Fist hung in mid air. The stump of his right arm was buried in what must have been a frozen explosion. Was the whole world frozen in time? Was I just dead, doomed to live in my last moment for eternity? Was this heaven or hell or some sort of limbo?

The crowd around us was mostly oblivious to what had just happened. There were one or two that I noticed that were just on the edge of wondering what was going on, what was that bright yellow flash of light or rumble from under the stage. The Red Dart looked as if he was jumping towards Wilma. Was he going to get involved in their fight? Grandpa had his hand on top of a water hydrant. The hydrant was cracking, and I could actually see little bits of water showing through. I couldn't see Ace, but I thought I could see the top of his car. Sydnafly was in the middle of getting up. He was wiping some blood from the corner of his mouth. Trash and splash and wisps of paper floated motionless on the frozen breeze. Walking through it was like walking on another world. I felt the frozen time against my skin. Nothing in the world moved. I was all alone in a world full of people. I didn't even have...

"Brand?" DD worked her way out of Wilma's frozen grip. "Are you okay? What's going on?" She waved her hand in front of Wilma's face and looked around in wonder at me looking around in wonder. We haltingly worked our way to each other, fighting time like the swell of a blizzard.

"I don't know." I turned to her in a daze. "I think we're both dreaming."

"In that you make your own reality?" Mr. Forest stepped out of the crowd of statues. "You could say that."

"Who the heck?" DD swung around like she was shoulder deep in a swimming pool.

"Mr. Forest," I said, and my head began to swim. "No, wait..."

I felt like I had drunk a bunch of cups of coffee. My hands were shaking. Something wasn't right in my head. He was Mr. Forest, but he wasn't Mr. Forest.

"Brand?" DD ran up to me in sort of slow motion and took my arm. "You've gone all white."

"I knew it would have to come to this." Mr. Forest walked up like the time-stream stop didn't affect him in the least.

"Did you do this?" DD reached back for an arrow.

"Calm down, my dear." Mr. Forest raised his hand. "I am going to need you on my side in a few minutes. We all are."

It was like my head was getting fuzzy. Their talking kind of turned into mumbling. I remembered a bunch of movies that I didn't remember watching. I was hot and cold and confused. People were talking to me, but not

152

people. It was like I was talking to myself. It was like a flood of memories coming in all at once, coming in and washing out all the old ones.

"Brand?" a woman said. "Brand?"

There was a girl next to me, holding my arm. She was dressed in a red costume and had a quiver of arrows on her back. Billy stood in front of me. He was holding a gnarled walking stick and he was old.

"Billy," I said.

"Close your eyes, Miss Deville," he said to the girl.

She looked at him and pursed her lips in a question. I noticed I was standing on chrono-affected water. Everyone around me was still. The universe had stopped. I wanted to get a closer look.

"Let's go big," I said, wondering what Billy had done this time.

"Brand?" the girl said as we went big.

As I expanded our consciousnesses to encompass all of reality, I heard the girl scream.

"Visualize us!" Billy shouted. "The girl is only human."

I recreated bodies for us, floating in space above the earth. The girl started retching into the void. The earth posed motionless, as if on pause, awaiting the press of a button. I felt odd, fuzzy, as if something was amiss.

"Oh, man, oh, man." The girl grabbed my shirt and pulled herself up. "Brand, what's going on?"

I looked around. "Who's Brand?" I said. "His name is Billy."

"She is speaking to you, Tulsi," Billy said.

The girl breathed heavily and tried to stand like a newborn deer on the invisibleness around her.

"My apologies, Miss Deville," Billy said. "You are experiencing one of the side effects of suddenly attaining cosmic consciousness."

"You..." she huffed, "you guys seem to be doing all right."

"Yes," Billy said. "Well, we've had some practice."

"So what is going on?" I said. "What have you done? I feel adrift. I can't quite remember things. You don't look or register quite right to me."

"Yes, that's the point." Billy pointed at Miss Deville. "Make a chair for the poor girl, won't you?"

I materialized a chair for her.

"Billy?" she said. "This seems... Are you...?"

"Billy's Bargain," Billy said. "I am the one who was supposed to have made the bargain."

Billy materialized a chair for himself. It was like the one in his living room, but I had never been to his living room. Why would I think that?

"What's going on with Brand?" she asked. "His eyes... They're all white! Is he blind?"

It seemed like she was talking about me.

"He is experiencing a re-revelation of sorts," Billy crossed his legs and leaned forward.

"You called him Tulsi?" the girl said.

"The battle," I remembered, "how goes the battle?"

"It goes," he said, "but not well. We need you back. Tarma is advancing."

"What battle?" the girl said. "Who is Tarma?"

"Who is this girl?" I asked. "Why is she here?"

"She is humanity," Billy said. "You need her."

"Why?" she and I both asked in unison.

Billy snorted.

"I hardly see..." I said.

"Why don't you remember me?" she asked, and she looked like I had somehow hurt her feelings.

"It's true," Billy said, "you hardly see. You should be thankful for that. Salvation is a murky glass."

"Why am I not dead?" the girl asked.

"It is not why you aren't dead," Billy said, "it is why you have ever lived at all."

I remembered fighting something recently. It was like

154

the wind, everywhere and nowhere. Was this the Tarma entity? Was I in space or under water? I sat down in my own chair and tried to remember. It was so aggravating, like a lost lyric or a forgotten name. We three sat there in the void of space, three chairs amongst the stars, our mental selves, observing the still, unblinking universe.

"You remember the stories," Billy said to the girl.

"What stories?" she said.

"Don't interrupt, dear," he said. "I wasn't asking a question. I was telling you."

"Tell *me*," I said, "what has happened? I don't remember the last thing I remember."

"I will tell you both," he said. "Then we may proceed."

I definitely remembered how maddening Billy could be. It was difficult to communicate with a man who knew everything. A voice inside of me told me that he didn't know everything, that he needed help to remember.

"I'm talking about the stories of the big battle," Billy said, "with all of the superpowered individuals clawing at one another."

The girl opened her mouth to speak but just nodded her head instead.

"It never ended," he said, letting the news sink in, daring the girl to say something.

"What do you...?" she said.

"Do not interrupt," Billy smiled. "The battle continues to this day, all over the earth, and the earth is tired."

"The earth..." I seemed to remember a battle-torn city, rivers burned dry, huge storms.

"You were there," he said to me.

"Was I there?" the girl said.

"Don't be silly," Billy snapped. "It was fifty years ago for you."

"Darlene," I found myself saying.

The girl perked up. Her name must be Darlene.

"Brand?" she said.

"No," Billy said, "his name is Tulsi. He is the living embodiment of a nascent universe."

"He looks like Brand," she said.

"He is Brand," Billy said.

Darlene cocked her head and looked at us. She was very pretty. I remembered humans. I remembered them suffering. There were so many suffering humans because of the war.

"He and I had an argument," Billy said, and I remembered that we did. I just didn't quite remember why.

"Can you start at the beginning?" Darlene said. "Why are we all here floating in space?"

"That is hardly the beginning," Billy said. "It's much closer to the end."

"He's the tree," I said as I recalled. "The tree from the Garden."

"Now, *that* is much closer to the beginning," Billy said.

"The Tree of Knowledge," I said. "Of Good and Evil."

"I guarded that knowledge," he said. "I helped to bring down the fall of man. I have been trying to stop it ever since."

"You're a tree?" Darlene said.

"It is harder for one on your world to understand," he said. "You have no miracles."

"We have miracles." She sat up straight.

"You don't believe that." Billy frowned at her. "You've never believed that."

She slumped in her chair. Somehow I knew that about this world. Humans felt this world was devoid of magic. This world...

"This world..." I looked at Billy.

"Yes," he said, and turned to Darlene. "As hard as it is to believe, I am not the person of import right now. Tulsi is."

"Why do keep you calling Brand Tulsi?" She took off

her mask and wiped her tears with her shiny red sleeve.

"You have to understand..." Billy said.

"Why does she have to understand?" I said. "What does it mater?"

"You don't think she has the right?" Billy asked.

"You know what I think," I said.

"Yes, I do."

I looked out into the stars.

"Every item and concept has a spirit representative." Billy pulled out some reading glasses from his shirt pocket. "There is a being that speaks for all glasses, for example. Another is the spirit of all glass. Yet another is the aspect of vision, and it continues for infinity, and the aspect of infinity."

Darlene looked at us both.

"They don't live here," I said.

"I'm getting to that." Billy put the glasses away. "Imagine someone who is the aspect of the entire universe."

"Like, God?" she said.

"No." Billy looked at me out of the corner of his eye. "A stand in, a representative, a mouthpiece."

"Okay..." She didn't really look like she understood. She fidgeted in her chair and looked around.

"When a new baby universe came into being, Tulsi here," Billy waved his hand in my direction, "was made to be its aspect, its representative, but more."

"I remember," I said. "That's right. I'm the embodiment of a new universe. The villains on earth were using another universe to battle me, another aspect."

"Tarma?" Darlene pointed at Billy. "Am I right?"

"Very destructive, you see," Billy said. "She is very powerful."

"I renamed myself," I said. "I named myself Tulsi, a plant that brings knowledge. I did it because you were my mentor."

"You also sought too much knowledge," Billy said. "You were an infant with omniscience, and it drove you mad."

"It did?" I couldn't remember that part.

"You got over it," Billy said. "But this battle threatened not only the human race, but the whole actuality itself."

"I took the humans," I said in sudden shock of my own actions. The memory came back so clearly, it was like someone had just turned on a camera in my head.

"You took the humans," Billy said, "*all* of them except the heroes and the villains."

"Took the humans?" Darlene said.

"And you made your own earth," Billy stood and looked down on the planet, "your own universe with new laws."

"I don't remember."

"A clean earth, a clean start," Billy said, "with no more powers, with no more magic, with no more miracles."

"But safe," I said.

"Safe enough," Billy said, "but the battle still rages on the real earth, on their real home. It's been fifty years here, but less than three minutes at home."

"I saved them." I stood.

"You condemned them." Billy tapped his stick on the nothing. "You cursed them beyond their curse."

I didn't understand. As usual, Billy was talking in riddles.

"Mankind chose to evolve," he said. "They chose knowledge of good and evil. They chose a flawed world that relied on the whims of miracles. You made them stuck and stale and defenseless."

"And safe!" I said again.

"You think they're safe?" Billy pointed. "Do you think she is safe? What happens when you leave?"

"I won't leave," I said.

158

"You have no choice," he said back.

"I am a universe." I could feel the rush of power in me. "I can do what I want."

"You've learned this lesson before, young Tulsi," Billy said. "Now listen to Brand."

"What about Brand?" Darlene said. "He looks like Brand, but he's not Brand. He doesn't sound like Brand."

Brand knows that humans need to be able to defend themselves," Billy said. "Subconsciously, he's been doling out powers down on earth."

"I've been..." I said. "He's been giving powers?"

"When Tulsi brought everyone here," Billy paced around me, watching me, looking into my eyes, "I followed to bring him back. Of course, I knew what he was doing. I also knew that this folly of his could redeem him. It proved more difficult than I..."

"Than you *knew*," I said and stepped away from him. "I'm not stupid. I knew someone followed me, and I must have made it difficult for you to know everything in this universe."

"You tried," Billy said and held out his stick. "But the whole lesson is that there are some things more powerful than even you. I could work things out with a divine branch of knowledge. You just had to keep living new lives."

"Wait," I had a sudden pang of memory hit me, "I died."

"You did this to yourself," Billy said. "You tried to hide this little pocket universe of yourself. You tried to make it so quiet and unobtrusive. You had to put a mask on yourself."

"I couldn't let the other universe, Tarma, find us," I said.

"She has her ways," Billy said, "and you are a product of your own imagination, after all, and the memory of billions of people. You became a hero."

"Mr. Mist," I remembered. "I just wanted to help do good."

"It was too hard with the new rules," Billy said. "So, you let yourself have powers, just a little. You just opened up the nozzle a little bit and changed the way the universe worked."

"And it threatened to reveal us," I said.

"So you used Martin Meeks to stop you," Billy walked up close to me, "to kill you, to give you a fresh start."

"You mean...?" Darlene said.

"Brand," I said. "I made myself Brand."

"And the powers drove Martin mad," Billy said.

"I took them back," I said. "I shut them down. I made myself forget."

"That kind of power bleeds through," Billy said. "Oil always leaves a stain, no matter the size of the canvas. Changing the laws of nature back and forth leaves scars, leaves traces. I tried to help you hide it, but you started doing little things subconsciously to bring yourself out. You kept hiding your impossible acts from yourself until it was just too obvious. You would heal. You would grant powers to others, all to remind Brand who you were. It was ridiculous. You should have accepted Brand. Eventually, you did something drastic. You set a bomb only you could detect and only you could stop by using powers. It brought everything to a head. Now you are here with me, trying to find yourself or lose yourself again. What did this prove? At least you, or Brand, learned the power and folly of helplessness."

"And the value of others," I looked over to DD.

"You should not have done it," Billy said. "It is all for naught."

"How can you say that?" I said, "I saved..."

"You need to come back," Billy said. "Without you, we will lose. Tarma will capture the whole actuality. She is just too clever and too powerful. This universe may be its

160

own, but it sits in the folds of the greater reality. You need to come back to defeat her, or else she will win and destroy this place."

"I can't," I said.

"I know." Billy knew.

"Why?" asked Darlene. "Go defeat this Tarma woman and come back. Come back as Brand."

Because..." Billy said.

"Because the only reason this universe can exist is because I'm here," I said. "It lives on my power. If I leave this place, it's like pulling the plug. Am I right?"

"Now you are starting to understand things the way I wanted you to," Billy said. "If you leave these powerless humans, they will die. If you stay, all of creation falls, including this place."

"And I can't bring all the people back to earth because it is uninhabitable right now," I said.

"Change it," Darlene said.

"I can't change it," I said.

"Forces more powerful," Billy said, "and all that."

"I would spend all my time chasing my own tail," I said, "running around mending fences while the enemy jumped the front line."

Much of what Billy told me rang true, but I was hearing dissent in my brain somewhere. It was more than a feeling. It was as if this Brand persona I had created had actually managed to manifest itself in my consciousness. Even in my addled state, I realized that was not a good thing. Not only was it bad for someone of my power to be compromised mentally, but it was increasingly hard to get my bearings. I couldn't get a read on myself, on my own universe. I had to be very careful who I listened to right now. I could do some very bad things without even knowing I was doing them. Furthermore, I wasn't even sure who I was talking to. These could be just aspects of my own mind. I had had a breakdown once before. Billy

161

could represent facts or authority. The girl could represent innocence or emotion or loss. Brand could be my conscience or internal strife, or the devil or the angel on my shoulder. I shook my body and thumped my head like I had water in my ears. I had to figure out what, if anything was real. It felt like there was a pressure on me, a physical pressure that I had to fight back.

"I want Brand back," Darlene cried. "I want to go home."

"Children," Billy said.

"Shut up," I said. "She needs me."

"She needs Brand," Billy said.

"They *all* need me," I put my arm around her shoulder.

"They really don't," Billy said. "You put them in this peril to begin with, then you changed the rules. If you hadn't left the fight, this would already be over. You had as much power as Tarma. You just didn't have the knowledge or experience. It is all a battle of the mind anyway. She has just proven smarter."

"If I leave..."

"Humans are resilient," he said. "Just open up the spigot and let the power flow in. The humans can take care of themselves. Change the physics so that they can have their miracles."

"No," Darlene raised her head. "It'll lead to another war."

"It's the same war," Billy said. "You really only have one ultimate choice. Time passes faster here. This world might have another hundred years as the next few minutes pass on the real earth. You could grow old and die with a wife and family. You could open up the powers and make yourself forget again. That way you won't be tempted. Your subconscious would be clear. Of course, your children and grandchildren would vanish in a moment of absolute universal sabotage, but Brand and DD could be happy."

Darlene's jaw dropped. I could feel Brand's memories and experiences fighting my own. He was scared. He was as confused as any of us. He just wanted to go home and hold DD in his arms.

"Maybe you should let Miss Deville decide," Billy said. "It is her life and her world after all."

"I can't decide the fate of the planet and all us people," Darlene said. "I'm just a girl."

"Then help him decide, girl," Billy said. "Time is of the essence. I need him to return to the battle. He needs to drop this fantasy of protection and let the powers flow back in. He has already opened the valve a little. Don't you want to be able to see great things? Tell him what you want. Tell him what to do."

"You already know!" Darlene threw her hands up. "Just tell us."

Billy actually looked taken aback.

"Which way does he decide?" Darlene held her palms up.

"He won't let me." Billy leaned over to her and held his hand up to me. "Tulsi's power is fighting mine. He won't let me know, so I can't let him know."

"Just do both, then," Darlene said in a near whisper. "Go do the fighting as Tulsi, and stay here with me as Brand."

I thought I might be able to do that. I could feel Brand inside of me like a separate person. Who was to say who was who? It was so hard to think with both of us in here anyway. I had the idea that if I could just purge this part of me, then maybe I could think things out. But who would I be then? It was so hard for both of us to remember. Was I Tulsi overwritten with Brand, or was I Brand taken over by Tulsi? Maybe I could clear both of our heads. It could work.

"It won't work," Billy said. "You know that. The minute

you left, this universe would collapse, and think of the harm you could do to yourself. You could lobotomize yourself. You could be a vegetable. You would be no good to anyone then."

"But I control the time," I said. "Maybe I could slow things down here or speed things up there, or... It's so hard to think straight."

"Then, listen to me," Billy said. "Without your full concentration, Tarma would overwhelm you. She would roll over your mind and soul like honey."

"You said I could decide," Darlene stood again. "I think we should gamble it all on him leaving us here together, going to fight Tarma, and then coming back before we die."

"I merely postulated the possible argument for your part in the decision," Billy said. "You have no standing for representation of your entire species."

"I believe in miracles." Darlene closed her eyes. "Even being born in a world without magic, I'm still human. That's miracle enough. Tulsi is miracle enough. Brand is miracle enough."

"Don't listen to her ignorance," Billy took my arm. He knew what I was thinking. "The stakes are too high."

"Not for the two of me," I said and waved my arm.

"You don't double your power when you double yourself." Billy shook his staff. "When you split yourself up, you halve your power. You become less, not more."

"Half of infinity is still infinity, and you know that," I said. "Besides, it's too late."

I felt a rush of darkness like the stars all blew away. Then a swirl of light wrapped me up like I was a part of the stars myself. Blurry dark clouds formed into focus, and I was standing with Mr. Forest and DD and a reflection of myself.

"The bomb!" I said to the myself standing next to me.

"Go take care of things," I said back, "and enjoy your

little miracles."

With that, they were gone. I stood above the earth with Billy. My mind was clearer than I ever remembered. All the truths were making themselves known. I looked Billy in the eye.

"Brand is a good boy," I said.

"He will never survive," Billy said, "unless you allow powers to come into this universe."

"He was never meant to be a life lesson in humility, was he?" I turned square on with Billy. I was refreshed. I was clear.

Billy stood quietly and stared at me. He frowned.

"He wasn't meant to teach me about humanity or helplessness or character." I stepped forward, nearly nose to nose with him. "He was meant as a distraction."

"Nonsense."

"I never brought humanity to a new earth." I felt angry and stupid. "I never came down to earth as a mere mortal to live amongst them."

"They are all going to die," Billy said, "unless you turn the nozzle."

"I never left the old universe," I said. "In fact, I never left the battle at all."

"How do you explain this earth, these people?" Billy backed up a step or two.

"The reality that is me," I said, "they are part of it. They are separate from the other earth altogether."

"You are sounding dangerously unhinged," Billy held up his staff. "You have had this problem before. You had best..."

"We've been keeping each other in check, haven't we?" I said. "You've poked and prodded and helped me create my own separate lie of a reality. These people were never who I or they thought they were, and neither are you."

"Ridiculous."

You've been worming around inside of me, excavating knowledge to use against me," I kept walking forward, and he kept walking backwards. "I've been fighting back subconsciously, the only way I knew how. You used the knowledge of my mentor against me. If I had opened up the possibility of powers, then I would have opened up the possibility for *you* to have powers here too. I've already caused too much damage with that. You figured you could win either way. Either I'm distracted with Brand, or I let your powers in like a parasite. It was your battle plan from the beginning. You're not Billy at all, are you... Tarma?"

"I'm not Tarma," Billy said. "You've got to believe me."

"I've believed you too many times already," I said.

I put my fingers on my chest, and like I was nothing substantial, I reached down into my core and brought forth a green-tentacled blob of energy. It jiggled and tried to bite me.

"See what belief built?" I said. "I pulled this out of my Brand self when I sent him to earth."

I reared back with it and threw it into him/her. It smacked him/her on his/her head, and sent him/her tumbling through the stars/planets.

"This was the infection you planted in my dreams," I said. "This was the hate parasite you were trying to use to control me. Take it back, Tarma. Take it back, green woman."

She stood with her back turned to me. Her back was hunched over and her head was in her hands. I could see the tentacled hate spread over her head and grow like long green hair that waved in the dark space. She growled in pain as the growth once again merged with her. She turned around, fully transformed into the green woman that I had seen in Brand's dreams.

"You fool!" she screamed and bared her fangs.

166

She was no longer blurry. Her hair was reticulated and sharp. Her eyes were blank, and her fangs were really bitey-looking. I was ready for her. She set to lunge, claws out, face taut, fangs still really bitey-looking.

"I kill you!" she hissed.

"Not a chance," I said. "This is my sand box and my rules."

Her muscles flexed and then relaxed. She stood up straight and sniffed.

"Sand box," she said, "little boy sand box... little help-less quiet little boy sand box."

She smiled. Her fangs weren't quite so bitey, but still were bitey enough to bother. She vanished, leaving the cold outer space, the mystery of where she had gone, and a trail of ozone leading me right to her.

CHAPTER NINETEEN

He couldn't know that I was watching him, of course, not that it would have mattered. Now that I was Tulsi again, he wouldn't know who I was anyway. Of course, I could make myself look like anyone I wanted to now. Time and space and everything in between was malleable putty. So, I made myself into a robin, and I sat in a tree and watched. I peered through the window of the house on this perfect spring day. I witnessed again the drama going on between those walls, quite literally between the walls. I could remember now. I could allow myself to remember. It was so important to forget before, but now the damage was done and needed to be dealt with. Now I could finally and openly remember the day my grandfather killed me.

Tarma was right about at least one thing. It was a difficult transition into universe-hood. It was hard to imagine that I had ever been anything else, but I once was. Attaining all powerful trappings is such a rush. It's also like rolling down hill in a red wagon. Once I realized the ability to look at things objectively, I could make things right. I was also able to recognize entities whose power levels were on my level. I had a nose for that and an acute ability to notice when something was a little off. It was a constant watch I kept on myself, so, I was particularly responsive back on the original earth, when Tarma was reborn.

I didn't know all that she had been through at the time, the children stillborn, the vacant husband, the loss of home. Even universes, it seemed, had domestic issues. When she acted out once too often, her husband murdered her. You can't really murder energy, though. You can just transform it. He apparently thought that her consciousness needed a good scrubbing, so he forced her essence through the very pores of another new universe, kind of like a strainer. He found out that if you run a consciousness through a strainer, it breaks into little tiny crazy pieces. It wasn't too good on the universe that was chosen as the strainer either.

At one point, her husband introduced us. I think I was still calling myself the Imaginary Man. He invited me to his home for a nice party with a bunch of Aspects and Powers that I couldn't even comprehend. He determined that it was too much for me, given my still delicate state; I wasn't much better than Tarma at that time. I didn't even realize that I was being checked to see how ripe I was, how good of a strainer I would be. Fortunately for me, he found another victim, and Tarma was disassembled and put back together. She was reborn angry.

She wasn't strong enough to destroy her husband, but she was determined to obliterate the little reality they were currently residing in. She threw a tantrum that threatened to wipe out every solar system, planet, dimension, and being in the universe.

She manipulated forces on earth in a bid to destroy the whole planet. She had to be careful not to take too heavy of a hand, or her husband would take note and stop her. She figured she wouldn't be noticed if she just nibbled away at the whole actuality until it died from a trillion cuts. She was wrong.

Her husband summoned me. I had been traveling, trying to make right some of the problems I had created. It was a journey of atonement recommended by Billy. Tarma's husband said he would help me in my quest if I would keep Tarma occupied until her little tantrum died down. He had grown fond of this reality and hated to see her trample it so.

I was to engage her in a limited battle to keep reality safe, but I wasn't to harm her. If necessary, as a last resort, he would step in, but he would rather not raise her ire any further. He wanted her to run to him, not away from him. I wondered if he was just scared of her a little bit.

Regardless, it proved very difficult to contact him whenever Tarma was on a rampage. She would sweep through and change what was real, all willy nilly, and then she'd make everybody forget what it was ever like to begin with. Sometimes she would leave a few miserable souls remembering what the world used to be before everything changed.

I would sweep in after her and change everything back. Luckily, reality has a shape it likes to fit into, but it's a little like putting a jigsaw puzzle back together with all the pieces turned upside down or missing or, as it happened once, turned into jellyfish, and there's no box to look at either. Babysitting this mad goddess became my full-time job.

She didn't take too kindly to my untying her knots. She attacked. I defended. She complained to her husband. I complained to her husband. He pretended like he had no idea what I was doing. It was a middle management nightmare.

Billy and the Tricks and I decided that we had to get rid of her, but not by 'traditional' means, whatever that was in a situation like this. We discreetly obtained permission from Tarma's husband, giving him plausible deniability in case it went wrong.

We baited her. We set her up. We presented a new universe ripe for the sucking. She could swoop in and claim the energy as her own, either before a sentience formed, or if necessary, aborting the new intelligence before it could mount any kind of resistance. I guess it was something that her kind—my kind—did to gain power.

The trick was that it wasn't a new universe at all. It was me disguised as a new universe, aided covertly by Tarma's own husband. I drew her in and trapped her there. Surprised by my command of the place, she was somewhat yielding to my rules. She was cut off from anything else, and the rules were mostly set before she even entered my domain. She had to obey my physics. I was to subdue her and lobotomize her, a universal surgery procedure.

To do this, I had to have surprise and standing and motive. If she broke into my universe and destroyed the place, I would have a good reason to take her out. I didn't own the other reality, the Tricks' reality. I didn't have authority. My bait was a nice new earth filled with billions of the humans she so hated, and a planet without those Tricks and their tricks and their connections. This conquest would give her another star, another mark. The currency of all powerful beings wasn't energy. They were already infinite. It was prestige and bragging rights. Her husband hadn't allowed her to conquer other realities for a long time. She could be in and out before he even realized.

Here's where my problem was, though. I had never created something like this before. This bait was more like a baby to me. I could no more allow Tarma to destroy this universe, as I could the other one. I also knew I would never get another chance. I had her husband's permission. I had her unawares. She would certainly be on guard after this if it failed.

In a split second, I had used all of my power to cancel out power of a certain consistency. This included superpowers and magic and certain otherworldly things. I quickly reworked physics to my specifications. And for it to work properly, I had to follow the same rules. That meant that I couldn't use any abilities that would supersede my new physics without rewriting them. I couldn't allow exceptions to exist, or Tarma would be able to use those exceptions to her benefit as well.

She instantly knew she was trapped, but she also knew it was my own downfall. I couldn't know what I had done. I just couldn't. With my problems in the past, knowing what I could still do in a powerless world would be too much of a temptation. It would drive me crazy.

So I created myself as a man, all in that one instant. I was Trevor Meeks, a good man, a sailor, seeing the world, having manly adventures. I was watched over by my father, Martin, a man finely attuned to and experienced with superheroes, except that it was all made up by me. The history was all a creation. Martin's main reason for existing was to be an alarm. I had stuffed all the power in the world down into a bottle, and tapped a cork on it. If that bottle cracked, or if that cork popped, Martin was then empowered and preprogrammed to take me out. He had to, to save the world and multiple other realities as well.

Tarma knew she couldn't reveal herself to me, because I might remember her and do something drastic. She was bound by my boundaries too. She had heard terrible stories of invading universes caught in the backlash of a dying universe. They could be forever trapped in the shell of the carcass, an eternal looping of infinite power. Having faced death and transference too many times herself, she wasn't in any hurry to do it again.

Now, here I perched as a little robin, watching myself get killed, wondering where Tarma was hiding and how she would strike. She must have been desperate to try to kill me now at Brand's birth. She had no real way of knowing what would happen, unless there was something I didn't know.

Omniscience was a temptation that some of the more foolhardy universes attempted. Most psyches were not quite as infinite as their power base. Most minds couldn't take knowing just everything about everything. I know mine couldn't. That was what drove me over the edge before. I tried to be like Billy. I didn't realize just how unique he was. I didn't dare look into the omniscience well to see if Tarma was hiding something. I could too easily fall in.

When Trevor first started realizing that water responded to him, he had no idea why or who he was. Super humans had been a part of the collective memory, but nobody realized that it was just a notion I had inserted into history. The whole world was only a few decades old. He did a few heroic things. It was pretty easy without superpowered resistance.

Brand would have to forget all of that. In a single spark of power, the rules would have to be reset, and Brand would have to keep forgetting no matter what.

Tarma gained power as Trevor did, and later as Brand did. Who knew what she might have hidden from me during those moments that I was so busy breaking myself. She couldn't even manifest herself while Brand was kept quiet. Only when the early vestiges of his power peeked through, was she able to make herself known in his dreams and quiet thoughts. I now remember those dreams, especially the later ones, that drove me to despair, and then to forgetfulness. That was quite a ploy, but I had been through this before. Subconsciously, I must have sought another way out. I didn't want to die again. I didn't want the power dampened again, no matter the cost. I sought a different way by giving powers to others.

I don't know what I was thinking. I jeopardized everything. Tarma could kill me. She could slip away from me. This universe and countless others could be maimed or destroyed because of my selfishness. If I got the chance, or found that I had to reset it all again, Brand would have to be erased. The very idea of superpowers would have to be cleansed from the human pallet. I will not let my selfishness endanger others again.

Basically, the house I was watching burst pretty much like I remembered it did. I forgot that the tree uprooted too and fell into the road. I flew over to the mailbox. There was Grandpa, a much younger man, immediately adept with his powers, because that was how he was created.

There I was as Trevor, picking myself up out of the mud, willing the water out of my costume, spitting the grass out of my mouth.

"Dad," Trevor said as he jumped up, "what has gotten into you?"

"You know, you know, you know!" Grandpa chanted, but I know that Trevor didn't know.

"Know what?" he said, pretty much like Brand a few years later.

Grandpa sat on a chair created out of water, surrounded by a force field of water, rolling through the broken debris of the house. He shot a beam of water like a battering ram. Trevor dodged it, but the garage next door got a hole above the windows in the side wall.

"He thinks he is a man," Tarma stepped up to the mailbox. "Hello, bird."

"I'm shutting you down," I said.

"So you say," she said, "but here is where I killed you once."

"You did no such thing," I said. "I would have sensed your power."

"You were so busy killing and birthing yourself, you would not have noticed even if I had floated out of the sky on wings." she crossed her arms. "Still, I took no chances."

Grandpa shot drops of rain at Trevor. Trevor covered his face against the gale onslaught.

"Listen to me," Trevor said.

"Last night I placed an inkling on the winds," Tarma

said. "I simply manipulated the ripples on the ocean that is reality. I breathed a few quiet words."

Grandpa smiled and raised his hands. The gale intensified. Trevor waved the water to the side.

"I gave up an idea," Tarma said. "I used no real energy. I just spoke so quietly that only a sleeping man could hear, a sleeping man who was plagued by the terrible burden of having to sacrifice his little boy."

"I remember now," I said. "You taught him a new trick."

I transformed out of my robin form and stood beside Tarma. Each of us were invisible witnesses to a moment that neither one of us wanted changed.

"You're not even here, are you?" I said.

"I am older than you," she said. "I am older than you and I am much older even than the universes from which you birthed. Age is important with us the eternal."

"But I am infinite," I said.

"As am I," Tarma said, "but I am more infinite. I was infinite before you were of infinite."

Grandpa gritted his teeth, and I winced at what was coming next. The rain that had been pelting Trevor and was now amassed all around him, suddenly, instantly, in one crack of transformation, became ice shards. Razor sharp teeth momentarily startled and confused Trevor.

"He thought he was a man," Tarma said.

The tiny knives shredded through him and dragged his soul out the other side. He slumped over into the puddles, now red, and died there in his front yard. Grandpa fell next to him in a sobbing heap. He would misremember this until it was necessary again. I would make sure of that.

"I always wondered how I was able to rebirth myself," I said. "Now I know that I was here from the future to do it. I didn't need to use the power from the present."

"And I and we stayed captives," Tarma said.

175

"I need to set this up," I walked towards my dead body, "and then, I'm coming after you."

"It is to be too late," Tarma said. "I am already killing you some time now. You are already being too late."

"Nonsense," I said. "It's time travel, not something difficult. I'm never out of time."

"You see?" Tarma smiled. "With age, we and you can always learn."

She slowly started to fade.

"Of course," she said, "I am never without the time too."

I wondered just where and when she went. I was afraid that if I followed her scent, it would just lead me off the path again. Then Brand helped me. I remembered the first time I saw Tarma, before the dreams, in a situation where I could be killed and her involvement would never be detected.

"Thanks, Brand," I said.

CHAPTER TWENTY

It was like we were in the eye of a scribbled tornado. We floated in white space while thousands of black scribbles zipped around in circles all around us.

"Do you smell hairspray?" DD said.

She grabbed my arm with both hands. A minute ago we were standing on the stars. Now we were floating in a scribble cloud.

"Oh, man," I said, "I must be dreaming."

"Don't be dreaming, Brand." DD's hair blew into her face as the scribbles flew closer. "Don't be dreaming."

"O-okay," I said.

A few minutes later, the scribbles turned and flew away from us like we had suddenly become poisonous. The white got darker, and shapes took form. A floor appeared under our feet, and walls around us. When the scene finally came into focus, I still wasn't entirely convinced that I wasn't dreaming.

I was in a large stone room with a rounded stone ceiling. It must have been an old church. DD stood beside me. Piles of stinking smoking blackened creatures were all around us. I didn't know what they were. They looked like winged reptiles. I wasn't sure if they were dragons or demons or dinosaurs, but none of them were moving. Behind us were church pews. Sitting in the front pew was a dirty little man. He held a black wooden cane with a serpent's head on the end. He had his head down, and the cane rested on his chubby little lap.

"Is that..." DD said.

"You've seen the movies," I said. "We've all seen the

historical news reels."

A door flew open up at the front of the church, to the side where the choir would sit. A limp creature was flung out. It landed by the pulpit and didn't move. I pulled my nozzle out of my pocket. People from my history books walked out in front of me.

"You must be the help that Billy told us almost nothing about," a woman said.

This woman walked up to me and shook my hand. She was one of the most beautiful and healthy women I had ever seen in real life. She wore a red and black flannel shirt and dark jeans. Her shirt was unbuttoned several buttons, and a smooth amber stone was glowing around her neck. Her long dark hair was pulled back in a messy ponytail.

"I'm Sarah," she said, then to the little man. "These guys are just kids, Billy."

"Uh," I said back.

"Who are you two?" a man behind Sarah said.

"Pleased to meet you," Sarah shook DD's hand.

DD gave a slight curtsey and looked at me out of the corner of her eyes. She held out her hand to the man, but he just nodded at us. He was about average height and build. He didn't have a smudge on him. None of the few hairs he had on his head were out of place. He didn't have a rip or tear anywhere on his clothes.

"Phil," I said.

"Have we met?" he said. "Sorry, it's been so crazy the last few days. I forget who I've met already. Were you in the park with *Chaltroon*!? I thought we had them there until they brought in that crack worm."

"That's the last one I could find." A man in leather walked through the door, holstering a handgun.

"Are you Millard from the Tricks?" I said.

I walked right away from DD and Phil and Sarah, right up to this black-clad man with long gray hair.

"Yes." He walked past me over to Sarah and Phil. "Are we expecting any more?"

"Heroes or demons?" Phil asked.

DD walked up to me. "They're talking real words," she said. "You know what I mean?"

"New words," I said. "Things that aren't recorded, things that aren't in a script or a book."

"We have fifteen minutes before a group of Russian super villains and three scientists beam in," the man on the pew said, looking up. "Yes, I'm Billy. Yes, it's true."

It was Billy. I couldn't hardly believe it was true.

"What did you find out about them?" Millard walked over to Billy.

"The Russians or these kids?" Sarah asked.

"Rit," Billy said, "burn a small hole above this south window and slice through the middle beam of the ceiling."

The stone on Sarah's neck shot out two light beams that destroyed what Billy directed.

"The villains will be no problem," Billy said. "Just move when I tell you."

"No problem," Phil said.

"Very little problem," Billy said, "and Millard, these are the children."

Millard looked me up and down. Then, he gave me a big old hug and lifted me off the floor.

"Excellent," he said.

Billy stood up as Millard gave DD a big hug. Sarah patted us on the backs. I could hardly look at her without blushing for some reason.

"Well, then, we're going to vaporize these K'thnark bodies before the Russians arrive," Sarah said.

She walked to a pile of demons. Her amulet, named Rit, shot out a precise beam that incinerated a pile of the beasts, but left the wooden floor intact. My head was starting to clear a little. I remembered the other me, Tulsi, talking about two earths, that there was never really a battle on my earth, but it was still happening right now on another earth.

"Yes," Billy said. "My mind is clearing too. You see, I know everything from all actualities, but this one was hidden from me. Tulsi had to keep it a secret to lure Tarma into a trap."

"Did it work?" Phil said.

"I don't..." Billy made a face like he'd bitten into a lemon. "We'll find out soon enough."

"We've got to get back," DD said.

Her eyes popped open and she grabbed my arm. "The battle in New York, the bomb!"

"We have a battle here too," Millard said, "and bombs going off in every corner of the city."

"But you have you," I said. "We're all we have at our home."

Billy shook his head and frowned.

"Please," he said, "we can do both. Now that I've recovered from that rush of new information from when you two teleported in, I can set my plan into motion."

Sarah rolled her eyes.

"Obviously, we don't have much time," Billy said. "Millard, give me your Eden Stone."

"What good are they going to do there?" Millard handed a small stone to Billy.

"They have to go back home," Billy said.

He handed me the stone. It was round and white, but flat like the stones I skipped on the pond in the park when Grandpa and I would go feed the ducks.

"Ah, good," Billy said, "we have another anomaly coming in."

"It's been fifteen minutes already?" Phil looked at his wrist watch.

"No, this is something else from Brand and DD's actuality." Billy sat back down and gripped his cane. He closed his eyes and braced himself. The Tricks stepped back to the walls. DD and I sat down next to Billy.

The scribbles made a tornado column right where we were first standing. It swirled for a moment and then vanished. Grim Fist now stood in the church with us. He stood straight and didn't say a word. Billy slumped over into my lap.

"Grim Fist!" DD jumped up.

She took his arm and jumped back in pain as an arc of electricity shot off of Grim Fist. She fell back into Sarah's arms as the Tricks rushed forward. Millard drew his gun.

"Hold on, wait!" I said.

I pushed Billy off of me. He slumped over the other way. I rushed over to DD and took her arm. She seemed to be all right. Whichever Trick was holding her let go, and DD put her arms on my shoulders.

"It's okay," she said.

Grim Fist just stood there.

"Who is Grim Fist?" Millard asked DD.

"Spark," Grim Fist said.

He flickered a little, like he was fading in and out.

"He's your ride," Billy said. "Wow, that brought in a lot of information. This isn't the man you know as Grim Fist. This is a tiny temporary byte of Tulsi."

"Did he get her?" Phil said. "Is Tarma defeated?"

"Apparently, she has set up a bubble around our entire actuality," Billy said. "She even hid it from me. Getting these kids back home is going to take a lot more work than I had planned. And sacrifice. It's going to take sacrifice."

Billy stood and limped a circle around Grim Fist.

"Spark," Grim Fist said.

"All of your plans involve sacrifice," Millard said.

"You of all people should realize the value in sacrifice," Billy said. "It's worth it."

"Not always," Sarah said.

181

"Sparky," Phil said to Grim Fist, "what is going on? What do you need?"

"Spark," Sparky said.

"He wants to take them home," Billy said. "I can help with that."

Sparky turned his head to look at Billy.

"Tulsi trusts me," Billy said. "Do you trust me, Sparky?"

Sparky remained quiet.

Millard raised his eyebrow and looked at me and DD.

"Do *you* trust him?" he asked us.

"He's Billy," DD said. "He supposedly ended the war. He supposedly saved the planet."

"That was before," I said, "back before we found out that our history was all a lie."

"Sounds like Billy," Millard mumbled.

"I didn't even know about this other world until a few minutes ago," Billy said. "Saving them and giving Tulsi purpose could be as important as anything. We don't want another Tarma on our hands."

"Then, what do we do?" Phil said.

"We get them to the Eden Rock," Billy said. "That anchor and lightman should almost be enough to send them back."

"Almost?" Millard said.

"lightman?" I said. That name sounded familiar.

"Not, lightman," Phil put his hand on his forehead, "lightman. There's a slight difference in pronunciation and in how he acts when you say it wrong."

"How do we do that?" Sarah said. "lightman is guarding the rock. He's sending Russian villains here in a few minutes to keep them away. How do we even get there in time?"

"No one is available right now," Phil said. "The Unbourne Heroes are keeping the onslaught contained in the city. The Fists Club is down on the docks fighting the Dark Water. The Hovering are spread out over three other churches. The Keys are in talks with the League of Aspects. Even the Lesser Ones are down in the sewers fighting the Remnants."

"Not to mention the rest of the Tricks," Sarah said.

"I assume you'll need the other Eden Stones to get them to the Eden Rock," Millard said.

"My thoughts exactly," Billy said. "Brand? Give this stone to Sparky here. If you and DD can help us, we will do all we can to get you home. Even in this mess, we have a lot of resources."

"Helping heroes is what I do," I said. "I'm a Trick."

Millard looked at Sarah.

I dropped the stone in Grim Fist's hand. We were all calling him Sparky now.

"These stones were used to help the Tricks," Billy said. "If they got into too much trouble, they could teleport to another stone."

"We can't take their stones," DD said to me. "That would leave them helpless."

"She's right," I said.

"We don't have time to argue," Billy said. "It doesn't do any good to argue with me, anyway. I know everything. Besides, they won't need the stones. They'll have you."

"Do it," Millard said. "I'm not too happy about going along with one of Billy's schemes, but we don't have much choice right now. Anyway, I always help a fellow Trick."

I looked to DD. She nodded.

"Concentrate on this energy signature," Billy said to Sparky and pointed at the stone in Sparky's hand. "Go to the next closest one."

"How can we help the Tricks?" DD whispered. "These

183

guys are real superheroes."

"Spark," Sparky said, and the three of us vanished.

CHAPTER TWENTY-ONE

Melvin Krumsnucker was an evil little man. No matter where he was, he was just a vindictive sociopathic rat. He was also very unique. He didn't know just how unique he was either, and I would bet that was on purpose. I had no idea of his specialness either until right this moment, or how I was the reason.

I told Tarma that time travel was easy, and for me it was, especially in this universe. I just didn't admit to how confusing I found it, as well. I wanted to home in to myself as Brand, just before he saw us in the basement during the Counterfeiter fight. Instead, I found myself standing next to Melvin moments before Alan crashed the bus through the wall. Nobody knew I was there, but Melvin was sniffing the air and holding tight to a briefcase. He was standing next to a very busy Gray Hand. The Red Dart was in another part of the building tackling the Counterfeiter, and the Dartettes hadn't gotten there yet.

"Out of my way, idiot," the Gray Hand pushed aside Melvin, and strung some wires to the door.

Melvin's face got red. He pushed his little rectangular glasses back up on his long thin nose and stomped.

"The cops come through here, they are going ta' get a real shock," the Gray Hand snickered. "You going ta' do anything, pipsqueak? I thought you was supposed ta' be setting the bombs."

He pushed Melvin's briefcase and knocked him backwards over a chair.

"You idiot!" Melvin spit and pushed his glasses up. "This is an explosive device."

185

"Then grow a pair and do your job," the Gray Hand said.

The Dartettes showed up on the balcony and pointed.

I was reading energy patterns off of Melvin that were interesting. The patterns were very low, and I doubted I would have even noticed them if I hadn't been looking for energy patterns outside of the ambient white noise. If I wasn't mistaken, these were energy patterns that hadn't been manipulated yet, hadn't passed through the proper stream. This energy, in other words, was future energy.

What's more, Melvin was not one of my universe creations. He was from the old earth. Some time in the future, I must have brought Melvin over to the current past. I had no idea why I would do such a careless thing to my universe, but here he was. I didn't recognize him during my brief encounter with him when I was Brand, but I sure did now.

Melvin was headed for the basement when Gina shot an arrow into the basement door to stop him. He stepped back just as the bus crashed through the wall. Melvin and the Gray Hand fell together on the floor.

"Move it, you worthless moron," the Gray Hand said.

He threw Melvin aside head first into a wall. Melvin smacked his head and bit his lip. A little drop of blood spilled out of his mouth.

"You are the moron," he said under his breath.

He grabbed the electric line that the Gray Hand had taped to the door, and shoved it into the Gray Hand's utility belt. The Gray Hand yelled and turned. As he did, the wires hit a metal canister and exploded. This set off a cascade of gas explosions that obscured the view of everyone.

Melvin walked to the basement door that had been knocked ajar when the bus hit the wall. He slipped inside, and I followed him. I remade my eyes in order to see properly in the large dark and somewhat smoky room.

186

Melvin placed his explosives and set the timer. He ran for the stairwell where Brand and Alan were just entering the room.

"Outa' my way, outa' my way, outa' my way," Melvin yelled.

He pushed them away and ran up the stairs.

Tarma appeared on the other side of the room, and I met with her immediately.

"No," I grabbed her hair and pulled against her.

"Help!" she called out.

"Stop it. You're through."

She slashed at me with her claws. We both became visible. She was calling Brand over to her.

"I will kill him before he becomes loud," she hissed. "Help!"

I grabbed one of her arms and pulled it around behind her. She twisted out of my grip and put her hands around my throat.

"Brand, help me!" she said.

"Nice try," I said, "but you're not getting anywhere near him.

I got her around her throat, as well.

"You... could not have..." she said. "How you here... first?"

"Intuition," I said.

"I slice your soul," she said.

"Hey!" Brand said to us. "We need..."

Tarma dove at him with her claws and fangs, but I was able to push her aside. I covered Brand with myself and shielded him. He was cut badly and had inhaled way too much smoke and gas, and yet, here he was, coming to the aid of someone he thought needed help. He had no idea how much time was left on the bomb. He had no idea how bad of shape he was in. He had no idea he was walking into a trap.

I couldn't risk revealing myself further, but I couldn't

just do nothing for the kid who would risk anything to help. I accelerated his healing in order to get him through this and to build his physical strength. He was going to need it in the next few days. I moved him to the door where Alan found him and pulled him up the stairs.

Tarma was gone. I couldn't sense or smell her anymore. I dampened Brand's energy signal to make it harder for her to find him in the future. I knew when she would strike again, but I didn't know if she knew, and I wasn't sure exactly what she was up to.

I saw the blinking from Melvin's bomb and wondered just how much trouble he might cause in the future... if there was a future. I gave a slight nod and turned his bomb into grain. Something for the rats to eat.

CHAPTER TWENTY-TWO

There was a poof of air as DD, Sparky, and I materialized somewhere outside in the middle of a crowd of people. Several people were pushed back and down, which allowed us to teleport in. There must have been hundreds of people all around, carrying bags and bundles and children and pets, murmuring and shuffling and crying.

"C'mon, c'mon, c'mon!" the loud voice of a woman called to the people from somewhere up ahead. "Move it! Faster! Don't run! Hurry up! Be careful!"

"Where are we?" DD said.

"There you are!" the woman's voice said.

Jumping up above the crowd from the tops of streetlights was a petite woman in a black unitard. She was incredibly fit and agile, as she hopped from the top of one light clear across to the next one. She swung around it a couple of times, and lit on top like it was as simple as walking down the sidewalk. I recognized her immediately, and pointed to her.

"Felicia," DD said.

She knew the Tricks' history pretty well.

"I bet Jeff's around here somewhere," DD said.

Felicia jumped up into the sky and spread her arms wide. She smiled and clasped her hands in front of her like she was doing a high dive. She fell through the air right towards us, and in a blaze of speed, at the last second, she twisted around and landed gracefully at our feet.

"Hey guys," she said, "Billy-boy said you guys were coming."

"What's going on?" I said.

"Hey, man," Felicia tapped Sparky on the shoulder.

The back of her hand zapped with electricity. She jerked it back and put her knuckle in her mouth.

"Jeez!" she said. "Man!"

She flipped her hand around in the air and turned in a circle. Sparky never even acknowledged her.

"Little warning, guys," she said. "I didn't know the robot was booby trapped."

"He's not a robot," DD said.

"What is he?" Felicia looked at his blank eyes.

"I'm not sure," I said. "I think we don't know."

"Spark," Sparky said.

I heard some whistling, like someone was trying to get our attention.

"We've got to hurry here," Felicia said. "I'm Felicia. Up there a ways is Jeff."

DD poked me in the ribs and smiled.

"It's so cool to actually meet you," I said, "but what can we do?"

"Jeff's taking people into his pocket dimension," Felicia said.

She jumped straight up into the air, probably fifteen feet. At the height of her leap, she twisted and shaded her eyes.

"Yep, he's calling for us," she said. "A lotta people have done a lotta fighting to give us this break. They're holding back a bunch of crazies to help us gather up these folks. I don't know how much longer we have. We got to get these people through that portal before the bad guys bust in, or before Jeff poops out. It's going to be close to see which happens first. Anybody left here when that happens is going to be sorry. Well, they'll be sorry for a few minutes, anyways. After that, there won't be enough of them left to be sorry."

"What can we do?" DD stepped forward. Her bow

190

blazed in her hand.

"Put that away," Felicia waved her hand. "Our priority is moving people. If it comes to fighting, the four of us won't matter much."

I put my hand on my water nozzle. Felicia grabbed my other hand. I reached out for DD as Felicia started dragging us through the crowd.

"Sparky!" DD said.

Sparky stood still and faded into the crowd. Occasionally, someone would yelp or cuss if they touched him.

"The militaries of several countries are trying to help," Felicia said as we pushed away, "at the edges of the fight, anyways."

"'Scuse me, 'scuse me," I said.

DD made her bow disappear.

"Hey," she said, "I made it go away just by thinking it. It was easy."

"We got zombies and vampires, mainly at night," Felicia said.

"And werewolves?" I said.

"Ha! There's no such of a thing," Felicia laughed and shook her head. "You kids and your video games."

DD raised her hand above the crowd.

"Look at this," she said to me as I pulled her along.

Her fiery bow appeared. Then it changed colors. Then it was electric.

"Wow," I said.

"I know, right?" She made the bow disappear. "It seems easy on this earth."

"A bigger problem than we reckoned was Fred the tech god," Felicia said. "He went and gave all the non-powered thugs alla these crazy guns. Now they got a whole army."

Somebody up ahead was waving and whistling. Beside him, people were pushing through a portal in the air that was surrounded by black dots. I could see grass and

191

trees and hills through the portal, and lots more people.

"There he is," Felicia said. "Let's go. I'm sure he's got a lot to tell us."

Suddenly a hand was in my face, motioning me to stop. One was in Felicia's face too. There was no body attached, just a hand surrounded by little black dots.

"What the what?" Felicia said. "Hold on a minute, guys."

"I wonder how many super people there are in this fight?" DD said.

"Have you seen the Hurricane?" I asked Felicia. "What's he doing, the Hurricane and Kid Mist?"

"They must be new," Felicia said. "I haven't met them."

DD and I looked at each other.

"Course we got a lot of super people pouring in right now, on both sides of the spectrum." Felicia cupped her hands and turned to Jeff. "What the heck is going on? You want me to come or stay?"

The hand reappeared in front of me. It was holding a two liter bottle with some sort of brass cap on it.

"Oh, looky," Felicia said. "Jeff's giving you a present. He's always doing that."

I looked at the bottle. It was filled with little black dots with shiny yellow auras around them. I took it out of the hand. It was very light.

"What is it?" I said. "What do I do with it?"

"Beats me," Felicia said. "He pulls all kinds of weird stuff out of his dimension. He's got little elves in there making strange things that nobody knows what they are."

I looked over the crowd. It was too thick to push through. Jeff was jumping up and down making motions with his hands.

"What does this mean?" I made the motion for Felicia.

"Screw it," she said.

192

"It must mean something," I said.

"Screw it," she said.

"Screw it on what?" DD said.

The brass cap looked familiar. It had wide threads that ran down probably an inch. I pulled out my hose nozzle. Jeff's hand poked through a little portal again. His thumb was pointing up.

"That's it," Felicia said. "The goop in that bottle is gonna get us home free."

"How?" I said.

"Spray the crowd." Felicia jumped up over our heads and perched on a lamp post. "Spray 'em! Spray 'em all!"

I took my black and white nozzle and screwed it on top of the bottle. I heard a *fsst*, and the bottle grew cooler. I started spraying massive amounts of water in a thin mist. DD was right. It was so easy on this earth. This was my power! It made perfect sense.

I arced the spray up, and every drop that touched someone popped them away into Jeff's dimension. The excess water just steamed away on the sidewalk. DD stood with her back against my back. Jeff collapsed his portal and let out a long breath. He plopped down on a black metal bench and held his head. Within minutes, everybody was gone.

"Yay!" Felicia jumped down. "You did it, Babycakes. Way to go!"

She grabbed my face and kissed me on the lips.

"WOOT!" she hollered.

DD jerked up and looked away. Jeff kept his head down and gave a thumbs up signal. Sparky walked up, holding the Eden Stone.

"Oh, yeah," Felicia said. "Hey, Jeffy, you got the stone for the kids?"

Jeff's hand disappeared, cut off at the wrist by floating black dots. It reappeared in front of Sparky. It was holding an identical creamy stone. It dropped it into

193

Sparky's hand.

"Spark, spark," Sparky said.

The stones melted together. Their color changed from creamy white to a smooth sand. Little black dots popped up all over it.

"Now, get ready for the dead people to attack," Felicia said, "and the thugs with guns, and the dead thugs with guns, probably. You ready honey?"

Jeff shook his head no and held up one finger. I unscrewed the bottle and set it on the ground. DD summoned her bow, and a bright green arrow.

"What's the green arrow do?" I said.

"I don't know," she whispered back, "but I bet it's something good."

"Spark," Sparky said, and we disappeared.

CHAPTER TWENTY-THREE

Brand was down in this crowd somewhere, admiring dinosaurs, chatting with Alan, looking for Grandpa, and thinking quite a lot about DD. I needed to find myself. Nobody noticed me in this crowd. I just looked like an ordinary person. Actually, the me now looked just like Brand. I mean, we ARE the same person, or we WERE the same person. Are we still the same person?

I made myself look a little older, but I looked too much like Trevor. I supposed if I got even older, I would look like Grandpa. I changed to look like a famous movie star that I liked, but figured that wouldn't do either. I would probably draw a lot of attention to myself, especially since the star had been dead for decades. I could look like Grim Fist. He was pretty cool looking, but he probably wouldn't want someone going around looking like him. Not that it mattered. With all the crazy outfits and animals and atmosphere, people weren't apt to notice much of anything. Plus, I was invisible and intangible. So that would do it too.

I flew up into the air to get a better look around. I didn't remember exactly where and when I was. That's what I got for dampening my own aura. I saw DD walking with The Red Dart and the other Dartettes. She waved in a direction. I followed her wave, and saw myself waving back.

"Ah," I said, "there I am."

There was a slight commotion on the roof of the building behind me. Several men appeared to be wrestling. I got closer and landed on the roof. Four police officers were hand cuffing another man who had a sniper rifle. I had no idea that had happened that day. I noticed too that the man they were hauling away was none other than Melvin Krumsnucker. He struggled for a few minutes and then relaxed. He sniffed at the air, squinted his eyes, and looked in my direction. It was as if he could sense me somehow, but not see me. I didn't know Melvin was a sniper. The man wore many hats.

As the police hauled him off, the murmuring of the VIPs on the roof trailed off. A woman screamed. I turned, and there on the ledge stood Tarma in all of her green woman glory. She was leaning way out, examining the crowd. Her back was turned to me, but I got the distinct idea that she knew I was here. I could tell that she was corporeal by the way she balanced on the edge, and of course, she was also visible to everybody. I walked up to her and reached out.

"You need to get..." I said.

She whipped her hair back and grabbed me by the head. In one quick motion, she threw me from the building and disappeared. As I fell, I realized that she had made me solid and visible. Plus, I still looked like Grim Fist. I went ghost and fell through the sidewalk.

Tarma was causing a commotion to draw Brand out. I had to stop her right away. A fight in a crowd like this could injure a lot of people, not to mention it could kill me. She stood on the sidewalk, pushing people around with her hands and her hair. I ran towards her, but I remained invisible. Occasionally, one of the people I phased through fainted, but I couldn't waste any time. I changed my energy to be able to hit her even if I was intangible to the rest of the world.

"Enough!" I shouted.

She looked at me and swore. Then, she vanished. This was not good. She wasn't even engaging me. She just hit and ran. Eventually, she would get lucky. I had to figure out a way to stop her before that happened.

CHAPTER TWENTY-FOUR

From what I understand, Jeff Montbloom was a really nice guy. I hardly ever interacted with him in any of my incarnations. He was always so quiet, distractively so. Still, I knew some very important things about him. I knew he loved medicine. I knew he loved to help people. I knew he loved his homeland, a pocket dimension from which he would pull the most amazing things. Mostly, though, I knew he loved Felicia. They were both Tricks together on the other earth. They fought against the worst of the worst, Yum, Monstrata, Steeler, and many others. It cost them dearly, but they never gave up.

I was so heartened when the people of my earth decided to build a hospital dedicated to the memory of Jeff Montbloom. I'm sure he would have been honored. Of course, he never really existed on this earth. He was just a memory I created when I created everything else. Honestly, I don't know if I could have created someone as noble as Jeff. I guess those types of people have to create themselves. I've seen a lot of good people on my earth. They've given birth to and raised a lot of other good people that I had no hand in creating. This earth and its population was a self perpetuating machine now.

Like any machine, though, there were occasional breakdowns. Regular maintenance was required. That was why it was especially heartbreaking to witness what happened to the still unfinished Jeff Montbloom Memorial Hospital. I knew Tarma had to have been there. There were just too many out-of-the-ordinary events that transpired that night. I felt it even as Brand. It seemed like more than what it seemed like. I had to investigate this further.

Sydnafly and Gold Fist were balanced on an I beam in the spotlight. A couple hundred people below cried and cheered. The two were exchanging blows, but neither one seemed to be hurting each other much. A pair of green eyes glowed in the background. At first I thought I had found Tarma.

"Nice show there, fellas," Grim Fist said from the dark. "Ya' practicing yer shadow boxing?"

He switched off his night goggles and stepped to the edge of the darkness.

"Stay out of this," Gold Fist said.

Sydnafly punched Gold Fist in the face.

"Hey!" Gold Fist stumbled back a step.

"You want I should show you how to really fight?" Grim Fist stepped up.

"Go away," Sydnafly said. He took a long swinging kick at Grim Fist.

Grim Fist dropped back in a crab walk position, and popped right back up after Sydnafly's foot passed harmlessly over him. Sydnafly, though, lost his balance and began to fall off the front of the hospital. Grim Fist slapped at his belt and pulled his hand up like he was drawing a six shooter. He tossed a lassoed rope around Sydnafly's flailing right hand. Then, he spun around an upright beam and clipped the rope to itself with a hook. Sydnafly fell and hung from the rope.

"Now, hows about I knock those stupid sunglasses offa' yer face?" he said, looking over to Gold Fist.

Gold Fist stepped to the edge of the light and engaged Grim Fist. These punches were much faster and harder than the blows between him and Sydnafly. Grim Fist dodged and punched right back. The two were really going at it. Sydnafly started climbing back up the rope, and the crowd erupted.

199

I heard more metal on metal as the cranes on the roof swung erratically. There was an electrical smell, and I was suddenly very thirsty.

"You cannot be saving them all," Tarma said.

She appeared in the sky between the cranes. Her arms and legs were outstretched. Her hair was flailing in rhythm to the crazy cranes.

"You cannot be saving them any." She shot out her power into the cranes, and they went nuts, smashing girders and shaking the whole structure.

I flew up to her, but she shot around the front of the building like a bright green comet. She went right into the body of Grim Fist. Of course, nobody else could see this but me. Grim Fist stood straight up like he was frozen. Gold Fist punched him a few times, but couldn't move him.

"What the... Ahh!" he yelped as his fist hit the stony chin of Grim Fist.

Grim Fist came back to life and smiled. His eyes and teeth glowed green. He caught Gold Fist's fist, and held him tight. Gold Fist couldn't pull his hand away.

"Let me go!" Gold Fist shouted.

"Join me or he dies," Tarma said through Grim Fist. "Take this one and battle engage with me."

"Who dies?" Gold Fist said.

Okay, this made no sense. Why would Tarma want me to fight her in a possessed body? She hadn't been doing very good against me by herself, but what could she possibly gain with this? This had to be some kind of trick. I looked around.

"He dies now." Tarma pulled back Grim Fist's fist.

"No," I said.

I flew down and possessed Gold Fist. I set his consciousness in a pleasant memory, the one where he made the sponsorship deal to advertise his gold sunglasses that were called Sin-Glasses in South America.

Tarma and I swatted at each other like the two untrained fighters we were. She seemed strangely happy about this.

"What do you possibly hope to accomplish with this?" I asked.

I heard Sydnafly's hand grab ahold of the beam a few feet away.

"You think power is so smart," she said. "I will show you that so smart is power."

Suddenly, Grim Fist became a much better fighter. He began punching Gold Fist/me over and over in the face.

"You feel that pain?" she said.

I did feel the pain. It hurt like, well, like pain, like getting hit in the face with a grim fist. I tried to strike back, but Grim Fist's reflexes were too good.

"Fight me," she said.

"I'm trying."

"Stop trying." She hit me in the nose.

"What do you mean?" I said

We both stood up straight and stopped fighting for a moment. Gold Fist/me had a bloody nose. Sydnafly pulled his other hand up on the beam.

"What you do is to fall back into the human," she said. "You let him use his moves and his training. You just kind of direct like, you know, a director."

"What do you mean?"

"You know," she raised her arms and made little motions, "a director, a director."

"A director..."

"Like in front of the orchestra," she said.

"Oh," I raised my hands, "like a director."

She hit me in the nose again.

"Yes," she said, "like a director. Now, fight me."

"I'm trying," I said again.

"Stop trying," she said again.

201

"I'm trying to stop trying," I said.

"Try to help me up," Sydnafly said. "This steel is slippery."

After a few seconds, I got the hang of it. I settled back and began fighting like Gold Fist would fight. Tarma was fighting like Grim Fist would fight. It was like a marionette show. She was really beating the tar out of me. Grim Fist was a much better fighter than Gold Fist.

"You be feeling comfortabler now?" she said.

"In a way," I said between swollen lips.

"Good," she stopped. "Now you are being stuck in that body."

"What?" I said.

I opened my one good eye as far as it would open. This must have been her plan, to get me stuck inside of Gold Fist.

"Now, I kill every person," she said.

She shot out of Grim Fist with a banshee scream that sounded like the twisting and moaning of angry steel beams. The building answered her in kind. Sydnafly fell back down on the rope and started climbing down the building. Tarma again used herself as a missile, blasting through electrical boxes, surging and exploding everything around us. Grim Fist collapsed in my arms. Rivets popped and ricocheted. The metal under my feet vibrated and whined.

Tarma had trapped me in this body that thought it was a man, just like Trevor had been caught thinking he was a man. When his body died, his consciousness, my consciousness became inert. I had to be there from the future to protect and restart myself. The same thing was happening here. Nobody but Tarma would be here to collect my unconsciousness this time, and she had already shown how good she was at controlling other people.

Grim Fist was pulled out of my hands, and I lost purchase on the beam. A huge girder that had been connected to one of the cranes flashed in the spotlights as it wobbled and fell. There were violent electrical explosions, and then it hit me.

No, the girder didn't hit me. The realization that I had been tricked hit me, and the moment I realized that, Tarma vanished. The trick would have worked, too, if it hadn't have been for Brand. Beings like Tarma and myself fear very little, really. Any physical thing we lose or misplace, we can just recreate. Any lesser being who dies can be brought back. We really have to work hard to care about much of anything. I was relatively new at this, but I had heard of realities that just shut themselves off in some cosmic sleep. It was actually more common than not. No wonder so many of us were crazy. Absolute power doesn't necessarily corrupt absolutely. It can also breed absolute apathy. This can be a death trap for a universal intelligence. If someone convinces a universe that reality is a certain way, then often times that is the way reality becomes. For someone like me to think something is so, makes it so.

What a fool I had been this whole time since my reawakening. I had been playing *my* game by *her* rules, and she knew it. She told me I couldn't save anyone, and so I couldn't. She told me I was trapped, and so I was. I just accepted it as truth, and it became truth. If I hadn't have been Brand in my life, she would have defeated me. I would bet this was something she had done many times, but the other realities didn't have Brand.

Brand had humanity. He loved and cared and lost. He carried that loss with him. He learned from that loss. He never had the power. He only had the struggle, and it was that need to struggle that gave him hope. Without hope, I didn't need to change reality. Without hope, I just resigned myself to the status quo. Without hope, I had to accept what I thought were the rules and the cages. I actually forgot that, not only could I break all of the cages, I *was* all of the cages. This sudden hope-filled realization changed the board.

I knew where she was headed next. I only had a fraction of a second to make things right here. It was all the time I needed. I left Gold Fist's body. Of course I wasn't trapped except in my mind. Down in the dark, where he would land, I created a cushion. I woke Grim Fist up, and placed his rope in his hands and his goggles on his face. I had no doubt that he could save himself, especially as I quadrupled his reflexes and strength for the next few seconds. He would chalk it up to adrenaline. A piece of metal struck a glancing blow on DD's shoulder down in the basement of the collapsing structure. I gave her a safe landing and caused the girders to fall in a formation that protected her on all sides. I grabbed Gina with a wire around her ankle and I shoved The Red Dart into a safe corner. I would have done more, but there were dozens of injuries and deaths outside I had to mitigate. Electric lines and gas lines and flesh were not a good mixture. There were some injuries, but nobody died. I had saved everybody, except one person.

In my blur of action, I had forgotten about Brand. Brand was me, after all, and I was fine. I was even thinking like Brand. I thought I was Brand again, and I got lost in myself and forgot myself. Brand had saved me, and I had failed Brand.

As I said, this state of being could be confusing to someone who wasn't always in this state of being. I found Brand's broken body at the bottom of the basement. There wasn't much that wasn't destroyed. This wouldn't do. I was tired of being tricked. I was tired of being treated like I was some sort of beginner. I was tired of being played.

With a whiff of thought, I brought Brand back. This would end now, Tarma. This had gone way too far. You were just a little fish floating around in my ocean, in an ocean made of me. I was done, and so were you. I fixed Brand right up. I placed a bit of unconscious power into him, just enough to move the giant girder that was protecting DD. I remade his crumpled flashlight and set it next to him.

Then I left this timeline. There would be no more games or tricks. I would end it immediately.

CHAPTER TWENTY-FIVE

DD and I ricocheted around the battles. We fought with a group of Tricks against the Obliterators and a Steeler robot. We saw the Red Rat get carried away by gargoyles. If DD hadn't had her energy arrows, Mac wouldn't have been able to hide in them and trick Steeler. We were needed there. If my Trick's training hadn't helped me notice the booby trapped god-machine at the airport, Skyway and all the heroes coming to help from England would have been killed. Again, we were in the perfect place at the perfect time.

"Welcome back," Billy said.

He walked into the church sanctuary from a side room. Millard was behind him. DD and I stood at the front below the podium. Sparky stood beside us, staring off into space.

"That was quite an experience," I said. "Can we go home now?"

"A long way around to end up where we started," DD said.

"You had to get the Eden Stones," Billy said.

"But you gave them out to be given back to us," I said. "Why didn't you just give them to us to begin with?"

"They are starting to figure you out." Millard gave a slight smile and zipped his leather jacket halfway up.

"I know everything," Billy said.

"Right," I said. "You're the tree from the Garden, from Genesis."

"Millard, that joke ceased being funny months ago," Billy said.

"What joke?" I said.

"I was going to say," Millard said, "that we have been having a lot of revelations from Genesis lately."

"He was," Billy said.

"Knowing Billy's beginnings lets you realize that sometimes the knowledge you get off of him is more trouble than just getting away from him," Millard said.

"The evil forces are pulling back," Billy said. "They're concentrating less globally and more locally."

"Which means I have to go," Millard said.

"Will there be any more monsters or villains tele-ported in here?" DD asked.

"Not for the time being," Billy said. "Lightman isn't go-ing to be seeing anyone at the Eden Rock until you get there."

"Oh," Millard reached into his jacket pocket, "I got this for you. I understand you may still need it. It's better than the plastic one you've been using."

He pulled out a solid brass hose nozzle and handed it to me.

"Wow," I said. "Thanks."

"No problem," Millard put his hand on my shoulder and gave it a pat. He turned and started walking down the aisle. "Use that tool well. It's special."

I looked down at the cool metal object in my hands. "What's special about it?"

Millard opened the church door.

"It was on sale," he said and left.

Billy held out his hand. "I'll take the old one and throw it away for you. It's no good anymore."

I handed him the black and white nozzle that Mr. Forest had given to me. He handed me another phone like the one Mr. Forest had given me.

"Trade me," he said. "Tarma was using the telephone she gave you to amplify your energy scent."

I couldn't believe how stupid I had been. I gave him

my old phone.

"Who's organizing all of these bad guys?" I said. "How can they all work together? In Trick's camp we understood that we had the slightest edge because of our altruism. We weren't as selfish and petulant as the Roadies."

"You wouldn't know him," Billy said.

He set the broken nozzle and the phone on a pew and pulled the notebook from his back pocket.

"But that is good observation," he said.

"Yeah," DD said, "I've found that most bad guys are motivated by greed or revenge, which is a type of greed."

His name is Joe Maston," Billy said. "I didn't want to tell you because I knew I would have to tell you."

"What?"

"Tulsi never mentioned him in your history," Billy looked at DD. "In a way, that's understandable. When you need to know him, you'll wish you hadn't."

"Who is he?" I said.

"I'll not explain now," Billy said. "I hate explaining, and anyway that's not what's been bothering you. You want something else explained. You're in luck. We have a few seconds before everything is where it needs to be. The gargoyles aren't in place yet."

"I don't..." I tucked the new nozzle in my pocket.

DD nudged me and looked in my eyes. She raised her head slightly.

"Spark," Sparky said.

"Exactly," I said. "These Eden Stones..."

"Yes?"

"How did you know to...?"

"Because..." Billy said.

"Because you know everything?" DD said.

Billy smiled and sat down.

"You thought I just used you to help the Tricks," he said. "How are these stones going to get you home?

208

Well, of course the answer is that they are not stones at all. They're a key to a navigational system."

"No," I said, "I wanted to know..."

Billy put up a hand. He was holding a pamphlet.

"Take this," he said.

"What's...?"

"I find that most people can't hear the answers I tell them because they are too busy trying to ask questions," Billy said.

"Okay," I sat down beside him. DD sat on the other side.

"To keep the shield around our actuality," Billy began, "Tarma had to anchor it someplace. The Eden Rock cannot be moved. Even if it's destroyed it remains. Even if it's moved, it stays."

"I don't get it," I said and then clamped my mouth.

"It must not be anchored physically," DD said. "Is it, like, spiritually fixed?"

"Pretty good," Billy said. "That's close enough to understand."

DD smiled and looked at me.

"Tarma knew that she might eventually be compromised in some way," Billy continued. "She's been around a long time. If she couldn't maintain the shield's position, it might fluctuate and lose its potency. Plus, if she were drawn away, she could find her way back with some sort of fixed beacon affixed to wherever she was lost."

"We don't have an Eden Stone," I said. "That I know of."

"No," Billy said, "but you do have something brand new, a fixed explosion of Tarma energy, a buoy of her own. I just learned about it when Sparky here joined your group."

"Where is it?" I said.

"It's that frozen explosion," Billy said. "That is pure Tarma creation force and an actuality anchor. You were sent to us through it."

"To the Eden Rock here?" I said.

"Then why did we end up here," DD said, "and not at the Eden Rock?"

"Lightman is guarding the Rock," Billy said. "Any creature coming near it gets zapped here to be taken care of by the Tricks. Also I had him send you here so I could use you for my own plans."

My jaw dropped.

"I knew it!" DD said.

"Yes, I'm a bit of a scamp, aren't I?" Billy said.

"I can think of a few other words," DD said.

"I know," Billy said.

"Our friends need us," I said. "They could be hurt. They could be dead. Thousands of people could..."

"Could be, could be," Billy said, "there's no could be with me. I know what is, was, and will be."

"Then, what?" I said. "What happens?"

"I'm not going to tell you," he said.

"Why?"

"Because that's my schtick," he said.

DD stood up.

"Sit down, DD," Billy said. "I mean that it's my responsibility, my burden."

"I know what you meant," DD said, "and you call me, Darlene."

"The stones needed to be sequenced and programmed," Billy said.

He held out his hand, and Sparky dropped the Eden Stone into it.

"From your first stop you got transdimensional power," Billy turned the stone over in his hands, "the very force of becoming there from being here. From the second stop you got raw ingredients, power and energy for the sake of energy. It's malleable and wild. It adapts. From the third stop you got god force, the power of faith,

210

pure belief energy, and absolutely necessary."

"What did we get here," DD said, "from you?"

"The power of knowledge," Billy handed the stone to DD, "a spark of the ultimate power."

"Spark," Sparky said.

"So how did you know," I said. "C'mon, how did you know?"

"You did it," Billy said, "or rather, Tulsi did it. I mentioned knowledge being the ultimate power. There are beings like Tulsi and Tarma who think they are incomplete without it. Tulsi, when he first came to realize what he was, simply willed himself to know everything and suddenly, he did know everything. He couldn't understand it, though, and he couldn't understand how to will himself to understand. It became a constant noise in his mind, scribbles in his consciousness, signifying something and nothing and everything and one thing."

"Scribbles, like..." I said.

"Yes, you saw scribbles on your way here," Billy said, "Tarma's umbilical cord, holding nutrients and power, Tarma's brain stem, holding information and reality. However, as I was saying, Tulsi couldn't function with this annoying buzz. He realized it was a useless bauble and he discarded it. He then decided that in order to know everything, he needed to experience everything. So, he went everywhere and everywhen instantly."

"Did that do it?" I said.

"You know what it did," Billy said. "It tore up reality like it was Swiss cheese. It ripped holes in time and space, and it drove him mad. Only through great... sacrifice, was he able to be calmed and helped."

"I don't know any of this stuff," I said. "I don't remember any of this. What was the sacrifice?"

"It was before your time," Billy's eyes welled up. "Another universe was destroyed. I haven't time for that story."

211

"Okay."

"So I've been sewing holes," Billy sniffed. "Tulsi left great gaps. He can't mend them himself. He's toxic to them. It's like using a lighter to mend a hole that was burned through paper. I know the proper ingredients to mend the rends. I have the glue. I know where all the holes are and where and when they lead, and where and when they open and bleed. I used one tear to go back and set things up with the Eden Rock, and who should have the individual stones and why. That is... I WILL do all this. I haven't done it yet."

"How do you keep things straight?" I said.

"It's my... it's my schtick," he said.

"And the notebook?" I held it up.

"You two need a teacher," Billy said. "Consider that a school book."

"But it's blank." I flipped through the pages.

"That will change," Billy said.

He struggled to rise, and I helped him up.

"So do we just teleport to the Eden Rock?" DD said.

"Not yet," Billy said. "Tarma is too strong. If it were that easily accomplished, Tulsi would have just pulled you home. You need to transform the brain stem and ride the reverse flow. You need one more form of energy, the universal force itself. You need pure energy from Tulsi in order to give the right code to tell the stream what to transform into. Otherwise, it would home in on you for the process and convert you to scribbles. Sparky is basically just pure Tulsi force, but he is just a spark. We need more to ride up the current of the entire river.

Lightman is a pure universal force, as well. He was created by Tarma's husband."

"Can her husband help us?" DD said. "Will he help us?"

"He's not around here anymore," Billy said, "and lightman's running thin. His batteries are almost depleted.

He'll be able to give you the boost you need to get going in the right direction, though. It'll be less like we will be turning the flow, and more like we are skipping you up-stream. We just have to make sure you don't sink until you get to your destination. I'll supply that final bit, an alien bit of universal force that will act as a poison. It will cause this universe to regurgitate you against the cosmic flow."

"That sounds not fun," DD said.

"You won't realize what's happening. Your mind wouldn't be able to comprehend it. The journey for you will just manifest in a shared delusion," Billy said. "Once you're past the tipping point, look for James. He'll lead you straight to where you want to go. Tell him I said hi."

So..." DD said again, "do we just teleport there from here?"

"No," Billy said. "You take a cab."

CHAPTER TWENTY-SIX

I knew the color of fear. It was a medium purple with a shock of dull pink in its hair. It might have been a different color for other people, but that was what color it was for me. Doubt was a kind of sea foam green with a dark green belt. Regret was pure clear azure with just a single dot of rust up in the right hand corner. I forgot the others. I was too busy tumbling through the emotional dryer that Tarma had waiting for me. Each barrage of emotion brought painful blindness, leaving only the colors associated with it. I couldn't focus. I couldn't think straight. I'm sure that was her intent. She was playing off my past insecurities, my mental breakdown. She was amplifying my hurt. She thought it was my weakness. Giddiness, it turned out, had a lot of orange in it.

I pictured a stone skipping across a pond, a day in the park that poets write about. It helped me calm down, to pour cool amber thoughts over my raging mind. It turned out that serenity was as clear as day.

"Stop it," I said.

I was down on one knee. My hands were out to my side like I was holding back a wall that wasn't there. I was on a stage. A small battle was taking place all around in front of me. Walls of water were rising up, forcing back the huge crowd of people who had come to celebrate the half-century mark of all the superpowers vanishing from the planet. I noticed Tarma's green booted foot just before it kicked me in the face. The force of it sent me back over onto my back. She was trying to keep my mind occupied. She was stalling me. I knew that at this time we both knew that she couldn't defeat me.

"You've taken advantage of me…" I said.

A brown sasquach came out of nowhere. It picked me up by the shoulders and threw me over Tarma's head to the middle of the stage. She stepped back as it took a running leap at me. I didn't even look at it. I just drew a small line in the air with my forefinger, and it disappeared.

"my naiveté, my ignorance…," I said.

"Ha!" She waved her arms around in her swirling hair.

I sensed a warmth beneath me. I remembered the bomb, but I noticed it in a different way than Brand had, or in a different way that he, right now, was noticing it. The stage moved beneath us with the water flowing in the road.

"my hospitality…," I said to her, "my inexperience."

"You trapped me here with you," she said, "and now you are to complain that I am here."

A dozen little weird chupacabras sprung up from the floor. What would the people battling down on the street have thought if they could see this odd show in front of them? The creatures clicked their tongues and growled at me. I just poofed them away.

"This bomb," I said, "this bomb you created is no ordinary bomb."

She cast emotions at me again. I shuffled them, compressed them, and converted them into a single gray, "Ah!" and threw them back at her.

"Ah!" she said.

This is a Tarma bomb," I said. "I can feel the compression, the detonation, the direction."

She shot out her hair like a thousand needles. I pulled a trick from my old friend Phil, and made them all just miss me. She never laid a hair on me.

"I want to go home," she kept trying to hit me, "to go home just!"

The bomb exploded. I froze it in mid explosion. Poor

215

Grim Fist got his arm blasted off. I gave him the power to regenerate. Tarma tried to flee again, but I shut down time and space for her.

"You will pay," she said. "My husband will find you, and you will pay. He is looking for me, even now."

"Your husband is..." I said.

She looked out at the frozen crowd with the eyes of a caged animal.

'The bomb is concentrated Tarma force," I said, "isn't it?"

"It would to remake your world," she sneered, "and stretch out and grow."

"Like the cancer you are," I said.

"Eventually, all would be me," she said, "and then I would be free."

"To kill and destroy," I said.

"What do you care?" She hung her head.

As she calmed down, I noticed an unfrozen strand of Tarma energy coming out of the frozen explosion. I tried to freeze it, but it kept casting off my power. It spread away from the bomb, not in any of the obvious four dimensions. It seemed to disappear into fifth dimensional space.

"What is that?" I pointed.

She looked at me and frowned.

I traced it back through dimensional folds, until it reached the edge of my reality. Tarma took the opportunity to wrap her hands around my throat.

"He doesn't think he's a man anymore," I said in a calm voice.

"Umbilical cord." She released her grip and dropped to the floor.

"What are you feeding?" I said.

"As long as I am alive," she said, "it will be alive. It is me too."

"It leads out of my reality," I said, "like an escape

rope. Why didn't you take it?"

"Because you, Mr. Big Jerk, did one rule even before you made the planet." She puffed her cheeks. "Your number one rule was 'keep Tarma in reality prison'."

"That was our whole point," I said, "to begin with."

"Well, nice trick, little boy," she said, "but you are sometimes being too smart for your own good."

"I'll just cut the cord," I said.

"No!" She reached out. "My insurance!"

"Insurance?"

"We live together," she said. "This line hooks the two universes. Everyone but Tarma can travel to and through, but it is a one way trip."

"I've been patient," I said, "casting a quiet line, but you are done here, Tarma. I won't kill you. I'll just absorb you, make your energy my energy, this escape rope my escape rope."

"I will eat you out from the insides." She stretched her neck at me and bared her fangs. "I have done it before. Once we get the taste for Absolute Flesh..."

"Oh, you would be cauterized," I said, "lobotomized, your essence pitted and dried."

"I would be a bitter taste," she said.

"I'd wash the taste out with a nice glass of lemonade."

"Hollow revenge," she said to herself. "Your own rules would trap you here in this universe."

"Why would I want to leave?" I said.

"You are stupid," she said. "It matters not, anyway. You will not kill me. I keep the gate open."

"What gate?"

"The rope," she said, "is a one way circuit. It leads to a mighty shield that encircles the other earth, a shield of Tarma."

"All the more reason to stop you," I said.

"A trap of Tarma," she said. "You kill me, it slams

shut and destroys everything in its final gasp."

"Your rules," I said. "I can change your rules."

"Here maybe," she pointed around, "but outside your walls, you are subject more to the rules of the rulers of other places. This is the only reason you can stop me or keep me here, because we are in your rules."

"I can't stop your shield," I said, "but I can cut your rope."

"Snap!" She clapped her hands together in warning.

I thought for a moment. There had to be a way out of this. I was all powerful, after all.

"And right now you sent them back," Tarma smiled. "This is what I waited you for. Now, in space you tell Billy he is Tarma. We begin our battle."

"What?"

"You send little boy and little girl back here," she pointed to the sky, "but I send them up the rope, the one way rope."

"What?"

"They are on old earth now." Tarma rubbed her hands together. "You can do nothing. Other rulers have their rules. They are in the battle now. They will die in the battle."

"Shush!" I said.

Tarma turned into a coin in my hand. I had gotten too overconfident. I had neutralized her power with just a thought. It was that easy, but I had messed things up. I should have just done it right away. I could feel her influence in the coin. This battle was over for now, but I could never let my guard down. Entities of Infinity never learn.

I sat on the edge of the frozen stage looking out over the frozen people. I placed the Tarma coin in my pocket. I traced the rope of energy to the edge of my universe. It still wriggled and moved like Tarma's hair. I hadn't curbed Tarma's power in my universe. There was too much hidden, too many booby traps. I would have to search them out and destroy them individually. If I left my universe, it would be too unsafe here. I could return to a wasteland. It could be a one way trip even for me. I could be locked out forever due to some failsafe lock.

I had to rescue Brand and DD from the other earth. They weren't used to powers and physics that would drive them mad. Maybe I could send an emissary, create my own temporary hero to help. Maybe I could send a message to Billy. Surely the Tricks could find a way. I had to at least try.

I sent a spark of myself into the rope. I dressed it up as Grim Fist, a hero the kids would recognize. It travelled out and into the other universe where I lost track of it.

"Good luck, guys," I said.

CHAPTER TWENTY-SEVEN

"I can NOT believe this," I said. "This is incredible."

"And I have shotgun!" DD turned around in her seat and smiled hard at me.

I stuck my tongue out at her. She stuck her tongue out at me. Sparky sat next to me and stared out the side window.

"Turn around," the driver, THE driver, said.

It was Ace. We were riding in Ace's cab. This Ace was the grandfather of our Ace at home. This Ace fought on the side of the Tricks and helped them in many adventures. This Ace was the essence of cool.

"I don't know why I have to drive clear out of my way to pick up these other people besides you," he said to us. "Billy never explains anything. He's lucky I was even able to snag you guys. There's folks trying to get out of the city, you know. I'm trying to help, here."

"He doesn't like to explain," I said. "He says..."

"Yeah? Well, he can find another cabbie," Ace said, "if he thinks so little of us."

"I don't think it's that," DD said. "What am I saying? I don't need to defend him. He treats people rotten."

Ace winked and nodded. A small building imploded about a block away.

"That would be her," Ace said and turned towards the demolition. He pressed a button under the seat, and the car started creaking. It actually expanded behind me. A new seat popped up. A door molded itself.

A large woman ran up to the door and ripped it off the hinges.

"Woops!" she said.

"Leave it!" Ace smacked his forehead. "We don't have time."

"I didn't mean to..."

"This is Ms. Power," Ace said. "Does more damage than the bad guys."

"I said I was sorry." A tear ran down Ms. Power's face.

Ace drove a few blocks. Every few seconds, Ms. Power accidentally broke something else.

"There won't be nothing left if we don't get there soon," Ace said.

"Sorry," Ms. Power said.

He stopped at a bus stop, and the cab expanded once more. Three colorful characters got in the back seat.

"Where we goin'?" the man in the middle said. He had a gray hooded sweat shirt over the top of his head. Bumps protruded out at unnatural angles. I imagined that he didn't look very pleasant underneath.

"I have no idea," Ace said. "These kids are headed to Harvestone's. Billy said I had to pick you up first."

"Typical," the man said.

"Hi, guys!" Ms. Power wiggled her fingers in greeting. The others nodded.

"Holly Courte, the Gate, and Buddy Towers," Ace said.

"Billy pulled us away," the woman named Holly said. "We were fixing the subway."

"At least we stopped the robots," the man on the far right in a striped blue suit said.

"We just fought robots," DD turned around and said, "at the airport."

"Those were just a segment of the whole," Buddy Towers said, "but I have a way with machines."

He moved his fingers, and Ace's cab healed itself.

"You're so cool," Ms. Power said. "You're so cool to have around."

The three nodded silently at her.

"Turn around," Ace said to DD, "and thanks, Buddy. Zero appreciates the mend."

We approached a brick building with a large shirtless man outside. He was punching holes in the wall.

"Thugmaster!" Ms. Power leapt up through the roof.

"Wait!" Ace said.

The car skidded as Ms. Power's weight threw off the center of gravity. Buddy Towers fixed the roof. The Gate waved his hand, and the road rose up beside us at a sloping incline. Holly surrounded us in a clear brass bubble, and when we hit the wall, we barely felt it.

"Power's out," Buddy said, "all around here. We have to make it to the substation."

"The kids gotta get in there." Ace pointed at the building.

"I sense internal damage," the Gate held his hands to his bumpy head, "to the structure."

Ms. Power and the Thugmaster pounded the tar out of each other.

"At least he's stopped hitting the building," I said.

"They'll need the outside power source," Buddy said.

Ace took off. "To the power plant then. Now I know why I hadda' pick you up."

After a couple of miles, we crashed the gate of the power plant. There was another large man standing at the door doing to the power plant what had been done to the building.

"Great Feena and Matina!" Holly said.

"Let us out." The Gate opened his door.

Ace slammed on the brakes. "It's Thugmaster's twin brother, Thugmaster."

The three in the back got out as fast as they could. Thugmaster grabbed the front of the car and swung it around like a shot put. Before we could even say any-thing, we spun through the sky like a propeller. Ace was cursing and pushing buttons. A moment later, we were steady and straight and flying through the sky in a flying taxi cab.

"Are you doing this on purpose?" DD looked out the side window.

"On purpose and with purpose," Ace arced through the clouds, "now that the skies are clear of evil thug ro-bots."

A hand tapped on the window beside me. It tapped from the outside. I recognized the hand.

"Jeff," I said. "Ace, Jeff Montbloom's hand is tapping on the window and pointing down.

Below us, Felicia jumped up and down and waved her arms. Jeff was pointing to a large portal above him. It was pretty clear that they wanted us to drive through it.

"Yep," Ace said and put the cab into a dive.

As we entered the portal, a silence fell over the car. The city became rolling green countryside. The sky was clear, and it seemed like we were frozen in place. The ground below was still. Then, it was like the entire world pivoted. Everything just turned ninety degrees, and I don't think it was us. We were now pointed in a whole new di-rection, though, and another portal opened up ahead of us. It came at us and swallowed us. The next thing we knew, we were back in a different part of the sky over the city, and we were on a collision course with a were-rat being carried by a flock of gargoyles. The gargoyles scat-tered, and a battered and lacerated Red Rat plastered himself across the bumper and hood of the cab.

"Good Lord!" Ace started taking the cab down to street level.

Before our eyes, the Red Rat began to heal. Large slashes closed. Hair grew back. Off kilter bones straight-ened. He dug a clawed hand into the hood and looked in

223

at Ace. We hit the ground hard, but he barely noticed. He climbed the hood as we slid to a stop. He raised a fist to the windshield, and was blasted clear off the car by a powerful jet of water.

"Good shot, Kid Mist!" the Hurricane said.

Before the Red Rat had hit the ground, the Hurricane zapped him with a lightning bolt. Kid Mist wrapped the Rat's head in a rope of water, as the Hurricane whipped up a mini tornado around the Red Rat.

"We'll hold him," the Hurricane said to Ace. "Get the kids inside."

"Go!" Ace yelled.

DD jumped out, but I couldn't take my eyes off of Kid Mist. This was my grandfather.

"Grandpa," I said.

DD opened my door. The wind was whipping everything around.

"Come on!" She pulled my arm.

"Go!" yelled Ace.

I ran to the building with DD. Ms. Power was pounding on an unconscious Thugmaster.

"Red Rat!" I shouted to Ms. Power.

"On it," Ms. Power leapt into the fray.

"I've got to help." I took a few steps towards Kid Mist.

"No," DD pulled on me, "that's not them, Brand. That's not them."

I ran inside with her and closed the door.

"Sparky is still in the cab." I slapped my forehead.

"I've got the stone," DD said. "Let's go."

It was obvious that DD had done this kind of thing before and I hadn't. I was a mess. I couldn't think straight. She just seemed to know what to do. Trash was thrown around the old building. Lights flickered. Doors were open.

"Go where?" I said.

"Spark," came a voice from upstairs.

We both ran towards the voice. Sparky walked into a room in the middle of the hall.

"Welcome, welcome, my good man," a voice from the room said.

We turned into the room and saw an old short man in a very wrinkled brown sweater and equally wrinkled brown slacks. He was placing a lei over Sparky's head. The telephone rang.

"This is the last one, I'm afraid, and he really needed it," the man said. "Would you tell that phone it's not working?"

"Answer it?" I said.

"Goodness no," he laughed. "That will just goad it on. Just tell it that it's disconnected right now."

"Phone, uh," I said, "you're disconnected."

The phone stopped ringing.

"There you go," he said to Sparky.

Sparky vanished.

"Where'd he go?" DD said.

"Who?"

"Sparky," we both said.

"I have no idea." The man grabbed my hand and shook it vigorously. "Who did you say I am?"

"Who *are* you?" I said.

"Henry Harvestone," the man said, "or Ed. No, Henry."

"We have to…," I said.

"Hold on," he said, "it's a busy day. What day is it?"

"I'm not sure," DD said.

"Then it's a very busy day indeed," he said.

He opened one of two doors in the side of the room.

"Six boxes of the peanut butter," he said and closed the door again.

He held a black hand mirror up to the window and wrote an X on the back in blue chalk. He put it in the top left drawer of his large wooden desk.

"Sit down," he said to us.

"There are no chairs," DD said.

"And that is why the lava pit is full." He pulled some thick glasses down from his head.

A knock came from the other door at the side of the room.

"That would be your ride," Henry said. "Go on in."

DD and I opened the door and looked in to see an old style bathroom with a claw foot tub and dripping faucet. We stepped in and the door slammed shut behind us.

"Hey." DD pounded on the door.

"What's the deal?" I looked around the small room.

"I think that man's crazy," DD said.

"I think you're right," I said.

After a few minutes, the door squeaked open on its own. Standing in a room that was not the one that was there before, was a panting and angry Red Rat and several tall piles of bananas. The Red Rat jerked his head in our direction. DD slammed the door and turned the lock. When we turned around, we were standing in a dimly lit cave.

"The door's gone." DD looked back behind her again. "The door's gone."

"Well, I guess he's not coming through," I said.

Florescent lights flickered from the twenty foot tall ceilings. The dark brown stone walls seemed to have all of the sharp edges worn down. We were in some little tucked away alcove. In front of us, the cave opened into what was probably once a majestic space. Stalagmites and stalactites were removed, leaving stumps and whatever ceiling stumps are called. There didn't appear to be any exit. The large room had one distinguishing feature. In the center was a large rock about ten feet tall and four feet around. It looked like melted wax. A very wrinkled man in a white jumpsuit and baseball cap was humming and polishing the stone with a red rag.

"Hello, lost children," he said without looking up. "You ready to go home?"

Soft violin music played somewhere between the rocks.

"We, uh," I walked into the room, "are you lightman?"

"What's left." lightman smiled a wrinkly smile, and tucked the rag into his back pocket.

"We have the Genesis Stone," DD said.

"I would hope so." lightman walked up to us. "Did you have a good time?"

DD handed the stone to him.

"It was," I said, "well, to be honest, it was pretty terrible. There was fighting everywhere. People were getting hurt. I was getting hurt. I'm worried about home. I don't know what I'll find when I get there."

"It was incredible," DD said. "Awful and wonderful and terrifying and thrilling."

"Yeah," I said, "all those."

"I wouldn't worry about home too much," lightman said.

He walked back to the rock and motioned for us to follow.

"You'll be getting back at the same time you left, well, just after. You wouldn't want to meet yourself. Believe me, I met myself once, and I can be a real jerk. Helps with the dishes, though."

"I think everyone here is crazy," DD said.

lightman positioned the Eden Stone on the side of the Eden Rock. The shiny black dots all erased from the face of the brown stone. lightman tapped it and raised an eyebrow.

"Some times it helps if you tap it." He tapped it again.

Three coin slots appeared in the brown stone.

"Hmmm..." lightman placed his wrinkly hand on his wrinkly chin. He took off his white hat that read, BLI-BRAWGY, in large black letters, and scratched his bald

227

head. The top of his head was the only thing that wasn't wrinkly.

"You have to pay?" DD said.

lightman put his hat back on and looked over to DD. "You always have to pay," he said.

There was a zipping sound, and the violin music stopped.

"Oh, you'll all pay," a high pitched voice echoed through the cavern.

DD made a bow and arrow. The Red Rat walked out from behind an outcropping at the far end of the cavern, up close to the ceiling. DD pointed an arrow at him. I pulled my new nozzle out. We both fired and missed. The Red Rat leapt down from his perch to the cave floor. He began running towards us, dodging my water ropes, slashing DD's arrows away, grinning and laughing and getting closer. He jumped at me with his claws out. I pulled back and closed my eyes.

"Ha-Haa-Haaakkk!" he screeched.

A second later, I was still alive. I opened one eye and saw his shadow squirming all around me. I looked up and saw him hanging in the air. A large hand was wrapped tightly around his neck.

"Spark," Sparky said.

The Red Rat tore at Sparky, but the wounds just sealed right up. Even when the Rat cut Sparky's arm completely in two, Sparky didn't move or release his grip, and the Rat didn't fall. Electricity danced all around the Red Rat. It shot into the floors and walls. I moved back out of the way and stood up.

"He just appeared," DD said.

Sparky took his lei off with his other hand and slipped it over the Red Rat's head. The Red Rat began to shrink. He squealed and squeaked and cursed and shrank until he was nothing more than a dirty brass coin in Sparky's hand, a literal coin. Sparky dropped it on the ground.

"I guess I see now," lightman said. "This is how we pay, but there is only one coin and three slots."

"Maybe there's a coin slot for each of us," I said.

"Spa..." Sparky said and instantly turned into a coin on the ground, right next to the coin that was the Red Rat.

"Nnnooo, I don't think so," lightman said.

DD started looking around the cave. She raised a silver arrow.

"Hold on, hold on," lightman picked up the coins, "we're not under attack. I get it now."

"This is the guidance," he held one coin up, "this is the gag reflex, and I am the power boost."

"How are you...?" I said.

He smiled and dropped to the floor as another coin. I picked all three up and looked at them. One had the head of the Red Rat on the front and a drawn curtain on the back. The second had Sparky on the front and a burst of energy on the back. The third had some sort of weird asterisk on the front and lightman's head on the back.

"I guess we put them in the rock," DD said.

"That's right," lightman said from his coin.

I tossed it in the air. "Man! you startled me."

DD caught it. lightman winked at her from the coin. She put it in the first slot. Nothing happened. I put the other two in. The cave walls melted up and became yellow. Then everything bled away. We were standing on an old stone bridge. A man on a stool smiled at us.

"Don't be alarmed," he said, but he was a little alarming.

His dark, misformed face tried to smile, but all the sharp fangs kept getting in the way. He had a pug nose and blazing eyes. His eyes were empty holes in his head that flickered with flame. Small lines of smoke rose up from them. He wore a long tattered purple and black cloak over blue jeans and a nice yellow button shirt.

229

"I'm James," he said.

"Billy said to look for James," I said.

"Didn't have to look too far." James slapped his knee. "I just need your tickets and I can proceed. Otherwise, I have to eat you."

"Tickets?" DD said.

"Eat us?" I said.

"Ha, ha, ha!" He slapped his knees again. "Classic."

We relaxed a little.

"But, seriously," he said, "I need your tickets."

DD drew an arrow.

"Or the password!" James put up his hand.

"How would we know the password?" DD said.

"Billy didn't tell you to tell me anything?"

"No," I said, "other than to say hi."

"Oh, well, there you go, then." James stood up. "That's the password. You can't be too careful in my line of work. I'm a doorman. My specialty is Reality/Actuality Passage."

He pulled a clipboard off the side of his stool.

"Your password is hi?" DD said. "That's not a very good password."

"That's fine with me," I said.

"This should be fun," James said. "Brand, I knew you before you were you. Heck, I knew Tulsi before he was Tulsi, back when I was a baby. Tarma was one of my mothers."

"Tarma is your mother?" DD put her weapons away.

"One of them." James read from a paper on the clip board. "It's a long story. Anyway, it says here that we'll be aligning the time flow. Did you know that?"

"I don't really know what that means," I said, "even."

"It just means that time will sync and flow at the same speed on both earths," James said, "starting just after you get back."

"Oh."

230

"Now, your mind will be a little foggy when you get back," he said. "You'll hardly know you've been gone at first."

"Why's that?" DD said. "Why shouldn't we remember what happened here?"

"It's not intentional," James took a pen from the stool, "nor is it permanent. It's just that you'll be stepping down from a higher actuality. Physics will change. Plus, it's your first time. It's always a little mind numbing the first time."

"Will it hurt?" I said.

"Well, you will be pushing upstream against a force that could turn a whole world into a cheese basket."

"So..."

"I'll be gentle," James said. "Just sign here and initial here and walk across the bridge."

"There's nothing to sign," I said. "It's blank, like that notebook Billy gave me."

"You'll fill it up," James said and turned to DD. "Keep the pen, honey. It writes upside down and under water."

DD looked up into his fire eyes and slowly put the pen in her pocket.

"You may pass," James said.

We walked to the edge of the bridge and looked out into nothing.

"See you later," he said.

We stepped off the bridge and began falling. It grew darker and colder until we could feel nothing at all.

CHAPTER TWENTY-EIGHT

The first thing I heard when the sun came back on and the world unfroze was Grim Fist's scream. It was a low, guttural roar in defiance of the reality of what had just happened. His attack on the bomb had made no sense, but it was what humans sometimes did when they were cornered, when there was no way out, when common sense was the last thing possible. He used his grim fist to attack an explosion. His fist was the first thing the explosion took.

There was a second there, or something like a second in that it was a feeling of time, a bit before everything released when I wasn't sure it was going to, and I wasn't even sure I wanted it to. My mind was scribbly. In the timeless time, there were no worries. I mean, there were worries, but I didn't have to worry about them. I knew that nothing bad could happen because nothing at all could happen. I'd like to say, as I transitioned from cosmic being to human being, that my life flashed before my eyes. I'd like to say that because then it might mean that my life was actually mine, and not some artificial construct of some unexplainable god-like being. Of course, when I put it like that, I realized that *all* lives were just constructs of some unexplainable god-like being, and that the difference between artificial and real was up to the constructs, really. That made it a little more understandable when my life didn't flash before my eyes, but everyone else's life did.

"My God!" The Red Dart shouted as the bomb exploded, then stopped. He had pushed Wilma back in a fruitless attempt to shield her. He was the next closest to the blast, but it never reached him.

There was a sound time made when it came back on. I didn't know how many people had ever experienced it. I think it could only be heard by the person traveling from limbo to linear. It was like a cracking, like the first hints of glass breaking, like the anticipation felt just before it shattered. Time was back in full swing, but the explosion hung in the air a few feet off the ground, still frozen, like a giant Christmas tree star about six feet tall and four feet wide. The explosion looked like time sounded. It was the crystalized shards of Tarma energy that we had been drawn through. Most of Grim Fist writhed on the ground below it. Everyone was dazed, but unfrozen. The sun shone briefly, but then the scene was covered in shadow. Our entire adventure on the other earth rushed back in my brain like a crushing river. I fell to one knee, and looked around for DD. One more battle threatened me, surrounded me, only I didn't have the Tricks to help me.

Grandpa made his giant walls of water all around us. The streets dried up and cracked as all the water rushed out to the sides of us. A small circle of sun shone from above, like a pop bottle top. Nobody from the crowd could get in, and nobody in the fight could escape. The water moved constantly, but it was nearly solid to the touch. The air even became dry. Almost without thinking, I pulled out my new brass hose nozzle and fired a rope of water at Grandpa. It went right where I wanted it to and hit him square in the chest.

At first, he stepped back as the stream pummeled him, but as soon as he touched his water wall, he took my water rope and added it to the liquid cage all around us. It just sucked right up and joined in with the wall. I was surprised that I was able to actually shoot the thing here on my earth. I was even more surprised when Grandpa just absorbed it. Then, he threw it back in a large ball of liquid that just narrowly missed my head and splashed into a light post behind me, bending the post clear over. Every splash and drop of water shot out to join in the wall.

His eyes were like, fogged over, like he was filled with water, like his brain was under water. Thin streams of water snaked out of his eyes like antennae. He looked like another person, or even like another creature. Had I done this to him? This was not my grandpa. This was not the man who raised me and cared for me and loved me. I needed to find that man again. He had to be inside there. Was this his real sacrifice? Did he just give up to the insanity?

The Red Dart holstered his gun and ran over to Grim Fist. He ripped off a piece of his cape to tie off the stump of Grim Fist's arm. Wilma jumped up and pulled out an arrow.

DD created a flaming crimson bow and a nearly white arrow. Her hands blazed with colors. Sydnafly was coming towards her, and she took aim. Then, she dropped her arm and the weapons disappeared. That seemed to spur Sydnafly on, and he started running to her. She pulled out a wooden blunt arrow and lined it up in her bow. It was second nature to her, and she fired it off before Sydnafly was halfway to her. It hit him in the chest and stopped him for a moment. Apparently, his suit was armored. He grunted with some pain and then started at her again. She fired again and hit him again.

Grim Fist threw The Red Dart back and jumped up. He seemed to be fine, even reinvigorated. I was sure he had lost an arm, but now he was fully healed. His costume was gone over his left arm and half of his chest. Wilma shot an arrow into his exposed shoulder. He howled in pain and dropped to his knees.

I shot some water at Sydnafly, who kept shrugging off DD's arrows, but Grandpa pulled out his pistols and sucked the water right into them. He wasn't saying a single word, even when I tried to talk to him. Any time anyone got close to the water wall, friend or foe, water would shoot out like a battering ram at them. His face flickered in and out of the water on all sides.

"Stop all this craziness!" The Red Dart shouted and wiped the blood from his nose and face. His mask had been knocked off by Grim Fist. He was reeling around, following the mad expressions in the dark waves.

"I'm down to real arrows," DD warned Sydnafly.

"Then I'm done playing around." Sydnafly leapt over some rubble and back handed DD. She fell to the ground and dropped her bow.

I tried to run over there but was hit in the shoulder by one of The Red Dart's knock out darts. I pulled it out, but I knew it was too late. My feet felt clumsy and wobbled around in different directions. I fell to my knees. I looked over to The Red Dart, but he was looking up. I felt dizzy and sick, but I fought to stay awake.

Above me, the sun dimmed as something managed to break through Grandpa's water wall. I looked up at a floating car, a taxi cab, flying in mid air in the eye of Grandpa's water walls, and on MY earth. A figure leapt down, his hand in the water wall, using it to slow his descent.

"NOOO!" the water screamed, and the faces all popped from view.

"It's a miracle," DD whispered to me through bloody lips, "and on *my* earth."

The sun was above him, and little sparks were swimming in my eyes when he landed right next to me.

"Brand?" he said.

The sun around his head made it look like he had a halo.

"Dad?" I said.

"It's all right, son," he said. "I'm here now."

235

Then I passed out in his arms.

CHAPTER TWENTY-NINE

When I opened my eyes, Alan was standing over me. I was disappointed.

"Where's Dad?" I tried to sit up, but a wave of queasiness swept over me. That better not have been some kind of chemical illusion brought on by The Red Dart's knock out darts. I could take the sudden arrival of powers. I could handle actually liking a girl. I could deal with my Grandfather's illness. I could get over being argued over by a couple of cosmic beings. I could even understand traveling to a whole other earth and helping fight a war. But if someone was causing my brain to trick me into thinking my dad was back when he really wasn't, then I was seriously ticked off.

"He's awake?" Gina hobbled into the room on one crutch. She was dressed in a T-shirt and sweat pants.

There were posters on the wall and stuffed animals all over the place. I was dry, and there was no sign of any battle around me, just little fuzzy multicolored pillows.

"What happened?" I held my head.

"Take it easy." Alan's eye was starting to look better but was still not too pretty.

"DD!" I sat straight up despite my stomach.

"Hey!" DD ran into the room and threw her arms around me.

I hugged her back, and before I realized it, gave her a kiss right on the lips. I flushed hot, and she smiled and looked down. She was out of costume and wearing her street clothes.

"Looks like you're feeling better," Gina laughed and

leaned up against a dresser.

"Looks like you're feeling great!" Alan put his face down next to DD's and compared black eyes. "Hey look, a matching pair."

"The fight," I said. "What happened?"

"You'll never believe it," Alan said.

"Let me tell it," DD said. "I was there."

"Fine," Alan rolled his eyes, "tell it."

DD sat on the edge of the bed and took my hand. She smiled her beautiful smile. I reached up and touched the back of my hand to her darkened cheek.

"Your dad is back," she said.

It was so weird to hear someone say those words. I heard them in my dreams all my life, but to actually have someone say them out loud was incredible. That was the kind of thing that only happened in the super days.

"Brand?" DD said. "Did you hear me? He's at your grandpa's house right now. I guess it's kind of a shock for him too. You were a little kid the last time he saw you."

"But... How is he back? I thought he died. I thought he didn't have powers. I thought he was in the Navy and died. I thought I was raised by... Grandpa," I said. "What happened to Grandpa?"

"He's in..." Alan started, but Gina put her hand on his chest.

"After The Red Dart shot you, everybody started fighting again," DD said. "When I got up, your dad, Mr. Mist, was slamming Sydnafly's head into the side of a broken lamp post. Sydnafly got up and took a few swings, but your dad dodged each one. I don't think he broke a sweat. Of course, if he had, it would have been absorbed into the wave wall. I was still down on the ground, so I did a leg sweep and knocked Sydnafly over. Wilma turned away from me because Grim Fist was almost on her. Your grandpa was trying to shoot Ace's cab out of the sky. Brand, Ace's cab can fly, like, really fly, like... you know. Your dad tossed Sydnafly into the water wall, and Sydnafly was electrocuted with water. He just got caught in the current for a minute, shaking like he was stuck in a waterfall. Then, he fell out onto the ground unconscious.

My brain was all squiggly from the trip. I had dropped my bow, but felt this warm buzzing in the back of my head. At first, I thought I was bleeding, but then I just seemed to know..."

Her fingers twitched like she was crumpling up balls of paper as she remembered.

"Her powers!" Alan said.

Gina popped him in the shoulder. "Would. You. Shut. Up?" she said.

"I was able to make my bow and arrows again, but I wasn't scared," DD said. "I just thought, and it happened. I felt in control of it, and when I shot, it was like I knew exactly where it was going. It was like on the other... time, Brand. I didn't have to worry about the wind or how far the target was, or even if I could see the target. I shot the water pistols right out of your grandpa's hands, right out. My arrow went in a curve until it hit what I wanted it to hit. I was so worried that I wouldn't be able to control it here, that I would kill somebody.

"Poor Grim Fist got shot a bunch of times by Wilma. She was using her REAL arrows. I don't even think she carries blunt arrows. He just jerked them out of himself and healed right up immediately."

"Powers!" Alan jumped up. "He's got powers too!"

"He punched Wilma right in the face, POW!" DD looked up at Gina, who suppressed a smile. "She hit the pavement right away.

Your grandpa went nuts then. He started waving his hands and screaming at your dad, no words, just screaming. This all happened in, like, less than a minute. He was screaming and waving his arms, and the water whipped around, smashing into us. It was crazy. At one point, the edge of the stage washed into the frozen explosion..."

"The frozen explosion?"

"Yeah, that's what people are calling it, the frozen explosion." DD looked me deep in the eyes and slowly nodded her head. "It's the explosion from the bomb, only frozen in place. Nobody can touch it or move it. It turned the stage into splinters. Anything that tries to go in it or destroy it just dissolves or explodes."

"Right," I said, "explosion."

"I can't believe what happened next."

"I can believe it." Gina moved from the dresser and sat on the arm of a pink furry chair and took her weight off of her hurt leg.

"Yeah, well, I can't hardly believe it." DD squinted.

"After all we've been through?" I said. "All the stuff on the..."

DD squeezed my hand tightly.

"What?" I swung my feet around and sat next to DD on the bed. We were still holding hands, and mine was getting sweaty, but I wasn't letting go. DD didn't notice, or maybe she didn't care, or maybe she thought it was *her* hand that was sweaty.

"The Red Dart shot your grandpa," DD said. "Knocked him right out, and the walls rolled in all over us. Any water that touched the frozen explosion just, poof! vaporized."

"He knew it was over," Alan said. "That's why he did it."

"I don't know," Gina said. "He's always been a hero deep down."

"Not always," DD squeezed my hand again. "They took him to prison. They took him and Wilma and your grandpa and Sydnafly away to jail."

"DD, my dad..." I said.

"But your grandpa hasn't woken up," DD said. "Even after the knock out stuff should have run its course. They

240

say he's in a coma."

"I should go see him," I stood.

"I don't think they're letting anybody go see him," Alan said.

"Where's everybody else?" I asked.

"Ace is talking to the police, I think." DD stood up next to me. "I don't know about Grim Fist."

"Ace said I could drive his car," Alan beamed, "his *flying* car."

"I think he was just being nice." DD leaned in to me.

"You should go talk to your dad," Gina said. "Like DD said, he's at your grandfather's house. I think you're all supposed to go down and fill out papers at the police station. He and Ace brought you here to escape the crazy mob and the crazy reporters."

"Where's here?"

"My room," DD said, "here at the hideout."

"I'll take you," Alan put on his black driving cap.

"Can I, um..."

"You need to go the bathroom?" Alan said.

"No," I bent my head towards DD, "can I have a minute, please?"

Alan rolled his eyes and left the room. Gina smiled. The way she looked over to DD made us both blush.

"I just..." I said.

"I'll wait in the car." She winked and hobbled out.

"This can't be," I said to DD as soon as Gina was gone. "Do you remember the crazy stuff in space and all the stuff with the Tricks and Billy and the other earth?"

"Yeah," DD said, "it took me a few minutes after we got back. I kept thinking about different types of potions I had made in the lab, like real life wasn't just happening all around me."

"Oh, thank goodness!" I plopped back down on the bed. "I thought it was some kind of dream or something. It seemed so weird."

"It's like, superhero stuff, huh," DD said. "Nobody but me and you remember your dad dying without powers. And that stuff with the other earth and the other you, I was worried you might not remember that. I am so glad you do."

"Should we tell anyone?" I said.

"It's the same old question as before," DD said. "Why do we have to decide what the world knows? Who are we? I don't know what it would do to people. Everything they believe is wrong."

"I guess," I said. "Maybe we should just kind of not say anything about it for a while. Let's see what's going to happen next. There's been weird enough stuff happen that we're going to have to talk about. Let's keep the whole other earth thing under our hats."

"Who would believe it?" DD put her finger on my chin. "I liked sharing an adventure with you, Brand Meeks."

I smiled. "I liked sharing an adventure with you too, Darlene Deville, and I liked..."

I blushed. I hated it when I blushed.

"This?" DD kissed me again.

"That." I kissed her back.

We soaked in the quiet time for a moment. The last few days had been very unbelievable.

"I can't believe my dad is back," I said.

"I don't understand what has happened to our world," DD said. "What's changed? Your dad says he was on a boat when a huge storm came up."

"When?" I said. "Where was this?"

"Years ago, when you were a kid," DD said, "out in the Atlantic, I think. But, anyway, this storm came up, and there was a huge water spout, and he tried to use his powers..."

"His powers?"

"I know!" DD said. "It's crazy. He tried to use his powers to control the water spout, but the spout came right up to his boat and talked to him."

"Wait a minute," I said. "The water spout talked?"

"That's what he said," she said, "and I believe him."

"Sure," I said, "why not? After all, I was also host to the representation of the entire universe. Why not a talking water spout?"

"Listen!" DD said and put her hand on my shoulder. "The water spout said he was the mighty water demon, Tulsi, and he was tired of a human controlling the waves."

"Tulsi?"

"... and that your dad would have to wrestle him to see who was truly the master of the ocean."

"Tulsi?" I said. "*Our* Tulsi?"

"I'm betting," DD said. "So, they wrestled for what your dad thought were hours, and when Tulsi spit him out on the shore, it was today."

"*Today* today?"

"Today," DD said. "Tulsi told him about what was going on here in the city, and that he had set things up with Ace to get your dad a ride, and that was that."

"That's so weird," I said. "That sounds like a tall tale."

"I think it might be the new normal," DD said.

"But do you think it's real?" I bent down slightly and looked her in the eyes.

"All I know for sure is what's here in front of me," she put her other hand on top of mine, "and that's real enough."

EPILOGUE

And that's what I did on my summer vacation. I can use a lot of this in my report that's due on Monday. There's a whole heaping lot, though, that I think I need to leave out. All the stuff about Billy and Tulsi and the superheroes still battling the villains, and the sentient universes fighting one another, and running around with the real Tricks, and the total upturning of all history can keep for another time. That seems a little much for a sophomore english class. I think I'll probably change the names, too. Although, people will probably be able to figure it out.

I wrote all of it down, though, the truth, the way it happened, because I'm starting to forget stuff. I know it seems a little hard to believe that I would forget any of this crazy summer or those incredible few days, but it's true. DD is forgetting, too. We have to keep reminding ourselves what happened, especially the stuff in outer space. James said we could remember. I want to remember. This was an amazing thing to happen, and I got to have this incredible adventure with DD. It was our adventure. It just wasn't fair to forget it. It might even come in handy in dealing with the new weirdness and events on our world.

Sydnafly escaped. He got loose on the way to jail. He had help from his network hierarchy, his own Tricks or, I guess, his own Roadies. Grim Fist is out on his trail. Grim Fist must have gotten my healing powers, because I sure don't have them anymore. I found that out the first time I skinned my knee.

I can still control water, but Dad thinks we should keep that quiet for a while. There were no witnesses to what DD or I did except the people in the water ring. No other powers have popped up since then that we know about. Only time will tell, I guess. The press has taken to calling Dad the Miraculous Mr. Mist. It seems fitting.

Alan is training with Ace now. I hardly see him except on TV. Ace is the biggest star since sliced bread, with his flying car. He and Grim Fist and Dad are all considered the world's only Grade A superheroes by the SGHV. Technically, DD and I are Grade A sidekicks, but we're laying low for a while. We're not doing a whole lot since school has started back up again. I kind of like just being a Trick anyway.

The Red Dart is still in jail, but he's cooperating, and everybody said good things about him. He'll probably get a shortened sentence for good behavior or something. I'm not sure how that works. I doubt Wilma will get any kind of deal. She's pretty hateful. DD got to talk to The Red Dart, and she said that he apologized. She's just not sure if she believes him or not.

The frozen explosion is still right there in the middle of the street. Even the government hasn't figured out what to do with it. They had to build a building around it, because people kept throwing their trash into it to see it just incinerate. People on TV are talking about trying to turn it into an alternative energy source. That would be cool. Other people are afraid it will unfreeze and wipe out the city. That's kind of scary. The Blackout Prophets are starting to worship it. They say the frozen explosion stopped the powers from coming back. There have already been several "suicide by frozen explosion" attempts and at least one "murder by frozen explosion" attempt. I have a feeling that this could be a problem down the road. I wonder what they would think if they knew what it really was. Maybe they would try to communicate

245

with it. Can we communicate with it? Maybe I should try to communicate with it. Oh, geez, I don't know. What if Tarma could get to me from it?

Grandpa finally woke up a few weeks ago, but he still won't talk to anyone. He keeps going in and out of consciousness. They still won't let me see him, either, in case he goes crazy again, I guess. He hasn't shown any more powers that I've been told about. Grandpa is the only classified super villain in the world. I don't think he should be classified a villain at all. He is sick. He needs help. He wasn't in control of his own actions.

DD and I are still girlfriend and boyfriend. We're still keeping things quiet. Now we go to the same school since The Red Dart isn't able to home school her anymore. She moved to an apartment with Gina. Gina isn't doing anything in the sidekick field anymore. I'm not even sure if she and Alan are still dating. He's been gone all the time, and she's started taking classes at night to either be a teacher or a nurse. She's really good at computers and works at a computer store during the day. I think she should go into computer stuff, but she says she isn't really interested in that. I guess The Red Dart had some money stashed away from his secret government jobs, so they don't have to worry right now. Plus it turns out that he had a side job selling chemical mixtures, gasses, knock out drops, fake flavors, and a bunch of other stuff, to heroes who needed that kind of stuff.

Dad got me an archaeopteryx, one of the few dinosaurs that mankind has been able to domesticate in the last fifty years. We remodeled Grandpa's house and are living there. I named my archaeopteryx Tulsi. Most people name their archaeopteryx Archie. I tell people that I just like the name Tulsi. Tulsi really makes our neighbor, Mr. Forest, mad when he roosts in his tree or gets on his porch.

That kind of brings me to what happened later that

day, the day of the frozen explosion, the day my dad returned. When we drove out to Grandpa's, Mr. Forest was out in his yard digging up dandelions.

"Billy!" DD pointed out the window.

"Mr. Forest?" I corrected.

"Your dad really wants to see you," Alan said, "but he didn't know how you'd react. So he didn't want to be all in your face when you came to."

"Don't you want to see him?" Gina pulled down the visor and looked at us through the mirror in it.

"Sure, I... Stop the car!" I yelled.

"Geez!" Alan put on the brakes. "We're right here. I just need to turn into the driveway."

"See that?" I pointed.

"Get out," DD said. "Let's go talk to him."

"Who?" Alan said. "Your neighbor?"

"You see that guy on the porch?" I said. "You don't see anything weird about him, anything familiar?"

"Just another old guy on a porch," Alan said, "probably Forest's brother or something. So, what?"

But it wasn't just another old guy on a porch. That's just what everybody else saw. In reality, it was me, or, as I suspected, it was Tulsi. I was pretty sure I was right when the world froze around DD and me and him the moment we stepped out of the car.

"Is it over already?" I walked down Mr. Forest's sidewalk. The frozen time didn't seem to slow me like before. It seemed to open up around me instead. "Did you win? Why is Billy frozen too?"

"That's not Billy," Tulsi said. "That's Mr. Forest.

"I thought Billy was Mr. Forest," DD said.

"It's confusing," Tulsi smiled. "This guy here is Mr. Forest. He's always been Mr. Forest. I had to do a little history housekeeping."

"I noticed," I said.

The person that you thought was Billy acting like Mr.

247

Forest was really Tarma acting like Billy acting like Mr. Forest."

"Tarma the evil universe?" DD asked. "The one you are supposed to fight?"

"Oh, man," I said. "Has he been her all along? Was he, I mean, she manipulating things my whole life?"

"It turns out that we've both been fighting her all along and didn't know it." Tulsi picked up a glass of lemonade and sipped on it. A little umbrella in the drink poked his cheek, so he took it out and laid it on the banister. "She was trying to trick me. I'm actually fighting her right now."

"Right now while you're talking to us?" I sat down on Mr. Forest's porch swing. In the frozen time, it didn't swing as much and just stayed wherever I put it.

"I'm in between moments right now," Tulsi said. "I have a feeling that I'll be fighting her influence for a long time, but at least it turns out that I have a lot more power and control here than Tarma led me to believe."

"So Mr. Forest never was Billy?"

"That makes sense," DD said. "We met the real Billy on the other earth."

"Yes," Tulsi looked out at the lawn. "She was just using the persona of Billy as a ruse, because he was once a mentor of mine. She thought she could manipulate me better that way. When she saw that I was bubbling back to the surface of your consciousness, she set up events that would lead me into revealing myself to myself. That's when *she* set the bomb. Then, she hoped to confuse me and trick me back into making some kind of decision that would take me out of the battle again. Either I hid myself back in your psyche, and thus stayed out of the fight, or I hurtled headlong into the battle, leaving powers for you to defend yourself. This would leave myself unguarded with her inside of me and able to use her powers. That's the kind of stuff she did fifteen years ago to your dad."

"Man, that's intricate planning," I said. "How many steps ahead was she thinking?"

"I'm afraid to find out," Tulsi said. "I don't even know if there are other things out there to watch out for. She may have had all kinds of tricks planned. You should have seen the wild ride she took me on. She kept trying to wring my mind out like it was a wet rag. I even went back to when Dad died."

"About that," I said, "how is he back when I'm him?"

"You know?"

"I read it all in a book that Billy gave me," I said.

"Well.. how am I here, when I'm you?" Tulsi asked. "I'm sorry. I don't mean to tease. I won't do that again. That, unfortunately, is the type of snarkiness we cosmic beings tend to display. That's what I learned from Billy."

"We experienced some of the real Billy's manipulation, too," DD said.

"Sometimes things seem so obvious to us," Tulsi said. "It's like somebody coming up to you and saying, 'excuse me, but how do you breath?'."

He sipped at his lemonade for a moment like he had forgotten all about us. His cheeks got red and his eyes puffed up a little.

"Sorry, my mind was elsewhere," he said. "Where were we? Oh, yes. Anyway, this Forest was always Forest. I was always me. You were always you. Your dad was always your dad. Time and history is just another part of me."

"So you really *are* God," DD said.

"Oh, Heavens, no," Tulsi lavhed. "He's much bigger than me. Just because I may be all the water in the ocean, doesn't mean I *made* the concept of ocean. I don't want to teach a class, here. This is a misunderstanding that mankind has always had. They think power equals God. That kind of thinking leads to earth-shaking super battles. That's the main lesson I had to learn. It's why

249

Billy became my mentor, and why I treated him so poorly. Billy knows God. He worked with God, and I, my friend, am no God."

"But you made heaven and earth and all the people on it." DD sat on the railing opposite of me.

"No, I didn't." Tulsi put his fingers on his chest. He picked up his lemonade umbrella and handed it to DD. "Put this in the little pouch in your quiver. This stuff is all just a part of me. It's in me. Also, on a metaphysical scale, I am the epitome, the very essence of it. I made this place kind of like how you made your kidney."

"So, basically you just changed history like a pair of socks and made everyone think you always wore those socks," I said.

"Basically," he said. "It's quite a neat trick."

"Why not change us?" I said. "Why do we still remember?"

"Why do the trick without an audience," Tulsi said. "Otherwise, things get very boring."

"Because it's not fair." DD jumped up. "Everybody gets to remember Mr. Mist and his heroics except his son, who gets to remember him die. Everybody has fond memories but the one person who should feel closest to him. It's just not fair."

"How many people get to witness cosmic miracles?" Tulsi asked. "And then would throw that away on false memories?"

"Don't pull that on me," DD said. "I'm sick of it."

"You need to make up your mind," Tulsi said, "on just what you want to believe and remember. You want to know how things are now or how they were then? Knowing everything's just not normal."

Tulsi looked out into the frozen sky. "Oh, what I wouldn't give for a little normal. I think that's why Tarma's trick worked so well. She was able to lock me into being a regular guy. She knew I yearned for that. I was in a

250

prison, but only I held the key."

He smiled at each of us in turn and paced across the porch.

"I'm sure you can work your little mortal dramas out," he said. "I have a cosmic war to win. I'll be back for real in a few thousand years. Keep good care of the place for me."

"I want to remember," I said. "I'm not saying I want to know everything in the world. I just don't want to forget what DD and I went through together."

"Me, too," DD said. "I want to remember too."

"I don't have a problem with that," Tulsi said.

"Wait a minute," I held up my hand. "Before you go, I did always wonder... I mean, why did you bring back the dinosaurs? Why did you clean things up and regrow the forests?"

"You have a final chance to ask me anything before I disappear for a thousand years, and this is what you ask?" Tulsi massaged the back of his neck and gave a little chuckle. "Why didn't you ask me about your nature? Don't you want to know if you are real? Don't you want to know what's going to happen, what has changed on our little planet?"

"Who says I only get one more question?" I said.

"I do," Tulsi's face relaxed. "I've learned the dangers of knowing too much. I learned from the best. Why don't you ask me about Grandpa?"

"I'm just a kid," I said. "I told you, I don't want to know everything. I don't need to be told these things."

"Yes, you do," DD said. "You're just as important as any adult."

"No, I mean, I don't need to be told these things be-cause they're part of me," I said. "I'm not trying to be wise or smart. I just figure that the stuff that's part of me will work its way out, that I'll figure it out or come to terms with it."

"And Grandpa?"

"Suppose I knew what was wrong," I put my hands in my pockets, "what could I do? I'm not a doctor. Are you going to tell me that he doesn't need a doctor?"

Tulsi smiled. "Trying to get two answers for the price of one?"

"I just kind of figure that you love him as much as I do," I said, "and if there was anything I could do, you would tell me."

Tulsi sipped the last of his lemonade. "Everything's part of you, Brand," he said. "Everything's part of everything. There's a lot of everything that is good, and there's a lot of everything that is tarnished."

"So you cleaned it all up hoping that humanity would keep it that way?" DD took my arm.

"If this is all part of me," Tulsi made his glass of lemonade disappear, "I'd like to be a tidy steward."

"And the dinosaurs?" DD said.

Tulsi covered his mouth and smiled. He looked down at the porch floor in thought.

"Let me tell you something, DD." He walked over to her. He was smiling, but his eyes were not. "This world really isn't a world without miracles. You were right about that. This world is a world of secrets... or at least it was."

"What secrets?" DD pulled in.

"I didn't have anything to do with the dinosaurs or the forests," he shrugged, "not directly. I just like them."

"Who did then?" DD said.

"But, oh, boy, boyo," Tulsi put up his thumb and smiled through gritted teeth, "you and I changed that, eh, Brand? There *will* be questions now that certain parties feel like their secrets are no longer secrets."

"Can you give us some more answers?" I said.

"In the loaf of cheese that is time, I don't see me doing that," he said. "I could possibly stand here and explain right now why I couldn't possibly stand here and

252

explain right now, but really, I'm busy. I know it sounds like a cop out, but in the grand scheme of things it's only because it kind of is. Plus, I can only carry so much and care so much, I mean, I don't want to be 'that guy' but if I'm not 'this guy', then who does that leave? I hope that cleared a few things up for you. Well, anyway, like I said, I think you guys can handle it. Good luck, you two. God knows you're going to need it."

And with that, DD and I were back in the car just before it came around the corner to Grandpa's house.

"Did we...?" I turned to DD.

She held up the little umbrella that Tulsi had in his drink.

Mr. Forest was pulling dandelions, but no one was on his porch. We pulled into the driveway and got out of the car. It was a hot day, but there was no moisture in the air. Dad stuck his head out of the attic window.

"I'm up here!" he shouted.

"We'll give you a few minutes," Gina said.

I took DD's hand and headed towards the house.

"No," she said, "you go talk to him. Go find out if it's real."

I nodded and walked in.

The house smelled really bad. The walls were caving in. The floor was bulging. Everything was ruined. I expected everything to be slimy, but it was all dry. This must have been Dad's work. I was only just beginning to wonder what powers he had. I walked up the stairs and found Dad in the attic, bent over a box of old stuff.

"This is just about the only place that wasn't ruined," he said with his back turned, "although, a good portion of your bedroom made it through."

He turned around, and we looked at each other. He opened his arms and I walked forward into a big bear hug. I didn't even realize that I remembered his hugs until I felt them again. I didn't realize how much I missed them.

253

I felt like I had been the one who was away from home. I felt like I was the one who was coming back.

"You are so big," he said. "I've missed so much. I've got a whopper of a story to tell you."

"I've missed you too, Dad," I said and tried so hard to remember more. It was like a hunger, but even then, I could feel the memories starting to trickle into my brain.

We sat in the boxes of memories and talked for, like, forever. He told me his water spout story. I told him about school and DD and my Tricks adventures here on our earth, but not my adventures with the Tricks on the other earth. We talked a bit about his plans. He'd been talking to some people and was hoping to put a team together with Ace and Grim Fist and Prez from the Dead Millards and a few other people. He wanted to name it after an old group from before the war. He wanted to call it the Tricks. He thought DD and I could help out sometimes, be Tricks or sidekicks until we got a little older. Nothing was sure. We needed to get a lot of normal stuff done first. We needed to rebuild the house. We needed to get to know each other again.

"Oh hey, Brand," Dad reached over into the piles of storage, "do you remember this old thing?"

He pulled out a little red wagon and set it on the floor. I couldn't believe I ever fit in something so small. It was bent and wobbly and probably not safe for anyone to use.

"You just about killed yourself in this thing," he said, "rolling down that back hill out at the old place. Remember that one time you almost ran right into the old station wagon? I had to run as fast as I could to catch you. Do you remember that?"

"I... do," I said. "I remember."

END

ACKNOWLEDGEMENTS

This is the part of the book, dear reader, that most readers don't bother to read. This is the part where the author rambles on about the influences in his life, those who helped spark his love of the craft, those who influenced this very book, those who wiped his nose and taught him to tie his shoes. In short, it's like an Oscar acceptance speech, except there is no little golden statue given out. You see, in many cases, a novel, and especially an early novel, is a work of love, formulated over years, sometimes a lifetime. This book is no exception.

This is not my first book. It's not even my first novel, but it is a part of what I have always considered my magnum opus. Since the early to mid nineties I have been growing these characters. Their roots trace back even further in my life. My children grew up with the members of the Tricks. They know them well enough to predict what they will do next. They can tell me if something is 'out of character'. The Tricks were in my life before my wife was. She learned them well enough to point out a discrepancy that forced me to scrap an entire book because I was forcing the characters to do something rather than allowing them to do what they would naturally do. How can I not thank my family? My siblings contributed to the very Genesis of some of the characters. My parents listened patiently to wild descriptions of worlds they could barely fathom. My best friends and siblings spent many late creative hours molding events and places and people and concepts that would creep into my stories. It's only right they be acknowledged. My teachers and instructors stoked the sparks of creativity that they found hidden under stones. They encouraged shining daylight on my hidden weirdness. I need to recognize them. Then, there are the world builders of the past and present who inspire my storytelling. They showed me it could be done. They proved that a voice with a story to tell could be heard. They carved out an audience, myself included. Why shouldn't they be mentioned? Finally, the enabler, the publisher, editor, and business end of the deal. If all above were true, but the final part was left out, you would not be wondering why in the world you are still reading the acknowledgements right now. And, finally, finally... you, the reader. I don't know your name. Well, I may know a specific individual's name, and I may know you, the person reading this page (Hi), but I don't know the name of the audience in general, because, of course, the audience in general doesn't have a name, unless it's, Audience, in which case, I DO know your name in general, just not in specific. Yeah... Thanks.

Let me tell you... no author writes in a vacuum. It may clean the carpet, but it's really dark and noisy in there and he couldn't breath.

Anyway... To my mom and dad, Carol and Bob Noe, thanks for putting up with me. To my siblings, Bryan, Melissa, Jennifer, Clover (and their wonderful spouses and families), thanks for being the type of family that promotes rather than mocks. To my friends, Mike Durbin and all the Durbin family, Jim Clevenger, Jim Poland and others. Your wild creativity, your eagerness to help, your opinions and insights have been invaluable. To Mrs. Tucker, Dr. Bagnall, Mrs Zapf and those teachers who encouraged me, look what you did! I hope you're happy with yourself! To the gang at Charlton Arrow who encouraged me. To my children, Sarah Marie Evelyn and Kelsey Lea Ann, who have turned out to be absolute geniuses and beauties and talents, my God, kids, look at this. Look at this. Thank you. And to my wife, Bobbie Jo... There are times when there are no words. To a writer, those are scary times. When I think of you, I don't need words. You take away the scary times. You, with your loveliness and your many, MANY talents, you are all the words and all the worlds I need.

In a perfect world, that would be the best place to end, but this is not a perfect world. This is MY world. This is the world full of tricks. I have some special acknowledgements to make.

First off, thanks to Julie Casey and Amazing Things Press. This is my first book with you. You have been a joy to work with, even in the very few times we have disagreed (and, dang it! you were probably right). I hope to have many more adventures with you.

Thanks to Kevin S, Halter. You took my characters and gave them an extra dimension. You are the first thing people see when they look at my book. It is quite a responsibility, and you pulled it off with aplomb!

Along with Kevin's cover, he also provided an interior page of a crazy Grandpa Meeks. "Above and beyond", my friend. Four other gentlemen took pen in hand and delved into the depths of my characters. Keep in mind, they had no pictures to pull from. There are no other illustrations of these characters. They had to reach into their own minds and put down on paper what descriptions I provided. That is no mean feat, and these guys are true talents. Thank you to Daerick Gross Sr. for his fabulous and snazzy rendition of Sydnafly. Thanks to Dana Black for bringing the Mysterious Grim Fist to light (or should I say, dark). Incredible! Thanks, too, to Sandy Carruthers for the remarkable rendition of The Red Dart. Right on! Many thanks to Truman Vasko, as well, for his rockin' rad, Mr. Forest. These fellows are rightfully busy and getting busier all the time. These are names you may have seen, will hear and read even more in the future, I guarantee! Please! Check out their web pages, their facebook pages, their artwork and anything they are working on. Look for the Charlton Neo comics, the Pix-C web comics, and even other great stuff we are working on together! To use a soon to be dated phrase... On Fleek!

Now, there are others. There are professional, established creators who, through no fault of their own, have become friends of mine. These guys took the time to read my novel even before the final edit. They saw stuff that ended up on the cutting room floor (figuratively in most cases). Mort Todd, Dan Johnson and Roger McKenzie, names you can check out on Wikipedia, blurbed me. That is, they read the book and provided back cover copy. These guys are busy making books every day. You would be doing yourself a great favor checking out their material. Just do a facebook or internet search for them. You'll be glad you did. Speaking of these gents...

Finally, a special thanks to the inimitable Mr. Roger McKenzie. I didn't list all the authors who inspired me throughout my life. That list would be full of people who are very far away from my real life, mostly people I will never meet or speak to in person, many of whom are deceased or live in another country, or a combination of both. This novel is like a comic book without the panels. I've read comics since the mid seventies. That's a long time. Before I started keeping track of the artists and writers I preferred, back when I just liked or didn't like a story and didn't know why, I found myself accidentally following an author. Suddenly, I liked the stories in Captain America and Ghost Rider and Daredevil. Why? What had changed? Roger McKenzie had changed the books. When I read Daredevil #158 and saw a life ending event in a comic book, I realized the power of writing. It was the right message at the right time in my life. It was a fulcrum between kiddie books and "real" books. It was one of those things that made me want to write. Well... Roger retired for many years. I was lucky enough to get some of his small press work, but mostly, I wouldn't hear from him until Charlton Arrow. I got in early on the Arrow. I wanted to script comic books. I soon found out that I needed to use different brain muscles for a comic script than for a novel. Roger was very encouraging. He went above and beyond what most people would. He gave me assignments. He critiqued those assignments. Let me stress this point, ladies and gentlemen. This is an extremely rare event! Roger, a published author with a legitimate fan base, a man coming out of retirement to an audience prepared to receive him, was taking time out of several of his days to tutor this unknown scripter, this wannabe writer, this comic book fan. Can you see how rare this is? I certainly could. Don't let him fool you. He's a humble and gracious man. If you ever get to shake his hand, shake it twice, once for you and once for me. Then, he agreed to write the foreword to my book. Mind blown.

So, in summary, family and friends... ACKNOWLEDGED! Mentors and inspirations... ACKNOWLEDGED! Crazy-good artists... ACKNOWLEDGED! Charlton Arrow, blurb-meisters... ACKNOWLEDGED! Amazing Things Press, Julie Casey... ACKNOWLEDGED! THE Roger McKenzie... ACKNOWLEDGED! Readers...? Readers? Oh YEAH! ACKNOWLEDGED!

Note: Bryan Noe first made the Red Rat. Mike Durbin first brought Ace the cab driver to life. Melissa Wells was the first Ms. Power.

Check out my facebook pages AND my website!

authordavidnoe.weebly.com is my website.

www.facebook.com/dave.noe.7 is my personal facebook page.

www.facebook.com/tradeofthetricks is the facebook page for this and other books.

https://www.facebook.com/typomagazine1 is a monthly magazine of short stories and poetry that I publish.

ABOUT THE AUTHOR

William David Noe lives in NW Missouri right between St. Joseph and Kansas City. His last name is pronounced, No'-ee. He has two daughters and one wife. His oldest daughter, Sarah is currently pursuing an acting career in NYC. His youngest daughter, Kelsey is a graphics designer in Kansas City. His wife, Bobbie Jo works in activities at the Gower Convalescent Center. Dave is also the editor of TYPO Magazine (www.facebook.com/typomagazine1). You need to go there! TYPO Magazine is a Laundreemat Press production.

He is writing a western for Charlton's Wild Frontier about a man known as the Alabaster Kid. He will also be reviving the shape shifting hero, The Shape with the prolific and talented, Mort Todd for the pages of, Charlton Action. He and Garry Hardman will have a short strip in the upcoming, Charltoons.

Dave has two other books for sale on amazon.com. One is a collection of short stories entitled, Odds and Ends, but Mostly Odds. The other is a mature audience thriller entitled The Notions of Minsa Van Whey/Psychic Biker.

He is also helping to form the fledgeling comic company, Anarchy Ink Press (you'll go AIP for Anarchy), with Dean Compton and other talented individuals.

He has an e-book available on Amazon Kindle. It's called, Guide To Ghosts. Check it out if you ever wondered just what it might be that went bump in the night. It's only .99 cents!

Finally, he will soon have a weekly online comic strip on Pix-C! It's called, Anagram For Crazy, and he desperately wants you to read the adventures of CC the Cat! (http://charltonneo.blogspot.com/2015/03/free-pix-c-weekly-web-comics-preview.html)

This book is not his only Tricks book! Aside from working on another novel featuring Brand and DD, Dave has several prequels in the works starring the original Tricks. Go to https://www.facebook.com/tradeofthetricks and like the page so you can be kept in the loop about all the new Tricks stuff coming up. Also, you will know when and where he will be for signings and readings and other fun stuff. Plus, there may be giveaways and prizes! Dave is also compiling some books of poetry that absolutely don't suck. You can bet he'll be talking about them, as well. Dave likes writing these bios in third person and he doesn't know why.

A MESSAGE FROM THE AUTHOR:

Thank you for taking the time to read my book. I would be honored if you would consider leaving a review for it on Amazon.

CONTRIBUTORS

Roger McKenzie (Foreword, Blurb-meister)

Roger has been in the comic book writing biz for many years, and has written such characters as Daredevil, Captain America and Ghost Rider. He is currently writing and editing for Charlton Neo and Pix-C (and several other top notch projects).

Kevin S. Halter (Cover, Grandpa Meeks, DD)

Kevin Halter was born in 1965, and shortly after began drawing. After decorating walls and his sleeping father with doodles he was given paper and hasn't stopped drawing since.

In the mid 1990's he worked briefly in the Independent Comic market.In 2014 he returned to his lifelong dream of dream of drawing comics working primarily at the resurrected Charlton comics. "Where else could you get the opportunity to work on westerns, horror stories, humor strips and superheroes in the same week?" Kevin lives in West Lafayette with his incredibly patient wife, Teresa, two wonderful sons Keegan and Ian, and the cat that won't go away, Topaz. He and Dave have many more projects in the works.

Dærick Gröss Sr. (Sydnafly illustration)

With nearly 50 years in the commercial art field, Dærick Gröss Sr. has worked as an illustrator, instructor, and art director. He has painted, drawn, written and edited comics for Marvel, DC, Image, Malibu, Studio G, Heroic, Revolutionary, Chaos, Innovation, Topps, and numerous other companies. His best-selling work includes the series Anne Rice's "The Vampire Lestat" for Innovation. Dærick also has his creator-owned series, Murcielaga She-Bat for both Studio G and Heroic, Brian Lumleyís Necroscope for Malibu, and the best-selling sex book The Guide To Getting It On. Currently, Dærick is venturing into a 're-birth publishing group' creating new stories of old CHARLTON COMICS characters, and some new, weekly 'downloadable' strips and cartoons through Pix-CC comics and his own Studio G. Among several ilustration and art achievement awards is the West Coast Comic Club's prestigious Russ Manning Award.

Sandy Carruthers (The Red Dart illustration)

Sandy is a Canadian artist and graphic design instructor, known for his work as the first illustrator of the original Men In Black comic book series and as creator of the webcomic series, Canadiana: the New Spirit of Canada. Sandy is currently working on a revival of Spookman for Charlton Neo and Ms. Molecule for Pix-C.

Dana Black (Grim Fist illustration)

Inspired by Star Wars and Dinosaurs, this New York native began drawing at age 5 and was published by age 9. Dana enjoyed all the arts but focused mainly on illustration,winning many local and state competitions and later attending the Fashion Institute of Technology.

Managing to avoid mainstream comics for the most part, the artist contributed his skills to various independent publishers as well as Dark Horse and DC comics. Always looking for a challenge , Dana ventured into storyboard and concept design for TV and Film, always returning to his first love, comics.

Dana is currently working on several comics projects, a Horror movie script as well as for Topps where he has fulfilled his lifelong dream of drawing Star Wars and Dinosaurs.

Truman Vasko (Mr. Forest illustration)

Truman is an illustrator/animator. Having a love of God, comics, and movies has made him what he is today. He lives in St. Joseph with his dog, Kiddo.

Dan Thompson (Blurb-meister)

Dan is a comic strip writer as well as a comic book writer. He is an assistant editor at Charlton Neo Media.

Mort Todd (Blurb-meister)

Mort is a publisher, writer and artist at Comicfix, Pix-C, ACE Comics and many others. He and Dave will be resurrecting the hero named The Shape.

Check out these titles from
Amazing Things Press

Keeper of the Mountain by Nshan Erganian

Rare Blood Sect by Robert L. Justus

Evoloving by James Fly

Survival In the Kitchen by Sharon Boyle

Stop Beating the Dead Horse by Julie L. Casey

In Daddy's Hands by Julie L. Casey

How I Became a Teenage Survivalist by Julie L. Casey

Time Lost: Teenage Survivalist II by Julie L. Casey

Starlings by Jeff Foster

MariKay's Rainbow by Marilyn Weimer

Convolutions by Vashti Daise

Seeking the Green Flash by Lanny Daise

Nikki's Heart by Nona j. Moss

Nightmares or Memories by Nona j. Moss

Thought Control by Robert L. Justus

Palightte by James Fly

I, Eugenius by Larry W. Anderson

Tales From Beneath the Crypt by Megan Marie

Vintage Mysteries by Megan Marie

Defenders of Holt by Julie L. Casey

A Thin Strip of Green by Vashti Daise

Fun Activities to Help Little Ones Talk by Kathy Blair

Check out these children's titles from
Amazing Things Press

The Boy Who Loved the Sky by Donna E. Hart

Terreben by Donna E. Hart

Sherry Strawberry's Clubhouse by Donna E. Hart

Finally Fall by Donna E. Hart

Thankful for Thanksgiving by Donna E. Hart

Make Room for Maggie by Donna E. Hart

Toddler Tales by Kathy Blair

A Cat Named Phyl by Donna E. Hart

Geography Studies With Animal Buddies by Vashti Daise

The Princess and the Pink Dragon by Thomas Kirschner

Sherry Strawberry's Coloring and Activity Book by Donna E. Hart

The Happy Butterfly by Donna E. Hart

From Seanna by Vashti Daise

The Boy Who Had Nine Cats by Irene Alexander

Meet Mr. Wiggles by Shivonne Jean Hancock

Amazing Things Press

www.amazingthingspress.com